Alondra

GINA FEMIA

FARRAR STRAUS GIROUX

NEW YORK

Farrar Straus Giroux Books for Young Readers
An imprint of Macmillan Publishing Group, LLC
120 Broadway, New York, NY 10271 • fiercereads.com

Our books may be purchased in bulk for promotional, educational, or business use. Please
contact your local bookseller or the Macmillan Corporate and Premium Sales Department
at (800) 221-7945 ext. 5442 or by email at MacmillanSpecialMarkets@macmillan.com.

Library of Congress Cataloging-in-Publication Data is available.

First edition, 2023
Book design by Meg Sayre
Boxing belt © by Martial Red/Shutterstock
Printed in the United States of America

ISBN 978-0-374-38845-4
1 3 5 7 9 10 8 6 4 2

Alondra

For Kimberlee & Carolina

Alondra

June

☆ **1** ☆

"YO, YO, YO, WHAT'S UP? THIS IS YOUR BOY PRETZEL COMING AT *you live from Coney Island with the match of the century, the fight of the summer—and it ain't even really summer yet! Do me a favor and lemme hear you make some noise!!"*

"*Who d'you think you're talkin' to, man?*"

"*Yeah, nobody's here but us!*"

"*I'm just setting the stage—you ever heard've dramatic openings?*"

It was hot.

Mad hot.

The kinda hot that made the air wet, that crawled its way deep inside Alonda's skin and, even worse, made her bangs frizz. She couldn't shake it, couldn't escape it, and damn, it was only June and already feeling like August. She'd glare at the heat if it had a face to glare at, give it a good cold stare and tell it to eff off or something.

"*You gonna call this match or what?*"

"*Hey, don't rush me, it's all a part of the process.*"

It was for sure too hot for whoever was making so much noise outside. Alonda stomped over to the window and looked out. If she couldn't glare at the heat, she could at least glare at them, whoever was disturbing her postschool, pre-Teresa afternoon peace.

Teresa was usually home by the time she got home, but if the trains were sucking (as the trains were known to do) it meant Alonda had some time to herself. And she had been reading, sprawled out on the couch in the living room; she especially liked how the late afternoon light hit the window as she read, the peaceful hum of the fridge as it turned on and off scoring the worlds she was visiting in her book, knowing that she wouldn't be disturbed by any of Teresa's nonsense—but how was a person supposed to concentrate with all that noise barreling through the window?!

"You know what else is a part of the process? Actually wrestling."

"Yo, gimme some time! Everybody loves the commentator!"

Being on the fifth floor didn't help with the heat—the apartment was stifling. She'd felt it as soon as she got home from school, walking up the stairs, the heat getting more and more thick and ominous as she went till she opened the door to her apartment and breathed in the stale, hot air. She'd pulled her thick black hair into a big messy bun as she stomped over to her book, trying to concentrate on the words but using the pages to fan herself every couple of sentences instead.

She pulled up the screen to the window and stuck her head outside it, far as it would go. She could almost trick herself into feeling a breeze that way.

She looked at the playground below—that's where they were, the disruptors of Alonda's peace, four of them, all about her age, looked like three guys and a girl, all of them yelling, but two of them in the middle of a wrestling match. Like, full-out pretending to wrestle—the girl, she was short, Black with dark brown skin, her long box braids flying in the air, sun bouncing off the neon pink tank top she wore with baggy denim shorts. She had her arms wrapped around the tallest guy's waist, pretending to try to flip him over but doing a sloppy job at it.

"Yo, you need to do a tighter grip!" Alonda could hear him say with an eye roll in his voice.

He was really tall, looked like a clear foot taller than the girl, Black with lighter brown skin, and even from the window Alonda could see how toned he was. He wore a tight-fitting gray tank top and gym shorts, looked more prepared for wrestling than the others there.

"All right, here it goes!" the girl said, clearly pretending to try to flip him over, but she was so obviously faking it, her grip was too loose around his waist, and he wasn't even trying to sell the move, so it didn't look like he was trapped or struggling to get out of her grip at all. He was just kinda standing there, half-heartedly waving his arms around. Alonda stifled a laugh. He kinda looked like one of those inflatable tubey-looking things that flap their arms around in the wind.

Looked like fun, though.

They were making a ruckus, but nobody around them was really paying attention, everyone going about their business unbothered. Like, Alonda could see Ms. Wong cutting through the park, coming back from the Key Foods probably, worn old Mets cap shielding her face from the sun as she pushed her cart overflowing with grocery bags across the way, Becky from B3 sitting on a bench, purple hair done up in a high ponytail and talking a mile a second into a bedazzled cell phone. It looked like Big Ricky from the apartment downstairs had fallen asleep on a bench that was in a clutch spot of shade, a paper bag in his lap and small boom box whispering out '90s hip-hop at his feet.

The playground area sat in the center of the public park on the corner next to Alonda's building. It was fine as playgrounds go, a little janky and usually abandoned, but not now. The wrestlers were all gathered in a spot between the jungle gym and the swings where there was mad padding, perfect for cushioning falls and skinning knees without breaking them. They were real, full-on wrestling— real WWE-style wrestling, not the kind that was in the Olympics and shit—or they were at least trying to. They was pretty sloppy at it.

But it was pretty cool.

Unlike this weather.

Alonda eyed the beat-up portable fan out from the corner of her eye. It was on the coffee table, but it was also Teresa's, and she had deep feelings about Alonda using what she deemed her stuff, so she didn't wanna risk it—Teresa could be home any second, and Alonda didn't wanna count on her having a good day, specially since she never seemed to have a good day on any day that ended with the word *day*. Only thing that seemed to make her less cranky these days was Jim, and he wasn't going to be around till the weekend, at least.

Alonda stuck her head farther out the window and tried to take in the view. She forgot how good Coney Island could look sometimes. Shit like that happens when you're in a spot long enough, and Alonda had been here pretty much her whole life. Seventeen years of the same view, the same crummy wallpaper, the same tired floors. Okay, well, technically not this crummy wallpaper or these tired floors; she hadn't always lived with Teresa. When Mami was alive, she'd lived on the floor below with her, where Big Ricky lived now, but Alonda could barely remember it. Besides, Mami and

Teresa had been over each other's homes so much, she couldn't really keep track of where her memories took place. Like, she could remember playing on the crappy linoleum floor with plastic blocks that were chewed around the edges ('cause she used to chew whatever she could chew on), and her mom putting on some salsa and dancing so hard that the neighbors downstairs pounded the ceiling, but Teresa was always there, dancing right alongside her mom, so who knew where it was, downstairs or here. And who knew if that was something that actually happened and not just something she dreamed up—Mami and Teresa both dancing, laughing, and happy.

Alonda shook her head, trying to get the memories to fall out her ears. It wasn't that she didn't wanna think about her mom, it was just that sometimes memories had a weight to them that she was too tired to carry right now.

"And King tries to swat the Incredible Lexi off his back—"

The commentator's voice drew her eyes back down where the wrestlers had resumed their match. The girl—she must be Lexi—had somehow climbed her way onto the tall guy's—King's—back. He was swinging her around, trying to get her off him, but she had her legs wrapped around his chest and arms wrapped around his head. Alonda smiled—it was a kinda funny picture.

"Get off!" King shouted, swinging the girl around.

"Say it in character!" Lexi shouted gleefully, not loosening her grip.

"—and it don't seem to be working . . ."

"My character's mad annoyed right now," King said, continuing to try to swing her off.

"Yo, you need to let go of him! Otherwise you're just gonna be spinning in circles forever," another guy shouted from the sidelines, pacing back and forth in frustration. He was shorter than King but taller than the commentator, and sweatier than all of them, his light brown skin looking shiny with sweat even though he wasn't doing nothing but watching.

"Good! Then I guess that means I'm winning, Spider!" Lexi shouted back at him. Alonda's mouth twitched into a smile. Spider seemed like a great name for a guy wearing a bright red Spider-Man T-shirt.

"Can't be winning if nothing's happening! You're really cramping my creativity, Lexi," the commentator shouted back, running a hand alongside his blond, heavily gelled hair. He wore a white T-shirt that looked like it was ten sizes too big for his small frame. Even from the fifth floor, Alonda could see the pink pimples that dotted his white skin.

She'd never seen them before, the wrestlers.

Well, no, that wasn't true; they all looked vaguely familiar, just like anybody who'd lived here most of their lives, which they probably had. Like, had she seen that guy—King, the one spinning with the girl on his back—the girl the commentator had called the Incredible Lexi . . . like, had Alonda seen King on a subway platform or seen Lexi hanging out on the boardwalk or even the four of them just chilling at that park on the corner before?

Probably.

But she probably never paid them any attention, especially if they were just walking around or whatever. She usually just blocked people out until they became part of the backdrop of her mind, like the buzz of the city. So yeah, all the wrestlers, they looked vaguely familiar, they were all as much a part of the scenery as Coney Island was—or as she was to the rest of Coney Island, just a fact she took for granted.

They'd never been wrestling before, though.

That, Alonda would've remembered.

That would've been a reason to pay attention.

Wrestling was Alonda's favorite thing in the entire world; it was an unspoken agreement between her and Teresa that every Monday night the TV was hers for three hours and she was not to be interrupted (just like how Alonda left Teresa alone for her Wednesday night *Real Housewives of Whatever City* marathons). Alonda'd sit in front of the TV on their fuzzy rug with a stack of Oreos and freezing-cold milk, and she'd watch wrestling. And it wasn't just on Monday nights, either; she filled all her spare moments with it, subscribed to YouTube channels and podcasts that talked at length about all the happenings in the wrestling world, the commercial world, the independent world, even had some action figures hidden under her bed, not that anybody needed to know about their existences or nothing. There was just a few, anyway, left over from when she was a kid, and though she had plenty of opportunities to throw them out, she couldn't quite bring herself to do it.

"Lexi's got King pinned to the ground—will he tap out?!"

Sometimes, she'd imagine it.

Like, imagine herself in the ring. For real, though, not like what the four in the playground was doing. She imagined herself doing it for real, in the middle of an arena with tens of thousands of fans screaming and cheering, lights flashing, music booming. Entrances were, like, at least a quarter of the fun of it all, and she'd come out scored to something super tight like to Snow Tha Product or Angel

Haze or the theme from *Jaws*, something dope like that. She closed her eyes, letting the image soak her brain.

The beat drops and Alonda enters, raising her hands to the sky, soaking in the cheers from the crowd. Everybody loves her, and she stops every couple of feet to kiss a baby or pose for a picture or just give an encouraging smile to an old lady. She gets to the edge of the ring and tightens her hair into a ponytail (her hair would definitely be pink!) before she leaps into the ring.

The music cuts off, and the crowd quiets down to a rustle as the announcer says,

"The following contest is scheduled for one fall."

"One fall!" the crowd echoes back, a tradition for the start of any match.

Alonda turns to look at her opponent: her most worthy rival, the Incredible Lexi. Lexi raises her arms as she turns toward the crowd. She's dressed in all neon-green leather, a stark contrast to Alonda's sparkly pink outfit.

"At the sound of the bell—"

The air is stretched thin with anticipation.

They turn to face each other.

Alonda hops from foot to foot, ready.

Lexi cracks her knuckles, ready.

"We want a good clean match, all right?"

Alonda can't help but notice how pretty Lexi is.

"...and here we go!"

The sound of the bell cuts the air in half, and the two are off as they run toward each other and—

"Christ, Alonda, you're smelling ripe."

The fantasy burst like a pimple.

Damn.

Teresa was home.

"You hearing me, Alonda, or what?"

Yeah, Alonda heard her, but she didn't wanna answer. If she could live inside the fantasy for a little bit longer, maybe she could make Teresa disappear, maybe she could go down and wrestle with all of them, maybe—

"What'd I tell you, you gotta put on deodorant when it's ninety degrees out—"

"I *did* put on deodorant."

"Then why do I smell you from here?"

"I dunno. It ain't me," Alonda said, squaring her shoulders and sticking her head farther out the window.

They were back to arguing out there about whose turn it was.

She could hear the hiss of a spray can followed by the lemony scent of fake flowers. Teresa spraying air freshener all over the place. God, she was being so extra!

"You really shouldn't have the screen up like that, you're gonna let all the bugs in," Teresa grumbled from behind her. When Teresa got annoyed, her vowels kinda exploded out her mouth even more than they already did. She had that old-school Brooklyn-Italian accent, and Alonda knew the deeper the vowels, the more annoyed Teresa was getting, and right now, they was going pretty deep.

"Heat's killing all the bugs."

"Yeah, you wish, their wings are like their own personal portable fans, makes 'em, like, cool down so they fly even harder in the summer."

Alonda rolled her eyes as hard as she could. "Yeah, I don't think that's how it works."

"You dunno that's *not* how it works."

Alonda shrugged and stuck her head farther out the window.

"Come on, Alonda, get your head back inside before you fall and smash your head against the sidewalk like a watermelon," Teresa grumbled. "It's too hot to figure out how to clean up all that mess."

"I'm fine," Alonda shot back. But she did pull her head a little farther back inside. She could hear Teresa shedding her work self for her home self, taking her shirt from her pencil skirt, kicking off her shoes, putting on her raggedy-ass slippers, and switching on her portable fan. She sneaked a glance over her shoulder. Teresa's dark-blond hair looked limp (and in need of a fresh perm), and her makeup was smudged around her eyes, a big glop of mascara stuck in one of the lashes, and she looked sorta sallow under her olive-toned skin.

Damn, it looked like she had A Day at work.

"Goddamn this heat," Teresa muttered, throwing her slippers off her feet. "Too hot for me to even keep my slippers on, goddamn, goddamn! Just gonna let my feet stick to the linoleum, I don't care or—no, even better, just gonna put my feet up so all they gotta touch is air."

Alonda made a noncommittal throat noise from the window. She was used to Teresa monologuing her grievances. As long as she acted like she was listening, Teresa would keep going and Alonda could keep watching the wrestlers, and the world, outside.

Alonda heard her pick up the remote.

"TV don't work," she said, still facing the window.

"What the hell, why not?"

"Rolling brownout crap. Been happening since I got home,

people all using their air conditioners and fans 'cause it's so hot, probably. We don't got internet right now, either."

"Damn, I hate the heat."

"Yeah, it ruins everything."

The wrestlers were still yelling at one another, but their words were getting sucked up by the breeze that had finally started blowing, like it remembered they was near the ocean or something and that there should be a breeze blowing out here. Alonda could almost see the ocean if she squinted hard enough and made her head go a certain angle, if she looked past the corner stores and pizzerias and bodegas; beyond all that, she could see Coney Island stretching in front of her like a kingdom.

"Starting to be a breeze out there," Alonda reported.

"Yeah?" Teresa asked, perking up a bit.

"Yeah. Looks like it might be a cool night at least."

Teresa sighed deep. "Thank God. I dunno how much of this I can take. It's this friggin hot already and it's barely June, what's summer gonna be like?" Alonda nodded at the world outside the window. What would Summer be like? Sure, Teresa was talking about the season, but Alonda was talking about the Summer. Like, capital-S Summer. Like, no school, endless days Summer. She could see it stretching out in front of her, as monotonous and never-ending as the ocean. She looked down at the wrestlers.

But maybe it could be different.

"Gonna be like sitting inside an exploding volcano, I think," Alonda said to the air. She heard Teresa snort behind her.

"Yeah, I think so, too."

Alonda smiled. She liked making Teresa laugh. Her and Teresa were like the waves of the ocean; sometimes they were chill. Other times, they crashed. And they could change from chill to crashing in the blink of a second.

"What've I told you, Alonda, you ain't a kid no more. You gotta remember deodorant, especially in this heat."

Like now.

Alonda spun around to face Teresa, crossing her arms. Teresa had the little fan under her shirt, probably trying to dry wherever the sweat leaked into her crevices, under her boobs, inside her armpits.

"For the last time, it ain't me. You're smelling, I dunno, the garbage or something, it's in the kitchen cooking in this heat, we should really get AC."

Teresa made a face. "We don't need AC!"

"No, but I—"

"And why's the garbage baking in the heat inside the kitchen and not downstairs and outside in the alley like it's supposed to be?"

Alonda felt her tongue roll up into her mouth. Because she hadn't taken it out yet. Oops.

"I mean, I dunno, it's just. Leftover garbage, probably."

"Leftover garbage probably, my ass," Teresa muttered, taking out her phone and holding it in her hands like it was precious metal. Probably texting Jim if the soft smile on her face indicated anything. She really seemed to like him.

Alonda took advantage of the distraction and nonchalantly whiffed her armpits, and . . . well, yeah, okay, there was a slight scent, but come on, everything had a slight odor to it right now and she was home, wasn't she? Nobody was here to smell her except Teresa and her sharp nose that could smell anything and everything, and she could be overly hypercritical of smells, so what's it matter, damn!

"You do your homework yet?"

"No." Alonda peeked outside, but the wrestlers had stopped fully, just sitting on the ground, chilling now. The guy wearing the Spider-Man shirt was holding his comic and gesturing wildly with it while the others watched. The wrestling had looked like fun, but somehow, this looked even better.

"You waiting for an invitation? To do your homework?"

"No." Alonda allowed herself one last glance out the window before retreating inside, turning her back on the outside world and resigning herself to the living room with Teresa.

"You planning on doing it anytime soon or what?"

"It's barely five o'clock—I got all night, damn! Besides, it's all easy stuff. Teachers are mostly already on summer break in their minds."

"You still got a few weeks of school left, don't think I don't know things, I know things, I read the memos from the PTA even though you don't show 'em to me—"

"Don't go through my stuff!" Alonda shouted, a little bit vindicated. She *knew* Teresa had gone through her shit but hadn't had the evidence until now.

"Uh, excuse me, they email the memos, now, too, just in case they get lost in transit. School knows what's up. You're not the only one hip to the twenty-first century, you know," Teresa said, eyes still glued on her phone. Alonda wrinkled her brow.

"Wait . . . *you* have . . . an email?" she asked, mock confusion in her voice. "An electronic mailing address? Wow, do you know how the internet works? Do you need a lesson? I know it was invented after your olden days."

Teresa gave her a sharp look. "You trying to be cute with me right now or what?"

"Who? Me? Cute?" Alonda scrunched up her face at Teresa, sticking out her tongue and wagging it around. Teresa swatted her away, but she started smiling.

"Don't make me laugh. It's too hot to laugh."

Alonda stuck her tongue out one final time before she turned and started walking away, out of the living room and toward her room.

"Hey, wait, where're you going?"

She stopped. Damn. Almost free. Turned back around to face Teresa, putting an angelic smile on her face. "Ain't going nowhere, Teresa, just gonna do my homework. Why, you gonna miss me?"

"Can you help me with this?" Teresa asked, pulling a tangled set of keys out of her bag. "I can't get the knots out as good as you."

Alonda's eyes widened at the sight of the mess of keys. "How the hell'd you manage to do that?" she asked.

"I know you're dying to work that knot out, come on, please," Teresa said, doing that same fake angel-voice that Alonda had done a moment before, complete with fake innocent blinking.

Alonda rolled her eyes, "Are you trying to manipulate me right now? Really?" she asked, mockingly annoyed, but Alonda's eyes twitched. She really wanted to work out that knot, damn.

"I'm not manipulating nothing! Just can't get this crap undone as good as you."

Alonda swallowed her sigh and walked over to the couch.

"Thanks, baby," Teresa said, handing her the jangling set of keys. Alonda immediately started picking them apart as carefully as she could. This was a puzzle, and she was gonna solve the hell outta it.

Quiet fell between them, just the sound of each other's breathing filling the space. It was nice. The type of quiet where Alonda could hear her thoughts for a bit.

It had been a lonely school year, though Alonda would never admit it out loud. Bad enough she started junior year in a new school after her teachers encouraged Teresa to send her to one that was more focused on math and science; worse that her best friend, Marlyn, who had lived in the apartment across the hall, moved all the way to California at the same time. Trying to fit into a new school junior year felt like being a fish trying to fly. And her and Marlyn's friendship had dwindled down to the occasional Instagram like. Maybe a comment. Same thing seemed to happen with her friends from her old school, everyone just kinda melting away, jokes in the group chat not making sense anymore, and so what if Alonda'd rather spend time with math than people, math was more interesting than anything anybody else had to say.

But the wrestlers—

"I had to go all the way out to Queens today."

Alonda didn't respond; she didn't want the quiet to go away.

"You listening to me? I had to go all the way out to *Queens* today. You know, the borough, *Queens*," Teresa said, stretching it out far as it would go.

"Yeah, yeah, I'm familiar with geography," Alonda mumbled. She knew the start of a rant when she heard one.

"All the way from Brooklyn! Had to pass through Manhattan— the entire borough of Manhattan—just to deliver some boxes— not just some papers but boxes of papers, too damn cheap to hire a delivery service. 'Why would we hire a delivery service when we got Teresa to deliver shit for us,' that's what that judge thinks, friggin Francis Kelly," Teresa said, spitting his name out like it was snake venom. Alonda nodded; she was very familiar with Francis Kelly, Teresa's work archnemesis.

"Paper's heavy, you don't think it's heavy, but when you get that many papers together, shit's heavy. *Heavy.* Had to stand the whole way there, took an hour just to get off the train and *then* had to walk fifteen minutes from where I got off all the way to where I had to deliver the damn boxes."

Alonda's mind had wandered away from the rant, and she was thinking about the wrestlers again. The guy—King—was as tall as the girl—Lexi—was short. But they looked like they made a good team. If only they could shut up long enough to actually keep wrestling.

"You listening?"

Teresa's voice brought Alonda back to earth.

"Yeah, I hear you."

"Long Island City, up-and-coming my ass."

"Yeah, it's just code word for getting-gentrified."

Teresa laughed in spite of herself. "Yeah, you're right, it sure is. All they used to have down there was warehouses, but developers came in, converted those abandoned buildings into industrial 'luxury' shoeboxes, probably charge five times the rent and call it cool." Alonda nodded and put the freshly untangled keys onto the coffee table.

Teresa was rubbing her foot, pressing her thumb into the center of it. Alonda could see that her feet were stiff with cramps, probably from being stuffed into her heels and running around all day. They also smelled like feet, which was gross. They were cracked and tired, but she did have a fresh pedicure on 'em. Pale lavender.

"You don't have to wear heels, you know, you can wear, like, flats," Alonda said, but Teresa was already looking at her like she had sprouted a second nose. Teresa had that old-fashioned mentality—couldn't leave the house without pantyhose or a full face of makeup and God forbid if she didn't have a fresh manicure every other week, let alone not wear heels to work.

"What, I'm just saying! They're destroying your feet! Obviously," Alonda said, reaching over and giving Teresa's foot a squeeze for emphasis.

"My feet wouldn't be getting destroyed if they didn't have me delivering boxes all over the goddamned city," Teresa started, and Alonda put her on mute, her voice a buzzing as Alonda's mind wandered again to the wrestlers outside. Alonda wondered if they were still there. They probably were, sitting together in the playground, waiting for the sun to make longer shadows on the ground, grabbing a breeze from the water.

"Hey, let's get pizza for dinner," Alonda said.

Teresa shot her a look. She probably interrupted her right in the middle of the big climax of her latest monologue. Alonda leaned into innocence.

"What?! It's too hot for the stove."

Teresa narrowed her eyes and pulled her feet away from Alonda's hands, back onto the couch. "Who's getting pizza, I ain't moving. Now that I got home, I'm staying forever."

"*You* don't have to move, *I'll* go get some from Tony's."

"You're gonna just go get pizza by yourself?" Teresa asked. Alonda felt a twinge of annoyance ripple through her body.

"Yeah, Teresa, I'm literally seventeen, I'm practically an actual adult, I can go by my-full-self two blocks down to Tony's to get us a couple of slices and bring it back like I've done many, many times before."

Teresa bit her bottom lip, chewing off her pale pink lipstick, thinking. Alonda felt her heart beating fast, but she kept her face looking as cool and nonchalant as possible. Teresa had always been overprotective, even since Mami died. It used to not be a big deal when Alonda was little, just a matter of life, but it seemed to have gotten worse the older Alonda had gotten, almost like Teresa couldn't bear to believe that she was getting to be an adult because it meant she couldn't protect her anymore.

But Alonda wasn't nervous about getting the pizza, she'd done that by herself tons of times . . . but she'd have to walk by the wrestlers on her way there and back, and maybe, just maybe, she'd be able to ask them what's up or something.

"We got pasta—"

Alonda was ready for that argument.

"Too hot to boil a full pot of water, come on, Teresa!"

"Nothing wrong with pasta—"

"Nobody said there was anything wrong with pasta. I'm hungry, and it's too hot to run water on the stove, and I really don't wanna make peanut butter and jelly. Come on, Teresa."

"Nothing wrong with peanut butter and jelly."

"Yeah, I know there's nothing *wrong* with it, but I don't want it!—come on! Pleeeease?" Alonda whined, stretching out the word and taking it to different decibels, almost like it was a bad pop song, until Teresa finally cracked.

"Okay, all right, God!"

Alonda clapped her hands as Teresa sighed and dug around the inside of her bra. She pulled out a ten and gave it to Alonda, who took it and immediately recoiled.

"Ugh, it's wet!"

"Use your own money, then," Teresa retorted, unbothered. "You don't like my money, you don't gotta take it."

"Nah, I love your money, it's the best money I ever seen. In fact, I wanna make out with it," Alonda said, pretending to make out with the money. Teresa swatted her away, but she was definitely choking back some laughs.

"I'll be right back," Alonda said, shoving her feet into her sneakers, getting ready to run out the door.

"Hey, what's going on with the job search?"

Alonda shrugged. "Nothing."

"You gotta get something—"

"Yeah, damn, I know! What d'you think, I wanna hang out around here all summer with your smelly feet? Not my fault Domingo's closed—" Alonda's heart still clenched when she thought of it, the bodega she spent most of her summers working at, which had fallen victim to high rents. Still couldn't get a good bacon, egg, and cheese anywhere, damn.

"Luna Park's hiring for the summer at least," Teresa said, floating her hand toward the general direction of the park.

Alonda's face recoiled. "And be around The Tourists all day?"

"They pay good, I hear," Teresa said.

"You heard from where?"

"You know Maria's son, Antonio? Well, she told me that he just got a job down there. They had a career fair—I told you about it—"

"I was at school probably—"

"It was on a Saturday—"

Shit.

"—And he got hired on the spot! If you'd had gone down there, you woulda been hired on the spot, too, probably—"

"Teresa, please," Alonda said, trying to keep the begging out of her voice but failing—she really wanted to see if the wrestlers were still there, and every second they argued was a second closer to them leaving!

Teresa opened her mouth, but the buzzing of her phone cut her off. She looked down at it, distracted by whatever it was saying. "Get one of those big bottles of Pepsi, too," she mumbled, responding to the text.

"Nice!" Alonda said, smiling even wider. The light was still streaming in the window, and the breeze started to float in. Outside was beckoning.

"Make sure it's cold, I don't wanna wait for it to get cold."

"Yeah, yeah, I know!" The wrestlers were probably still out there. She'd pass right by them.

"Pepsi, not Coke."

"Never!"

"Exactly. Hey."

Alonda stopped.

"Gimme a kiss."

Alonda rolled her eyes, but she went over to Teresa and gave her a quick peck on the cheek. It was nice.

"When d'your grades come out?" Teresa asked.

"I dunno. Soon, though."

"Yeah? And how you doing?"

"Good, good."

"You're smart."

Alonda looked at Teresa, trying not to be as surprised as she felt. "Yeah, I know," she said, trying not to show her anything.

"Yeah. I think you can probably be whatever you wanna be. You know?"

Alonda smiled hard. Gave Teresa a huge hug. They lingered like that for a moment before Teresa broke it, turning her head back down to her phone.

"All right, go get the pizza, I'm hungry."

Alonda pocketed the money, unlocked the locks on the door, and turned back to look at Teresa. She was on her phone, looking at some meme or something. Alonda wasn't even sure what she wanted to say but just let it evaporate into her heart, and opened the door.

She swore she could hear the sounds of a crowd cheering as she stepped outside, following her down the hall.

☆ **2** ☆

OKAY, SO ALONDA HAD PUNKED OUT ON TALKING TO THE GROUP.
A couple of times . . . Or, like, more than a couple of times, more like a few times. Sure, she had walked past them to get the pizza, but all four of them had been laughing about something so hard, they was gasping for air, and it seemed like it was *real* funny, so she didn't wanna interrupt whatever it was.

I'll just . . . say "what's up" on the way back, she thought, passing them, trying not to stare. But by the time she was walking back, they were all sitting on the benches chatting normal, but, well, it was still hot out and she had cold Pepsi—*cold Pepsi*—and Teresa had specifically requested she bring it back cold; she couldn't risk it getting warm in that heat, you know? *I'll do it tomorrow*, she thought, scooting past the group. *Tomorrow will be the day I say hey.*

That was Monday.

Today was Friday.

Every day was a tomorrow that never happened.

Turns out it's harder to start a conversation in real life than in one's own brain. Like, Alonda could think of a million ways to say hey, even practiced in the bathroom mirror after a shower, her reflection foggy and confident, but every time she opened her mouth in proximity of the group on the playground, all her words stuck to the roof of her mouth and she couldn't quite figure out how to get them loose with her tongue. Excuses not to talk to them danced in her head every time she passed—she couldn't start a conversation today, she had to get home to do her homework, had to buy some rice for dinner, had to wash her armpits; every excuse seemed like the most important one yet, so she'd scurry past them before they could even notice her and then would just watch them from her window, wishing she was with them.

Mami could start a conversation with anyone, the world just full of friends she hadn't yet met. She'd always tried to get Alonda to pick up that skill, but Alonda had always been shier, more content to dance behind Mami's legs instead of risking a hello. Mami'd be making fun of her if she was around to see her, running past the group.

"What's there to be afraid of," she'd say, "¡yo vivo sin miedo!"

She'd always say shit like that, "I live my life without fear." 'Cause she did.

Alonda tried shaking her mom outta her head, but somehow her voice wouldn't leave, just kept getting louder and louder every day she didn't talk to them.

And they were always out there, always wrestling. Not getting any better at it because, well, they really did need a fourth person to make the pairs even. A triangle of wrestlers meant there was always somebody left out. She knew that if they had four, things would be more even, they would get more done . . . and she'd be great at it.

That was the thing she knew more than anything in the world: She'd be great.

"It's not gonna work—"

"You dunno that it won't—"

Alonda was walking by slowly, her daily eavesdropping on the group. It looked like they were in the midst of a more heated debate than usual.

"Uh yeah, I do know it won't 'cause it literally can't work, 'cause it hasn't *been* working right, and—" King was saying, waving his hands in the air for emphasis. But before he could finish a thought, Lexi cut him off, her energy much more contained to the sketchbook she had open in her lap.

"Right, but it's not that serious—" she started to say, but this time Spider cut her off, his voice lazily floating from under a bench. He was lying under the wooden planks, making shade for himself.

"I mean, it's kinda serious . . . ," he said from under the bench.

"Not if we're doing it for fun!" Lexi retorted.

"Hold up, tell me real quick, which one sounds better," Pretzel said, jumping up and interrupting as though they weren't in the middle of a conversation. "*Innntroducing.* Or, or, or, what about if I did, like, *introDUcing.*"

"Not now, Pretzel!"

Alonda rolled her eyes slightly at Pretzel, the self-appointed announcer. He took his announcer duties way too seriously. The trio obviously had other things on their minds, but Pretzel was standing, staring at the others, his toothpick arms crossed across his scrawny chest, looking at the group expectantly.

"Well?" he asked impatiently, pushing his square-rimmed glasses up the bridge of his sweaty nose.

"'Well,' what?" Spider said, his voice snapping a little, neck craned to look at him from his spot under the bench.

Pretzel looked at him in disbelief. "Well, what?! What do you mean 'Well, what.' Well, which one sounds best?!"

"Which what sounded like what?" Spider snapped back, barely looking up from his comic. Pretzel looked like he was a steam whistle on a teakettle about to burst, his pale face turning red with annoyance.

"Which 'introducing' sounds the best, like the most legit?!"

"There was a difference?" Spider muttered to his comic.

Pretzel looked scandalized. "Uh, yeah, they was all *completely* different, so."

King just shook his head. "Come on, we gotta figure this out 'cause I'm telling you, this shit's not gonna work—"

"You're being so negative, man," Lexi interrupted. She had abandoned her sketchbook and was hanging upside down from the monkey bars, her long braids cascading down. She had tucked her yellow T-shirt into her shorts and was swinging back and forth.

"Yo, I'm not being *negative*," King said, emphasizing his words with a shake of his head, "I'm being a *realist*—"

"How d'you know it's not gonna work if we haven't even tried to do it yet?" Spider asked, peeking his head out from the bench and retreating back into the shade as soon as the sun hit his face.

"Because there's just no way to make it work!"

"It might work," Pretzel said, putting his hands on his hips.

"Pretzel, seriously?" Lexi said, shooting him an upside-down look.

"What?"

"Don't take his side just 'cause you want us to pay attention to your announcement voices or whatever—"

"Just tell me which one's best!"

The three rolled their eyes in unison. It was pretty impressive, Alonda had to admit.

She slowed to a stop, straight-up eavesdropping now (even though, was it really eavesdropping if it was a loud conversation happening on public property?). King raised his hands again, as though he was trying to physically gather their attention in his hands.

"Okay, so here's the situation, right, lemme lay it all out."

"Here we go," Lexi muttered.

King shot her a look. "You got something to say?"

"Nothing," she said, smiling big and swinging back and forth a little bit. King opened his mouth to continue, but Spider interrupted him.

"What's the situation, just say it."

"I'm trying to say it, but y'all keep on talking over me!" he said, his voice getting close to a whine.

"Fine, fine," Lexi said, somehow crossing her arms still upside down. "Say what you're gonna say, we're not gonna interrupt you."

King gave Lexi a look, but she just pretended to button up her lips. "Okay," he continued, "so there's only three of us. And we got Spider being a heel, Lexi being a face, and me, the antihero."

Oooooh, Alonda suddenly understood what they were going on about. In wrestling, characters had different archetypes. Faces were the heroes, the characters who fought with some kinda honor to them, who rarely cheated, who played by the agreed-upon rules, while heels were the villains, characters who often lied, cheated, and manipulated their way to victories. And then, much less common were the antiheroes, characters who weren't on either side, just out for themselves. Usually characters switched between the archetypes (if their careers were long enough), so nobody was ever pure "good guy" or "bad guy." It had more to do with a character's motivation to step into the ring and fight than anything else.

"Come on, we'll figure this out later," Lexi said again, swinging herself to the ground.

She landed heavily, her feet thumping on the padding, though she seemed a little woozy. "Whoa, head rush!" she said. "I feel like I'm floating!"

Alonda held back a giggle. Lexi had her arms out like she was trying to catch a breeze and fly away.

"You're always saying we're gonna figure it out later, and then we never do!" King said, throwing his arms in the air. Instead of his voice getting louder, it seemed to get higher and hit a pitch that was a full-on whine.

Alonda understood the annoyance. With three people, it made things mad lopsided. Like, you could never really get a good feud going because one person would have to be doing double duty and it just wouldn't make sense.

"Why're you so hung up on being an 'antihero'?" Lexi said, putting huge air quotes around the word *antihero*. "You really think that Stone Cold Steve Austin went into his shit being, like, I'mma be an antihero? Or maaaaybe that's just what he, like, evolved into naturally—"

King was already shaking his head. "Even if *he* didn't say 'That's what I'm gonna do,' it's what *I* wanna do."

"So what you're saying is, 'We really need a fourth.' Just like I been saying all year," Spider muttered, aggressively shutting one comic, picking up another, and starting it.

"You sure Tania said she didn't wanna wrestle with us?" Lexi asked Pretzel. He was sitting on the ground, probably playing some kinda game on his phone from the look of concentration that etched itself across his forehead. He shrugged without looking up.

"Uh, I dunno, what does 'I'd rather walk out into the middle of the ocean till I meet the mermaids and they make me one of their own' mean? Is that a yes or a no, what do you think."

"I honestly have no idea. Who says shit like that?" Spider asked.

"It's a pretty solid no, gotta say," Pretzel said. "What about that guy you're seeing, Spider?"

"What guy," Spider said flatly.

King and Lexi exchanged a glance, but Pretzel didn't get the memo. "You know, your boyfriend . . ."

"Shh, Pretzel, damn!" King said.

"Oh, you mean my EX-boyfriend?" Spider asked, throwing out the word like it was a poison dart.

Pretzel flinched. "Sorry, man," he said.

"There's gotta be someone else we can ask," Spider said, clearly choosing to pretend like that last bit of conversation never happened. "What about that guy, real white, kinda short, lives in your building—" Spider said, looking to King.

"Max?"

"Yeah!"

"Can't, he's got summer school."

"What about that kid Matt—" Pretzel started, but King answered before he could finish.

"Said it sounded too dangerous."

"Why're you just naming cis-dudes, damn."

"All right, Lexi, you know anyone of any other gender who might wanna partake?"

"I'm just saying, your circle's, like, mad limited."

"I can do it."

The group stopped what they were doing and looked at Alonda as though she was a tree that had suddenly started talking.

Oh shit, had she actually said that out loud?

"You say something?" King crossed his arms, looking at Alonda. She was suddenly very aware of how sweaty her face was and how damp her underarms felt. Teresa's voice filled her brain: *"You gotta be more careful with how you smell—the heat makes you stink!"*—or whatever nonsense she was saying earlier in the week. She folded her own arms across her chest and tried to look cool despite having a gigantic backpack on her back.

"I . . . uh, was just . . ."

It was impossible to be cool with a gigantic backpack on your back. She felt like a turtle, and a sweaty turtle at that, droplets of sweat rolling down her back and into her butt crack, but she was determined to pretend like none of that was happening, like she was cool, like she was composed.

"Just say hello." Mami's voice echoed in her ears.

Dammit, Mami, okay.

No going back now.

She cleared her throat. "I said, I can, I can help you out if you need help or you know . . . whatever."

King licked his lips and walked closer to her. "Oh, so you know about wrestling?" he asked. His voice was low and smooth, ran out his mouth and hit her ears like a tickle that ran up her spine, making her stand taller.

"For sure. Probably as much as you. If not more," she said, trying to be as chill and nonchalant as possible.

"I mean, that's cool," Spider said, rolling awkwardly forward from underneath the bench. Close up, she could see that he was the type who sweated, even when he was doing nothing but standing still. His skin was a little bit of a lighter brown than hers and he kept his honey-colored hair on the longish side; he had it pulled back into a small bun at the top of his head. He shook his hand a little, trying to get the comic that stuck to it off his skin; she could see it was a Spider-Man comic, and that the pile by his feet all contained the web-slinger.

"Fine!" said King, turning back to Alonda. "Then, like I asked before—what do you know about it?"

Alonda squared her shoulders and cleared the squeak out of her throat. She knew what she was talking about. This was her moment to shine.

"Three's a bad number for wrestling. For anything, really, never quite balances out. And you don't wrestle," she said to Pretzel, who abruptly stopped laughing and nodded.

"Yeah, I don't *do* sweat," he said, running a hand alongside his perfectly gelled hair. "Can't mess with perfectch," he said, cutting the word *perfection* off as though it was a thing. She just gave him a look before turning back to King, a smirk dancing across her face.

"And when shit's not even, someone's always left out, so you can't really build matches or feuds or even fights because nothing's even. I mean obviously you all can't help but suck. That part's not your fault. Just seems like you'd get a helluva lot more done if you had a fourth."

She couldn't tell by their expressions if they was impressed or if they thought she had sprouted an extra nose or something.

Oh shit, *had* she sprouted an extra nose?

Alonda felt like the sun was crawling inside her face, and she suddenly had no idea what the hell she was supposed to do with her arms. "So, yeah," she said, fiddling with the straps of her backpack, "I'm just saying if you need someone else, I'd be down. I'm chill. Or . . . whatever . . ." She trailed off, losing steam.

Ugh. How hard would it be to will a hole to open in the earth and swallow her up? They were all still staring silently. She took a deep breath and nodded.

"Well, okay, guess not! I should go—"

"Who the hell are you again?"

King's voice was deep and great, even if it sounded not the friendliest right now. It melted Alonda's insides.

"God, King, what the hell is that!" hissed Spider from beside him.

"What?" King shot back at him.

"Why you gotta say it like that, like '*Who the hell are you again,*' ew!"

King rolled his eyes at him. "How else I'm supposed to ask it?!"

"Like normal, like 'I didn't catch your name, what is it?'"

"Don't censor the way I ask things!"

"I didn't say," Alonda squeaked out. She cleared her throat and tried again. "I mean, I didn't say what my name was, actually," she said. "That's why you don't know it."

"Yeah, okay, so you don't got a name?"

"King!" the trio said in unison.

"What?!"

"You are being so RUDE!" Lexi said, turning to Alonda. "Seriously, don't mind him, I think he's just got sand in his pants today. It's making him itch."

"I do not!" King started to say, but Lexi kept going, talking over him.

"I'm Lexi, hi," she said, her dark brown eyes warm and friendly.

"Alonda," she whispered, her voice sticking to her throat like sandpaper. She cleared it again. "My name is Alonda. And I . . . I actually . . . seen you? From my window? Wrestling?" she said. She didn't mean to make that last statement into a question, but here she was. She gestured toward her building, on the corner next to them. "Yeah, I mean, I live right there, and so I got a pretty good, you know, view of all y'all and, like, can hear you 'cause you're all mad loud or whatever—"

"You been stalking us, Alabama?" King asked her, interrupting her rambling. He held his gaze steady with hers, raising his thick eyebrows at her.

"Jesus, King," Lexi said, rolling her eyes.

That pissed Alonda right off. Her name didn't sound nothing like Alabama! King was just messing with her. Her eyes narrowed. She suddenly got it.

This was a test. And she was gonna pass it.

She was mad good at passing tests.

"I don't gotta go outta my way to stalk you, I got better things to do with my time. Nah, it's like I said, I live right there and you're all so loud, s'hard not to notice."

"Been watching our sick moves, right?" said Spider. He was sitting again, fanning himself with one of his comics. He hoisted himself to his feet with a grunt and a stretch, then walked over to stand beside Pretzel, dusting orange crumbs from his shorts. "Damn, I sat on my Cheetos!"

Alonda scoffed. "I would be watching your 'sick moves' if there was any moves to be watching. Spend more time arguing than doing any actual wrestling." Pretzel made a noise like a cough getting stuck in a mouth. Sounded almost like it was a laugh.

King's eyes flickered over to Pretzel before they narrowed steadily on Alonda.

"That ain't true."

But Lexi started laughing, too, adding to Pretzel's laugh. "Yeah it is! We're mad good at arguing, though, so at least we got that going for us," she said with a shrug and a grin.

Lexi's laughter gave Alonda some more courage. "Yeah, if arguing was wrestling, you'd all be airing on TV right now. Too bad it ain't. Besides, the wrestling you do, when you do get to it, is really sloppy."

"Oh yeah, that's super true," Spider said.

"Yeah, that's because none'a you practice as much as me!" King whined again, losing the sharpness of his tone, but the three kept on laughing.

Alonda used the laughter to her advantage.

"Right, and it's hard to practice when there's not enough people to keep it even, to practice with. So . . . ," she said again, trailing off and vaguely pointing to herself.

"Yeah?" King snapped, crossing his arms. "And you're suggesting you?"

"I mean, you know, like . . . yeah . . . ," said Alonda, gesturing to herself, a move which looked really cool when she imagined it in her head but in real life looked more like she was trying to swat away a rabid wasp. Shitshitshit, what did people do with their hands?! She decided to try to hook them in her jeans and act like she wasn't being the most awkward person in the universe.

The three guys stood shoulder to shoulder, all their arms crossed, sizing her up. Lexi gave them a look and rolled her eyes.

"You're all being so aggro right now—calm down!" she said. She turned to Alonda.

"I think what they mean to say is we're pretty serious about this. And we don't know you. And we're looking for someone who is equally, if not more, serious, too," said Lexi. Spider nodded, his eyebrows dancing up and down into his forehead like he was The Rock.

"Here's the thing, though, we don't even know if you're cool," King said, throwing the words out like they was daggers.

Pretzel and Spider nodded. "That's a good point," Spider said.

Alonda froze up. There were a lot of things she thought she was— she was smart as hell, sarcastic, cynical, realistic. But cool? What was their definition of the word *cool* anyway? Alonda opened her mouth to ask that, but closed it again in a hurry. Cool people didn't ask shit like that. Alonda wanted to be cool; she desperately wanted to be cool. But . . . they couldn't know that.

"Oh well, but the thing is," she said, jutting her chin out a little, "I am cool."

King smirked. "I dunno, you seem pretty basic to me."

Alonda glared. "I am not basic."

King doubled down. "Do you even like wrestling?"

"Uh, you're right," Alonda said lightly, looking at her nails as nonchalantly as possible. "You're right, I don't like wrestling." Spider's and Pretzel's faces fell, but King's looked triumphant. Lexi just watched silently, waiting.

"I don't like it, I love it. Ask me anything."

"Fine," said King, stepping forward to size her up. "I got one for you. Who's your favorite wrestler?"

Alonda smiled. Oh yeah, a classic question, one of the most important ones. Any good wrestling fan spends hours poring over wrestlers, comparing their best matches, thinking about their pros, cons, and choosing themselves a favorite. And she bet she knew what King was gonna assume she'd say.

She cracked her knuckles. This was gonna be fun.

She let her backpack fall to her feet, stretched out her arms, and put on the sweetest voice she could muster. "John Cena . . ."

She watched the guys dissolve into nonsense; they put their arms up, shouting, "Faaaake!" and started to walk away, and that's when she hit them with a ". . . is what you *think* I'm gonna say!"

They turned back to her, varying degrees of surprise and hope on their faces. Lexi smiled so big, looked like her whole face was gonna split with joy.

"I like you," she said to Alonda, her words warming Alonda's heart in the way the heat couldn't touch.

King raised his chin. "Fine. I'm listening."

Alonda smiled.

"Because he's soooo popular, he's the face of WWE right now, like people who don't even know wrestling know John Cena, he's all over merchandise, he's even a movie star, he was in that summer blockbuster last year—"

"Yeah, he was mad good in that movie, too!" Spider interrupted excitedly.

"Right!" Alonda said, but King elbowed Spider and she got herself back on track.

"But, uh . . . yeah, I mean, most people know who John Cena is right now, so that would be a pretty easy answer to fake, and it's undeniable that he's good. He's mad good, kids love him and cheer for him, grown-ass men pretend to hate him but secretly they love him and cheer for him and his larger-than-life optimistic shit—I mean, come on."

They were all watching her, waiting to hear what she had to say next. Alonda felt powerful, confident. Maybe Mami had always been right and talking to people wasn't so bad. She hopped on the bench and started walking across the edge of the seat like it was a balance beam, a practiced move that looked dangerous, but she knew she looked nonchalantly awesome. She continued:

"But I'm not gonna say John Cena. 'Cause *that's* basic."

She hopped from one bench to the next, continuing her balancing act.

"And hey, I'm not gonna say Triple H or Steve Austin or The Rock because this ain't the nineties—though that was a great era, let's be honest. And even though Undertaker is an all-time great—maybe the all-time best—"

"Pour one out," Spider said solemnly, and Pretzel poured out a little bit of his cherry Gatorade while the rest took a moment of silence for respect. The Undertaker wasn't dead, but he *was* retired, which was almost as bad.

Alonda continued. "But I'm not gonna say Undertaker, either, because you didn't ask me for that, you didn't ask me who the all-time great is, you asked me who my favorite is. And, funny thing about favorites, they don't gotta be the best or the greatest or even good, they just gotta be your favorite. And a favorite's a thing that makes you happy. That, when you think on it, it gives you a warm feeling in the back of your brain, makes you smile."

"So?"

Alonda started, almost losing balance and falling off the bench; she was about to make her grand finale finisher of a revelation, but Lexi's voice startled her. She turned to look at her, excitement coming out her eyes. Alonda's heart did its loop-de-loop, and her breath got caught in her throat. The corner of Lexi's mouth curved into a smile as they made eye contact.

Alonda's heart skipped. "Tell us, who's your favorite?" Lexi asked.

Alonda regained her balance and her stature and paused for dramatic effect. The four of them all leaned forward, waiting to hear what she had to say.

She might have paused a little too long, the four of them looking a little confused.

"Are you . . . gonna say it or . . . ?" Pretzel tentatively asked, genuinely confused.

"Eddie Guerrero," she finally said, hopping off the bench spectacularly.

The others nodded their heads with respect. Eddie Guerrero was one of the greatest wrestlers. He could make anyone look good in the ring, not just himself. But even more than that, he could wrestle any style, be a face or a heel, be super acrobatic and hop off the ropes of the ring in the middle of the air, or be a strong base for his opponents. Some of his matches were Alonda's favorites, and she had them memorized and everything. He died kinda young, before he really got a chance to fully show the world how great he was, but that didn't stop Alonda from binge-watching YouTube videos of him and basking in his greatness while studying his moves. Maybe she could be as good as he was one day.

Maybe.

Alonda looked at the group. "So? Am I in?"

They all looked at one another. "We do need a fourth," Spider offered out. Alonda's heart floated to the top of her head, and a smile spilled out on her face. She was in! She was actually in, but before she could say "Cool!" a voice rang out.

"Can you wrestle?"

It was Lexi, giving Alonda a really skeptical look. Her question melted the smile off Alonda's face. "What?"

Lexi looked at the guys. "I mean, that's the real question we should've been asking, not forcing her to prove her 'coolness' or whatever," she said to the guys, rolling her eyes at them. "I swear, y'all never think of the thing you should be thinking of! 'Cause it's one thing to know stuff about wrestling, but it's another thing to actually have the guts to wrestle. So," she said, turning back to Alonda, "can you wrestle?"

Alonda scoffed. "I dunno, can any of *you*?"

King made a face. "I obviously can!"

Alonda put her hands on her hips. "It's not good enough if one of you thinks you know how to wrestle! Don't get me wrong, you're all sloppy, but you"—she pointed right at Lexi and felt the words tumble off her tongue—"you are the ultimate sloppiest of them all!" The boys all let out a collective, low ooooh! and even Spider seemed to pay more attention to watch the two of them argue.

"I'm not *that* sloppy," Lexi said a little defensively, but Spider shouted out, "My knee would beg to differ," and she gave him a small glare.

"That was one time," she said outta the corner of her mouth.

"Again—tell that to my knee," Spider said.

"Told ya," Alonda said.

"All right, let's see if you can do better, then." Lexi stood and walked toward her, stretching her arms as she went.

"Yeah, I can do better. I can do better than better, in fact, I can be the best!" said Alonda. Somewhere in there she realized how silly she was sounding, but her words were like a runaway train, racing out her mouth.

"We're definitely gonna have to work on your vocal delivery," Pretzel said.

Alonda stood about a full head taller than Lexi, but she was definitely intimidated. "I—I'm not warmed up," Alonda stuttered out.

"So warm up!" Lexi said, jumping up and down a little, wiggling her whole body like she was made of Jell-O. "C'mon, what are you, scared?" Her voice dripped with fake innocence. "'Cause you know, can't wrestle if you're scared." She threw out that last statement as a fact, stretching more.

Alonda's eyes narrowed.

"I'm not scared."

That was technically true—Alonda wasn't scared, she was terrified. But she wasn't gonna admit it.

"Yeah, I may be a little bit overenthusiastic sometimes," said Lexi, stretching out her arms. "I may get too excited and forget what I'm supposed to be doing. And yeah, maybe sometimes that makes people slip outta my arms—"

"I didn't slip—you dropped me! Multiple times!" Spider shouted, but Lexi just talked louder over him, "BUT if you're scared, you don't even stand a chance. Fear don't belong in the ring 'cause it can't. Simple as that. So if you're scared, you can't wrestle." She was gathering her long braids up and tying them together tight to put up and out of her way.

Alonda lifted her chin and tried to make herself look even taller than the five and a half feet she really was.

"I already told you. I ain't scared."

"All right, then prove it! Let's go!"

The guys were moving to the side, clearing out a playing space for the two of them to take over. Lexi kept stretching her upper body, getting her muscles warmed up. Alonda nodded and started stretching, too, trying to kinda copy what Lexi was doing; she didn't know how to stretch anything besides what they did for warm-ups in gym class, but she wasn't about to let any of them see that, so she kept on stretching, pretending like she did this shit all the time.

"All right, Alonda," she whispered silently to herself, "now's the time to put your late-night YouTube-wrestling-wormholes knowledge to use." She'd spent many a long night searching for—and memorizing—videos of how wrestlers did some of the more basic moves—just for fun, just because she wanted to see how they was done. She liked understanding things, looking at the mechanics of a thing to see how it worked. People liked to say that wrestling was all fake, but that wasn't all true—wrestlers knew what the outcome of a match would be, sure. They knew who was gonna win, who was gonna lose—that was all scripted and decided in advance—but that didn't mean the moves they did to get there were fake. Doing those moves required skill and athleticism, and Alonda had studied them so she could spot 'em in real matches, whether she was watching on TV or live in an arena or a rented-out school auditorium. So she knew how to do some moves, knew how to do them pretty well, but it was different practicing by herself rather than doing them with a real stranger, right?

Lexi was bouncing from foot to foot. "Set us up, Pretzel."

She'd worry about that later, in, like, three minutes. Alonda turned to face Lexi. It was now or never. "All right, all right, okay, let's do a . . . a lock up, a knee drop, and then I'll toss you in a fireman's carry."

The guys all looked at her. "*You're* gonna do a fireman's carry?" Spider asked, his voice equal levels skeptical and awestruck. It was a move that would require Alonda to hoist Lexi over her shoulders before throwing her onto the ground. And yeah, okay, maybe she'd only practiced on chairs before, but Alonda was strong, mad strong, and she could do it, she could totally, totally do it. She could tell Lexi would work with her, and that's all that mattered, really.

"You sure about this, Alabama?" King asked.

"Alonda, man. My name's Alonda," she snapped at him, so sharply he had the decency to look chagrined. "And yeah. I'm positive. Unless you're scared?" she said, turning her question to Lexi.

Lexi was full-out smirking at her. "I've never known the taste of fear!" she said gallantly, putting her hands on her hips and puffing her chest out. She was getting into her superhero character, transforming into the Incredible Lexi right before Alonda's very eyes. Which made Alonda self-conscious, because all she knew how to be right now was an awkward disaster.

"I hear it tastes bland, and I'm not about that life!" the Incredible Lexi continued, her hands on her hips and stretching herself out as tall as her five-foot frame could stretch. "Let's see what you can do."

Lexi's eyes made Alonda feel warm, as though the heat of the day had crawled its way inside her heart. Alonda held her gaze, momentarily forgetting there was anybody else on the playground with them. The way Lexi was looking at her, it felt like she might be the only person in the world.

Pretzel's voice broke the spell. "*InTROducing* the undefeated champion, coming at you straight from Coney Island, New York, give it up for the Incredible LEXI!" Lexi raised her arms to the sky and pretended to enter the ring slowly, soaking up invisible cheers.

Spider half-heartedly clapped his hands and let out a small pathetic little "Woo."

"Try harder!" Lexi shot at him out of the corner of her mouth. "The Incredible Lexi is superpowered by your cheers!"

King threw his arms up in the air and cradled his head in his hands. "Just get on with it already!" he begged. "You're taking forever!"

"Right, okay. And her opponent, fresh outta the apartment building on the corner, apparently, it's"—Pretzel stopped short and whisper shouted to Alonda—"yo, you got a wrestling name yet?"

Alonda shook her head. Out of all the fantasies, that's the one that hadn't formed in her head yet. "Just call me Alonda."

Pretzel nodded. "You gonna wanna give it up for ALONDA!!" Alonda raised her arms to the sky and pretended she was entering the ring, but it was weird, like she suddenly didn't know what to do. So she kinda half waved, but her hand jerked itself into a weird fist bump and she choked out a weird-sounding "Yeah!" and she could see outta the corner of her eye the others cringe.

"Okay, uh, we're all just gonna ignore that . . . all right, so, the following contest is scheduled for one fall. At the sound of the bell, we're gonna wanna good clean match, all right? Ready? Set, ding-ding, baby!"

Alonda didn't even have a second to think about how ridiculous Pretzel's fake-ass bell sounded; the two girls ran at each other and immediately got tangled up in each other's arms. Alonda wasn't sure where to put her hands or her arms, but Lexi helped her out. That was the thing about wrestling—the opponents in the ring actually couldn't be mortal enemies in real life, they couldn't for real hate each other 'cause they had to work together, work close together so that they didn't hurt each other, so that they helped each other out in the ring. They had to make each other look good, make sure each other is safe. And that's what Lexi was doing, moving Alonda into the positions so that she could carry out the moves.

First, a lock up. Alonda grabbed Lexi and locked her up in her arms, covering her face and head while Lexi struggled against her. Lexi pretended she couldn't move, acting like she couldn't get out, but she was more in control than Alonda was. Then Alonda lifted Lexi up slightly and pretended to knock her down to the ground—a knee drop. Again, Lexi was the one doing most of the work. Alonda lifted her, sure, but she didn't just drop her down. Lexi collapsed her own body, was in control of when she was gonna fall to the ground that whole time. The thwack she made against the ground sounded more painful than it actually was, but looked super, super cool.

Lexi grabbed Alonda's head in her arms, acting like she was grabbing her head for a move but really, grabbing it so she could secretly whisper into her ear.

"You ready for this?"

Lexi's breath felt moist against her ear, getting caught in Alonda's hair. Her voice sounded rough and wild with the hint of a smile in its whisper.

"You trust me?" Alonda whispered, asking Lexi for real.

Lexi smiled. "I trust you."

Alonda looked her right in the eye.

Smiled.

"Let's go."

Alonda steadied her hands, took a deep breath in, and picked up Lexi and lifted her up, up, up, high over her shoulder.

But Alonda didn't stop there, she kept Lexi's body moving,

soaring through the sky before landing her on the ground, hard but safe and sound.

The guys were all shouting and running toward them, excited because what they just did together, it looked dope as hell. Alonda knew it, she didn't have to see it to know it, she just knew it, felt it in her bones.

They surrounded Alonda, each talking over the other, fighting to be heard, King making plans on how and when to use that move in a match, Spider asking how she did it, and Pretzel asking if she had any water because he was thirsty from all the commentating. Alonda stood in the center, trying to field the tornado of questions whirling at her.

But all she could really see was Lexi's smile, her eyes looking back at her.

"**KNOCK KNOCK.**"

Alonda sighed deeply, scratching the back of her neck.

The sound of sirens racing down Surf Avenue floated through the open windows.

". . . hey, uh. Alonda. Alonda, knock knock?"

Alonda coughed into her arm. Maybe if she kept ignoring him, he'd disappear.

"Yo, knock knock!"

"Come on, Alonda, answer the man!"

"You just gonna keep me hanging?"

No, Alonda did not have any intention of answering him. But she was only prolonging the inevitable. She glanced across the kitchen table. Teresa was looking at her like, *Please just answer him*, as though he was really knocking on her door and Alonda was keeping him out in the cold.

"Yeah, come on, knock knock! Knock knock!" Jim wrapped his knuckles against his glass of Pepsi. Alonda shoved a huge piece of pizza in her mouth and chewed slowly and deliberately, suddenly very interested in their water-stained ceiling.

"Alonda, come on."

She pointed to her mouth and chewed more slowly.

"Hey, hello in there, I'm knocking on the door and I see your light on, I know you're at home!" He started banging on the table, making the paper plates dance. "Come on, knock knock, knock knock!"

Alonda rolled her eyes and stifled a sigh. Jim O'Donnell was the corniest human adult man who had ever stepped foot on the earth's surface, Alonda was sure of it. He loved telling jokes, and his jokes all sucked. It was like he scoured the internet, went to BadJokesDotCom to download this corny shit and regurgitate it back at Alonda like she was five instead of seventeen. But Teresa was looking at her with that look she usually had when Jim was around, that "Please, just play along!" look in her hazel eyes. Alonda hated to admit it, but Teresa seemed to have a full-on crush on this guy. Teresa didn't really bring guys around, and Jim was the first in a really long while. Even if he was a corny white guy, he seemed to make her happy. Damn.

Jim was still knocking on the table, his knocks growing in increasing frequency, more like he was a drummer in a band, so Alonda swallowed her mush of pizza left in her mouth and sighed.

"Who is there?" she asked as flatly as she possibly could.

Jim's blue eyes crinkled with the anticipation of telling his horrible joke. "Turnip."

"Sorry, I dunno any Turnips, I think you got the wrong spot!"

"Alonda . . ." Ugh, she could feel Teresa's glare on her shoulders.

Alonda looked over at her, a picture of pure innocence. "Yes?"

"That's not how the joke goes."

"Isn't it?" Alonda feigned shock and surprise. Damn, she could definitely be an actor if she wanted. Teresa narrowed her eyes. Alonda let out a breathy, garlic-riddled sigh. Okay, fine, she'd play along. She slapped a huge fake smile on her face and looked at Jim.

"Turnip who?"

Jim put his hand toward his ear and straight-up shouted, "Turnip the volume, that's my jam!" and started doing the corniest kinda dance Alonda had ever seen in her whole life, all while sitting and making sounds like his mouth was a bass and everything.

Alonda's mouth fell open into a gape because she could not believe the corny audacity of it all. Jim's cackles filled the air, his pale skin turning bright pink with the force of his laughter. She hated that laugh; it sounded like a cartoon llama was trying to escape his esophagus and crawl through his nostrils, especially now that he was congratulating himself for a joke that wasn't even that good or nothing, shit.

Teresa was laughing, too, snorting her laughs into her hands, wiping away her tears with a piece of paper towel they was using as napkins. Her laughs were more infectious than Jim's and sounded better to Alonda's ears, more like music. She hated to admit that Teresa had rarely laughed as much before Jim came around, only at sitcoms, and even then, she usually would squeeze out a chuckle of acknowledgment, not the full-body laughter that was happening right now.

Still, his joke really wasn't funny.

"You get it?! Do you get it, Alonda?" Jim was still banging the table, giving her a headache with his noise.

"I dunno, maybe you need to explain it to me," Alonda mumbled to her food. Jim's laughs were still dripping out his lips. He took two garlic knots and shoved them in his mouth at the same time. Alonda made a face. So gross.

"Aw, lighten up," Jim said, chewing the knots and smiling his charming smile. "Sometimes things can be funny just 'cause they're funny."

Jim flashed her another smile, this one accompanied by a wink of one of his crystal-blue eyes. Ugh. The man could be charming. Alonda got why Teresa liked him, he was fine looking as far as humans went, she guessed, and he did fix shit around the house, which was definitely convenient. He had a bunch of colorful tattoos on one arm, all making one huge epic painting as they crawled up past his elbow to his shoulder, disappearing under the sleeve of the plain white T-shirt he wore. He called the tattoo painting a sleeve because it covered that arm like a whole sleeve. Had plans to get the second one tattooed, too. He had a scar over one eye and a lot of muscles—Jim worked at JFK airport out in Queens and he'd spend the day lifting luggage and throwing it from the plane to the carousel, from the truck to the plane, all day long. So yeah, Alonda could see the theoretical appeal of Jim, even if he wasn't funny. His humor seemed to have brainwashed Teresa, though, who was still sitting over there giggling about Turnips.

Alonda turned her attention back to Teresa. "I'm done, can I leave?" she asked Teresa. This was a new law that Teresa put into effect and was only for when Jim was around. Alonda hated it—she didn't know why she couldn't just leave the table when she was done eating. Or, like, why they was eating at the table at all, when usually she and Teresa would sit in the living room, watching whatever was on TV and making fun of commercials together. Alonda hated when Jim came over. It meant they'd be behind on all their sitcoms and it'd take forever to catch up again.

Teresa raised a freshly waxed eyebrow at Alonda. "Not everybody's done eating so you're gonna have to wait." Alonda felt her insides start boiling, like her body was making a stew. She still had to do some work for chemistry, but, more importantly, she needed to get to YouTube to study up on how to do a hurricanrana. It'd be a sick move to do if the group could figure out how to pull it off. Alonda had already studied it a couple of times, and it honestly looked like they would be able to pull it off if they could get their shit together long enough to try it out. It was technically a beginner move, but it was tricky as it required being launched into the air and spinning, and Alonda wasn't sure any of them would be able to do it. But King was determined they practice the hurricanrana when they met tomorrow, so she wanted to be sure to memorize the how-to a couple of times before bed, and her chemistry homework was gonna take an hour at least and the night was ticking away and she was stuck at this table fake laughing at Jim's dumbass jokes.

"But . . . I'm done," she said as politely as her mouth could muster.

"Yeah, and not everybody is," Teresa returned overly politely with a hint of edge in it. Alonda looked at Jim's plate, which contained another whole piece of pizza. She groaned internally. He'd already eaten, like, three pieces! The pizza wasn't even that good.

That was a lie; it was mad good.

Alonda looked back at Teresa.

"I understand, but I'm done."

"Just wait."

"Yeah, but—"

"Wait."

"But—"

"So, Alonda!" Jim said, breaking up the verbal volleying. "School's almost out, huh?"

Alonda blinked at him. The go-to subjects: School, the Weather, and Future Plans. She hated them all.

But Teresa was sitting there giving Alonda the "You gonna answer him or what?" look, and Alonda could see her time on YouTube disappearing in the rearview mirror of her mind if she didn't answer. Might as well try to make the best of it. She turned to Jim.

"Yeah," she said, adding a "Two more weeks," for good measure. Jim nodded sagely.

"Getting excited for summer?"

Alonda shook her head no. Teresa made a noise from across the table, prompting Alonda to say words.

"No, Jim, I am not excited for summer," she said robotically. Teresa opened her mouth, and she quickly added in her natural cadence, "I actually hate summer—it's too hot."

"Summer's hot," Teresa said.

Alonda glared at her. "Yeah, but it's *too* hot. We should get AC."

Teresa opened her mouth, and Alonda knew that "We don't need AC!" was gonna come out. Alonda and Teresa argued about it every summer, so much that Alonda could recite the points along by heart. But before she could get the words out of her mouth, Jim butted in. "It's gonna be one of the hottest summers in all of history. I was reading it in this book called the *Farmers' Almanac*, you ever heard of it?"

Alonda shrugged. She could Wikipedia it later. But Jim plowed on with an explanation.

"It's this kinda book that predicts the weather for the year. Farmers use it to predict crops and shit like that, and it takes you through all the seasons. When it got to the summer section, it said all about how this year is gonna be the hottest yet, that the atmosphere is burning up and stuff, that more days are gonna be hot and humid and drier than usual, so yeah, you're probably gonna wanna get an AC."

Teresa nodded. "Yeah, been thinking about it," she said nonchalantly. Alonda had to bite the inside of her mouth to keep it from dropping open. Oh sure, if Jim wants an AC, Jim'll get an AC! That wasn't fair, after she'd spent her whole life asking! Well, if she was gonna play that way . . .

"I wanna dye my hair pink," Alonda blurted out. Jim turned to her, eyes wide, and Teresa threw her hands up in the air with exasperation.

"Not this again," she said, but Alonda cut her rant off.

"I'm just telling Jim! I wanna get his opinion on it." Teresa gave her a look but didn't say nothing.

Jim was looking at Alonda with interest. "Oh yeah?" he asked, chewing around a piece of pizza. Alonda nodded at him.

"Yeah, I think it'd be cool. But Teresa don't want me to do it for some reason."

"Cool, sure, it'll be cool as a cotton candy," Teresa muttered out of the corner of her mouth.

"It will not! It'll look cool," Alonda said. She'd always wanted to dye her hair pink, but she wanted it even extra now that she would be wrestling. Lots of wrestlers had different-colored hair, different from, like, just black or blond or brown; they was usually purple or green or fire-engine red, and Alonda wanted to fall into that category of wrestler.

"Nobody'll give you a job with pink hair!" Teresa said, but Alonda was ready for the argument.

"Actually, that ain't true. Luna Park already gave me a job!"

Teresa looked surprised. "They did?"

"Yeah, I went and applied and they said yeah or whatever," she mumbled. It really hadn't been that hard to get the job; seemed like they wanted to hire a lot of people for the summer and she had all that experience working at the bodega for the past few years. "Sometimes the people we hire at the beginning of the summer decide it's not for them by the middle of the summer," Roberto, the guy who interviewed Alonda, had told her, "so we'll start you on part-time, but there's definitely opportunity for more hours."

Alonda had nodded along, smiled, and said things in her charming adult voice. Her first shift was Saturday.

"When were you gonna tell me this?"

"Right now," Alonda said, but she kept pushing. "And I saw that some of the workers down there have different-colored hair and—"

"Next thing you'll be wanting is a tattoo," Teresa muttered.

"What's wrong with tattoos?" Jim asked, flexing his sleeved arm.

Alonda rolled her eyes. "Not talking about tattoos, I'm talking about *my* hair and—"

But Alonda felt all her words turning into peanut butter inside her mouth. She wanted to argue more but couldn't get the words to unglue from the bottom of her tongue. It wasn't fair. Mami would've let her dye her hair pink, she was sure of it. Yeah, Alonda knew that pink was a weird color for hair, technically not even in the rainbow, but it was her favorite color because it reminded her of Mami. Their place used to be full of pink flowers. Not red, not purple, pink. All different kinds, any kind as long as they was pink. Some of them wasn't even real, they was fake but those were good, too, because that meant they never died and was always around. Teresa didn't like clutter, didn't like flowers, so everything was super neat and bare and there wasn't anything ever around, but Alonda remembered those pink flowers. She'd been wanting to dye her hair pink because of that, too, because maybe making her hair pink would be like getting a hug from Mami on the regular. Like she could be carrying Mami on the outside as much as she was always carrying her on the inside.

Not that she'd tell Teresa that.

Not that she'd ever say it out loud.

"You dye your hair," she muttered in a last feeble attempt.

"Yeah, because've all the gray hairs you give me!" Teresa said, self-consciously running a hand through her blond hair. She went to the salon once a month to get her roots touched up and to gossip. Blond wasn't her natural color, Alonda knew—it was more of a chestnut-y brown with lots of gray streaking through.

"I think you should do it." Jim's scratchy voice broke Alonda's spell. She started a little and looked at him in surprise. Teresa looked taken aback, too, like she wasn't expecting him to take Alonda's side.

"Really?" Alonda asked, skeptical. She didn't trust it. Maybe he was gonna make this another one of his jokes that involved slamming the table again. Maybe he was just making fun of her. But Jim was dead serious, nodding his head and considering her hair.

"Yeah, listen, I know nobody asked me, but I'm sitting right here so I got an opinion and I, personally, I think it's unique. You gotta stand out in this world. Pink, that's a big, bold statement, you know?" Alonda nodded. Hey, the man was making sense. He continued, "I think it'd look nice, like it would bring the rose of your cheeks out. Not that I know any of those technical terms," he quickly added, suddenly a little self-conscious. Alonda puffed up a little bit, happy, turning to Teresa.

"See?!" she said triumphantly. Teresa just folded up her paper plate and shook her head.

"All right, you can leave now," Teresa snapped at Alonda, but

Alonda just smiled more mischievously. Maybe Jim wasn't so bad to have around after all.

"I dunno, I think I wanna stay now and talk more about fashion with Jim," she said, settling down in her seat.

Teresa glared at her harder. "If I hear the words *pink hair* one more time tonight, I'm gonna scream!"

Jim chuckled a little and took a sip of his Pepsi. "Now, come on, Alonda, listen to your mother."

His words knocked the air out of the room. Alonda's blood went cold. Teresa was quiet. Jim realized what he said midsip and tried not to choke on his drink. "Uh, I mean—"

Alonda pushed her seat away from the table. "No, it's all good. Pink hair would look bad, Teresa, you're right. I'm gonna go to my room."

"Clear your place, please," Teresa said quietly. Alonda nodded and grabbed the paper plate and dirty napkins.

"Hey, Alonda," Jim said. She stopped and looked at him. "I really do think you'd look good with pink hair. You should try it if Teresa lets you."

Alonda's mouth tried to twitch into a smile, but she couldn't quite get it all the way there. "Thanks," she said, turning her back to the two and heading to her room. She could hear the two of them murmuring, talking low, but she closed her door slowly, muting their gentle murmurs with a quiet *click*.

"What's up, this is your main dude, Freddy Rocks, here to demonstrate how you can perfect a hurricanrana . . ."

Alonda was trying to concentrate on the video in front of her, but her mind kept wandering away from it, back to what Jim said. It wasn't his fault, a slip of the tongue. Most people lived with parents, right? In the TV world they did, anyway. The image that was pushed to the front of everyone's minds, and even though Alonda knew that image wasn't a true one, it still hurt.

"First thing you're gonna wanna do is make sure you've got a clear runway..."

She always knew that Teresa and her mom weren't blood related—Mami being Puerto Rican and Teresa being Italian—but she also knew that you didn't need blood to be family. And Mami and Teresa, they were sisters.

"... then you just lift the other person up into the air and..."

The way they acted together, people really thought they were sisters, even though they looked nothing alike—Teresa's hair was always bleached blond, even when she was younger, and stick straight when she didn't perm it, and she had green-hazel eyes and olive skin that soaked up the sun in summer as a tan. Mami's skin was always light brown—in summer, a deeper, more golden brown, with the longest, curliest black hair and dark brown eyes that turned a lighter shade in the sun. But when Alonda was younger, Mami and Teresa were always laughing, always walking arm in arm, running up and down the stairs to each other's apartments with gossip or ingredients, whatever.

Alonda slammed her laptop shut. Her mind was unraveling, going all over the place. Her room felt too small. She could hear music softly playing from the living room, slow-ass romantic music, and knew Teresa was out there with Jim, slow dancing to their corny oldies. She opened her chemistry textbook, trying to get caught up in numbers, concrete facts and figures instead of the mysteries that danced around her head.

They never talked about her dad when Mami was alive. No photos, no stories, no conversation. Questions were deflected, flies swatted away. Alonda used to think it was because something terrible happened, that her dad did something unspeakably bad, but she cornered Teresa one day, in the middle of one of their epic fights, the ones that used to explode out regularly right after her mom died, demanding to know about him and all the good he did or all the obvious bad he must've done to not be talked about, that got him ripped away from the backdrop of her life like this. She'd run into her room, slamming the door behind her so hard her portable radio had tumbled off her desk into her wastepaper basket.

Teresa had come in after the fight with some watery instant hot chocolate and the truth. She told her it wasn't that he'd done anything horrible or abandoned them or anything. They just never talked about him because there weren't any stories to tell. No memories passed along, no photos, nothing. It was just one night, with a stranger.

Which was its own kinda sad, the not knowing, the maybe never knowing.

Screw this, Alonda thought, tossing her textbook to the side. The music was still seeping its way in and her brain wouldn't settle and everything felt too tight, the room, her chest, everything. She couldn't take it; she opened her window to the fire escape, pausing to make sure Teresa hadn't somehow magically heard. Nope, music still playing. She carefully climbed out onto the platform of the escape and climbed up the shaky ladder on its side the few steps that led to the roof. Yeah, it was technically not allowed and technically probably dangerous, but she'd been doing it since she moved into this room ten years ago. It was like her own secret passageway, the kind she read about in books or saw in movies, except hers wasn't hidden if you knew how to look.

She climbed over the lip of the roof, landing hard on her feet, and breathed in the night air. There was a coolness clinging to it, a little bit of damp from the ocean. On the roof, she felt like she could really breathe, could feel the whole world rushing into her lungs, could think again.

She dragged out one of the folding chairs that were stashed up there for such an occasion and set it up so she could get a good view of the Parachute Jump, the tall old ride that was no longer a ride but a national landmark instead, all lit up and glowing. The sight of it soothed her, standing there straight and tall, unmoving but bright. She took in its weird-looking shape, a solid base that extended into a long stem to a circular top. It calmed her. She breathed in deep, closing her eyes and letting the nighttime embrace her and letting her thoughts go where she normally hid them. There was more air up here on the roof. She could see the whole neighborhood, the whole world from up here. It eased her memories, let them come at her, slowly and then all at once.

Mami had been healthy. She didn't go to the doctor a lot because she didn't trust doctors. "They don't listen," she'd always say, not as a complaint, as a statement. "I tell them the truth, they think I'm telling a lie. I speak in paragraphs, they pick out three words only and make a whole diagnosis around it. Who has the time?"

The clot that killed Mami, that formed and made its way through her bloodstream until it hit her lungs, it was probably undetectable. That's what they said. So even if she had gone to the doctor, they probably wouldn't have been able to see it.

That's what they said.

She had aches. But so did everyone. She ignored them. 'Cause aches and pains, they were just part of living, pushing through a sharp sting in her chest to the side because it'd go away soon. They were just signs of being alive.

She had a cough, but that was because she smoked. It was her one bad habit. Didn't drink or anything, but cigarettes? She ran through them. And sometimes that cough took her breath away, made it harder for her to breathe, the smoke wrapping its hands around her lungs and squeezing.

There was no way to see it coming.

That's what they said.

Alonda'd looked it up, memorized the signs and symptoms Mami'd probably ignored, pushed to the back of her brain, talked away. She was always saying she was gonna quit smoking, and sometimes she did, but she could never stay fully away.

Mami wasn't at home when it happened. She had collapsed at Waldbaum's, right in front of the frozen vegetables. There used to be a Waldbaum's until it closed. They gutted it, repainted it. Now it was the Key Food. Alonda still couldn't step inside. Even though she wasn't even there when it happened, even though it was brand-new, she couldn't go inside.

It was ten years ago. Alonda had just turned seven. She was at home, Teresa watching her. "Just gotta pick up some groceries real quick." A peck on the head Alonda'd ignored 'cause—why? She was playing with dolls? 'Cause when Mami'd leave, she'd be right back?

Everything after was a blur. At some point, Teresa had been made Alonda's Just In Case of Anything Horrible Happening Legal Guardian since there was nobody else, no other family around. When it came to Alonda, Ava was always prepared. She always thought of worst-case scenarios, even though she never thought they would come true. If she had, she would've stopped smoking. She would've gone to the doctor when her coughs wouldn't stop. She would've had them x-ray her chest just in case. Just in case of anything.

Just in case.

There was nothing magic or poetic about death. Her mother's death sat on her chest like a hole in the center of her body. She sewed it up over and over again, but there was always a hole beneath those invisible stitches.

She pushed her thoughts to the side again, out of her mind, and just looked at the Parachute Jump, blinking brightly in the night, almost like a lighthouse guiding her thoughts to less rocky waters, guiding them back home.

☆ **4** ☆

"YOU AIN'T DOING IT RIGHT!"

"What, no, you're doing it wrong!"

"Maybe you're both just doing it wrong."

"Shut up, Pretzel!"

Alonda held back a sigh and resisted the urge to check the time for the tenth time. They'd been here for, like, fifteen minutes, but nobody had done nothing but argue. She'd never seen such a group of friends that liked arguing with one another as much as they all liked hanging out with one another. It'd only been a few days, but she felt like an extra limb they didn't need, a bent puzzle piece that couldn't quite fit into the picture. She usually just hung back and let them bicker their way to action, joining in whenever they got to that point.

Which always seemed to take forever when they were arguing like this.

"You don't listen to me!"

"Nah, you ain't listening to ME."

King and Lexi stood in the middle of the playground, both of them sweaty and hot from their many attempts at doing the hurricanrana; as Alonda had suspected, it was taking more work than just watching a YouTube video and none of them had figured out how to do it yet. Since King stood over six feet tall and Lexi just barely brushed five feet, he was attempting to launch her off him and into the sky. Lexi was supposed to go spiraling into the air before landing on her feet. But every time they tried to do the move, Lexi couldn't get herself into the air at all. She kept falling to the padded ground like her body was made of bricks. And it didn't matter that it was a tricky move and that it probably took real wrestlers a bunch of times to master it, they were each blaming the other for their failure.

"Look, you're supposed to leap OFF me!" King said, exasperated.

"Yeah, I know what I'm supposed to be doing, but you're making it so that I can't do it!" Lexi grumbled back.

"Maybe take a break so someone else can wrestle?" Spider's voice floated up lazily from the ground, and Alonda turned to look at him.

Spider had given up watching the two and was lying under his bench again, eating Twizzlers and reading. "Some of us wanna turn, too!" he shouted to the two, not taking his eyes off his comic. Spider was always reading comics. Alonda didn't know they made as many comics as Spider could read, but it looked like he always had like ten different ones a day.

"No, we're gonna get this—we've gotta!" King said, a whine starting to creep into his voice. For the one who was the biggest and the strongest and the most dedicated, he could also be the whiniest. "I just wanna practice this move the right way, but we ain't even close to getting it right!"

"Yeah, because you're doing it wrong!"

King let out a groan. "Man, Lexi, it's like you didn't even watch the how-to. How're you supposed to know what to do if you don't watch the how-to?"

"I did, too, watch the how-to!"

"Then why aren't you doing it?!"

"I dunno, because it's not my fault! I'm not the one messing up! I got good instincts!"

"You do not!"

"Do, too!"

"Oh damn, King. You are doing it wrong." Alonda didn't realize she had spoken until she realized the others were staring right at her.

Lexi had a smirk on her face. "I knew it!" she said triumphantly. King glared at Alonda.

"You're lying."

Alonda scowled. "Am not."

"Just trying to make me look bad."

"Man, you don't need any help with that," Alonda shot back at him, which raised a chorus of ooohs from the group. Even Spider looked up from his comic to watch the burn sizzle as it landed.

Pretzel laughed. "She got you, man!"

"Shut up!" King said to Pretzel, but he was looking at Alonda, not with fury in his eyes but with something else. "What d'you mean?"

The words threatened to evaporate in her esophagus, but Alonda shook them loose. "Just that Lexi's right, you are doing it wrong." Lexi snickered. She'd already plopped herself down next to the bench and taken out her sketchbook, doodling something. King glared at her before turning back to Alonda.

"All right, if you're so wise, then how's it done?"

Alonda sighed and got up, walking toward the pair. The sun was beaming again. Made the sweat tickle its way down her back. Maybe Jim was right; it was gonna be a hotter-than-actual-hell kinda summer. She cracked her knuckles nervously. "Okay, so first of all, your hands are all over the place and none of them is the right place. Lexi, where you're putting them is right."

"Okay, so show me," King said. Alonda's heart started beating a little faster. She was gonna have to touch him. Which was fine, that's what wrestling was, but it was still nerve-racking and weird. Like, she still barely knew anyone in the group, not like how they all knew one another, and she wasn't really used to touching anyone yet. It wasn't like she went around touching people on the regular, not like *that* at least. Like people was always bumping into her on the subway, and yeah, she hugged Teresa every once in a while, but she never grabbed anyone's hip or waist. Especially not a basic stranger.

"Everything cool?" King asked, noticing Alonda hesitate. Lexi's words rattled around her head—you can't wrestle if you're scared. So don't be scared.

"Yeah," she said, clearing the fear from her throat, pushing it as far down as it could possibly go. "Yeah, everything's cool. In fact, it's super cool."

King raised his eyebrow. "I dunno if I trust nobody who says super cool," he muttered. Alonda squeaked out what she hoped sounded like a casual laugh as she placed her hands on King's hip and shoulder. His shirt was damp from trying—and failing—at the move so many times. She could feel his muscles. God, he had a lot of muscles. Her heart started pounding. Had she even ever felt muscles before? Not like this, that was for sure.

She shoved her racing thoughts to the side. No, stop it. She was about to wrestle, and wrestlers didn't get distracted by bodies, they used them to do their job. And this was what this was—a job.

"All right, so, I gotta be like this, right?" Alonda said, her hands still in position.

"Yeah, right," said King, confirming.

"And you gotta put your hand on my thigh," said Alonda.

King made a face. "Yeah, see, that's what I been doing!" He moved his hand down to her thigh, and Alonda immediately knew what the issue was.

"Oh, you been holding Lexi wrong!"

"What, no I haven't!" King said defensively, stepping away from Alonda so she almost fell. She crossed her arms, annoyed.

"Dude, why can't you just admit when you do something wrong so you can fix it, instead of just arguing and still being completely wrong?!"

She heard another chorus of ooohs from the group, and Lexi straight-up laughed. Alonda felt a smile creep to her face, though she tried to smash it out with her lip. Come on, this was serious business! "Here, look, I'll show you."

King made a little bit of a show, rolling his shoulders like five times before he got back into position with Alonda. She ignored him and went on, "Okay, so you're grabbing Lexi's thigh, it's true, but you gotta actually be getting, like, the thigh and the . . . her . . ." She felt her cheeks getting warm as she gestured down. "Her ass, you know?"

King just nodded. "Oh, I get it." He started to move his hand toward where she gestured but stopped himself. "Oh, uh, are you comfortable with me putting my hands here?"

"Oh, yeah, yeah, for sure, yeah," Alonda said quickly and as lightly as possible, though she might have said one too many yeahs to be casual. It was weird having the first person to touch her butt be for wrestling, but it was all for a reason. As King moved his hand down, Alonda glanced over at Lexi, who had abandoned her sketch, watching the pair instead. She could swear she saw a flicker of something pass through Lexi's eyes. It made her heart flutter more than King's hand did.

"Like this?" King's voice snapped her back to the present. She nodded at him.

"Yeah, yeah, that's where you gotta be because you're gonna have to help launch Lexi up to your shoulders. Like that's all, that's the only thing you gotta do to get her up there before she tightens her leg and pulls back so you both can fall to the ground or whatever."

King nodded gravely at her. Up close, she could see that his dark brown eyes had little flecks of gold in them. They seemed to go on forever.

"So you gonna do it or what?" Lexi's voice snapped Alonda back to reality, and she stepped away from King.

"Oh, uh, nah, you guys should try it. You been trying." Alonda wanted to try it, was dying to try it, had imagined herself flying through the air while she watched the YouTube last night, but now, confronted with actually doing it? She'd rather be anywhere else. She'd rather be on the moon. Or in bed. Or under her bed, damn, anywhere but here. She started to walk back to the benches.

"Oh, so what, you punking out on me now?" King's words crashed into Alonda like a wave.

She turned slowly to face her accuser. King was standing with his arms crossed and his eyebrows raised, looking directly into her eyes. She looked around. She was surrounded by eager stares, Spider, Pretzel, and Lexi all around.

"I'm not punking out. You two've been messing with it, so you should do it, that's all."

"This move don't belong to nobody," said Lexi. She made a grand, sweeping gesture toward the center of their makeshift ring. "Try it!"

"I mean, I dunno, I—Spider, you wanna try?"

He shook his head, excited. "Nah, I wanna watch this!" It felt like there was a fire rising inside Alonda's stomach, rising up through her body. She turned to Pretzel, but before she could open her mouth, he held up his hand to his freshly gelled hair. Okay, Alonda had officially run out of bodies to ask, unless she wanted to go tap in Big Ricky, who was sleeping soundly on one of the benches, definitely on his way to getting a nasty sunburn by how red his skin was turning, and yeah he was sleeping off his midafternoon high, but still, maybe he could—

"Hey, if you don't wanna do it, you don't have to. It's whatever, for real." King's deep voice cut off her wild thoughts, stopping them in their tracks. He said it rough, but when she looked at him, his eyes looked kind. He wasn't smiling, but his eyes looked so kind. Alonda didn't realize that an eye could look kind, but here she was, staring right at him and his kind eyes.

Lexi snorted. "Just a waste of time, then," she muttered, aggressively erasing part of her sketch so hard it looked like she was gonna tear a hole in the paper.

Alonda felt herself flush. Lexi's words filled her up. She wasn't wasting time. She set her mouth in a straight line, took a deep breath, and walked toward King.

"Nah, obviously I'm gonna do it, I was just acting," Alonda said, putting King's hands back in position on her. "Got you all good, didn't I?" she continued, putting her own hands in position on King.

Lexi snorted. "Yeah, you really got us good," she said a little bit dry.

"I didn't know she was joking," Pretzel said.

Spider punched him in the arm and hissed, "That's because she wasn't, obviously!"

"Ignore them," King said. He looked at Alonda. Damn, he was so tall. "You ready?" he asked.

"I was actually born ready, so yeah, yeah I'm a hundred percent ready," Alonda responded.

"We're gonna have to work on your in-ring talk," Pretzel called from the side. "You can be really long-winded and boring."

Alonda ignored him and placed her hand on King's thigh. They made eye contact again, this time all business. "On three," he muttered low enough for only her to hear. "One, two—"

She could feel his muscles tense up as he lifted her to his shoulders, her legs over his shoulders. Damn, she'd never been this high! King stumbled a little bit but regained his balance, holding on to her thighs. "You cool?" Alonda called down to him.

"Yeah, ready whenever you are," he responded.

She took a deep breath in and pulled herself back, pulling King along with her, down, down, down as they tumbled to the ground. It happened so fast she could barely see it, but she felt it, felt the world turn upside down, felt the air open up as she flew through it, taking King along with her.

She landed hard as she kicked her legs out and found the ground. She stumbled a little bit, the ground came up faster than she expected, but she hit it, the ground was there under her feet and she was right side up and she had just flown, she had flown.

"Holy shit! I'm alive!" she yelled, raising her arms to the air. "I mean, I did it, no sweat," she added as chill as possible.

"Oh damn!" Spider said, shooting up. "You can fly!"

She looked over at King, who had landed on his butt. "You good?" she asked. He nodded, a huge smile on his face. "That was awesome."

Lexi was looking at her, eyes wide. "Easy?" she asked with a small smile.

"Yeah," Alonda said, still a little breathless. "Yeah, it was totally easy. Once you get the hang of it, it's totally, totally easy."

"Yeah, that was pretty dope," Pretzel said sagely.

"All right, lemme try!" Lexi said, throwing her sketchbook into her bag and getting into position with King.

Alonda walked back to the bench, her heart still fluttering with adrenaline, though she wasn't sure it was just because of the hurricanrana.

Time flew by quickly after that, and before Alonda realized it, the small breeze that was blowing was cooler and the sky was starting to turn pink with dusk.

"Shit, I gotta go, it's gonna be dark soon," Spider said, carefully packing his comics back in his bag like they were precious sheets of metal instead of paper.

"Yeah, we're good for the day," King said. Sweat was dripping down his face, but he was smiling big.

"What are you, like, dismissing us?" Pretzel asked. "Since when are you the group president or whatever?"

"You know I been president," King said.

"I dunno if *president* is the right word for it," Lexi said, but King wasn't listening, he was deep in his phone.

"Oh shit, I gotta run, I was supposed to defrost the pork chops for dinner!" he yelled, and darted away before anyone could say goodbye.

"Yo, Spider, is everything set for the parade?" Pretzel asked.

"Yeah, for sure! My sister said she'll be able to drive us over around noon."

"That early?" Lexi asked, shoving her sketchbook into her bag. Spider made a face at her.

"It's not *that* early—"

"Parade don't start until one!" Pretzel said.

"Yeah and it's gonna be mad crowded! We should really be getting there around eleven to make sure we get actual good spots, but whatever," Spider added under his breath.

"Alonda, you going?" Lexi asked lightly.

"Which parade?" Alonda asked, unsure of what they were talking about. She only really kept track of the Puerto Rican Day Parade in the City, which had already passed, and the Mermaid Parade in the neighborhood, which wasn't for another couple of weeks.

"Brooklyn Pride's Saturday," Spider said.

Oh, right. All of June was Pride Month. The big parade in the City was the last Sunday of the month, but there was events throughout the boroughs all month long.

Alonda shrugged, feeling unease drift into her body. "That's out in Bushwick, right? Kinda far," she said. It was a pain in the ass to get all the way out to Manhattan for those parades, but getting to Bushwick from Coney Island wasn't any easier—even though they were both in Brooklyn!

The group was still looking at her expectantly, but she tried to ignore them. She knew it wasn't really an answer, but she didn't really wanna talk about this right now. She wanted to go, but . . . she didn't know if she'd actually belong? Obviously anyone could attend the parade. It was more like, it was something that she was constantly unsure of, her own . . . self? Inside? And she didn't like to think about things that didn't make sense, didn't know where to put her confusion except inside a box inside her chest, which she'd then lock and never allow out. Simple.

"My sister's gonna drive us; she's borrowing the car from her boyfriend!"

"It's really cool, it's so queer and joyful," Pretzel said. "You should definitely come with us!"

"Don't you—I thought you had a girlfriend," Alonda said.

"Well, yeah, but so what?" Pretzel responded, a little sharply. "That don't mean I'm not queer. And anyone can go, anyway, it's not like there's rules against it!"

The secret box inside her chest gave a rattle.

"So you wanna go?" Lexi asked.

"I . . . it's Saturday?" Alonda asked. "Oh shoot, no, I'm actually working." Which was true; it was her first day. In the excitement of everything, she'd forgotten to be nervous about that.

"Next time, then," Lexi said. Was it Alonda's imagination or was that a flicker of disappointment?

"Oh yeah. Next time, for sure." Alonda nodded, trying to keep that secret box inside her chest locked, aware that she'd just discovered some kinda key she didn't quite understand.

THE ARCADE, OR THE FUN-CADE AS ITS SIGN PROUDLY BOASTED,
was loud and bright and small and packed with games that made
a lot of loud noises. Alonda hated it immediately. She was gonna
have to get earplugs or something to make it through a day without a headache; seriously, how was it okay for one small space to
be so loud?! The sounds were reverberating against the walls, and
she could practically see the echoes in the air, shit. Even if it was an
arcade and part of its appeal was being loud . . . she could feel Teresa
making fun of her for acting like an old lady for thinking all that. But
so what? Just because she was young didn't mean she wanted to be
surrounded by noise.

It was awesome that she had got a summer job so easy and was
working for Luna Park, but damn, why couldn't she have been
assigned to a food stand, or one of the midway games or even taking credits for the rides? What bad luck did she draw to be stuck
here, in the middle of all these intensely blinking lights and sounds,
surrounded by brats.

She adjusted her neon-orange shirt (another reason to be
cranky, it made her feel like a traffic cone) and tried to force her
face into a pleasant expression. It wouldn't be good customer service to show her intense discomfort at being surrounded by people

and machines in such a small space. It was only 10:00 A.M., but the Fun-Cade was already slowly filling with people wandering to the various video games, playing the basketball shoot-out game or Skee-Ball or—

"Hey, yeah, hello, where do I get coins?"

Alonda turned to face the speaker. A frazzled-looking middle-aged white lady was standing in front of her impatiently, holding the hand of a kid who was pulling her hand like he was trying to win a game of tug-of-war with her arm.

"Uhhh," Alonda squeaked out.

"Mommmyyyy, I wanna playyy with the zombies!" the kid whined, pulling his mom's arm with all his little might.

"Well?" Mommy responded, running her free hand through her frizzy blond hair.

Alonda felt frozen—she really wasn't sure what to say.

"Hi, how can I help you?"

Relief flooded through Alonda. Someone had come to her rescue.

She turned around and saw a smiling Asian girl, a little older than Alonda, wearing the same crappy neon-orange shirt. Her name tag read MICHELLE NG—MANAGER.

"Yeah, I've been trying to figure out where to get some coins—"

"MOMMY!!"

"—for my son."

"Oh, our machines don't take coins anymore; we use these cash-less cards instead. For your convenience," Michelle said, flashing a huge smile and showing her a plastic card.

The mom glared. "How's it supposed to be 'convenient' if I need to buy one—"

"It's no problem. Let me help you with it," Michelle continued, politely (if not a little intensely) talking over the woman and leading her to a card machine. Alonda watched, taking mental notes. Math class sure hadn't prepared her for soothing cranky-ass customers.

She let her eyes wander around the room, already trying to memorize where everything was; the machine where guests could buy the cards that would hold their money, their tickets, the different games that the arcade had to offer. Her gaze wandered over to the big glass case that held the prizes, lingering over different ones they had to offer—small brightly colored rubber balls, neon plastic spiders, erasers that looked like different foods, making her gaze up toward the big coveted prizes, small stuffed dogs sticking out their rubbery tongues, baseball caps, giant teddy bears with their arms stretched wide for a hug.

She paused on the giant teddy bears, a memory threatening to come loose at the seams.

"Hey, you're Alonda Rivera, right?"

Alonda started and looked over to see Michelle had returned.

"Yeah, that's me."

Michelle's face broke out into a huge smile. "Great, it's so nice to meet you!" She held out her hand to shake, and Alonda saw a pretty big tattoo of what looked like some kind of purple and green feather on the inside of her forearm.

"It's a peacock feather," Michelle said.

"Huh?"

"I see you staring," she said, waving her arm around.

Alonda grimaced. "I wasn't staring," she started to say, but Michelle just shrugged her away.

"It's cool, I mean, I got it so that people would see it, I just prefer to end the internal guessing game early," she said with a laugh. Alonda smiled back a little, her nerves starting to settle. Michelle had a way about her that made Alonda feel instantly at ease.

"Does it mean something, your tattoo?" Alonda asked.

"For sure," Michelle said, adjusting her glasses. "Means I like peacocks."

Alonda laughed out loud at that, and Michelle winked at her. "I know, everyone thinks that tattoos have to have some big, huge meaning behind them, and I guess some of them do, but I was like 'I just like peacocks' and wanted to see something that made me smile every time I saw it, which is now every day for the rest of my life."

"Makes sense," Alonda said, nodding a little.

"You got any ink?" Michelle asked, straightening out some of the bright rubber prizes behind the glass cases.

Alonda shook her head. "Nah, I think my . . . mom would go ballistic," Alonda said, deciding at the last minute that she didn't wanna get into her backstory with Teresa, just easier to call her "Mom" to this practical stranger. "She's already gone ballistic 'cause I told her I wanted to dye my hair, can't imagine what she'd say if I told her I wanted a tattoo."

"No, I know, my mom lost her shit when I got mine; she's still got that old-school mentality, like nobody's gonna hire me because I got a tattoo, which obviously, that didn't happen 'cause I'm working here"—she gestured at the Fun-Cade—"or that it's, like, scarring on my skin, which it's not, it's art."

"Right!" Alonda said, smiling.

"So, this your first summer working here?" Michelle asked.

Alonda nodded. "Yeah, I used to work at a bodega, but it closed—"

"The one over on Surf?!"

Alonda shook her head again. "Nah, it was over by Mermaid—"

Michelle grunted, cutting off Alonda's sentence before she could finish. "God, they're all closing, it sucks. I hate how they're all disappearing or getting turned into bougie delis."

Alonda opened her mouth to agree, but Michelle kept barreling over her.

"*Or* it's like they don't even get taken over by anything, they just sit there empty and rotting for years till someone swoops in, buys them, and turns them into luxury apartments that nobody ever moves into and— Hi, can I help you?"

Michelle's tone changed midspeech, and Alonda turned to see a timid-looking customer was waiting, quietly trying to get Michelle's attention.

Nothing Michelle was talking about surprised Alonda. Teresa talked about it all the time, how the developers were coming in and making everything so expensive instead of just letting the people who wanted to live out here live out here in peace. Like, Teresa'd lived here her whole life—the apartment they lived in together now used to be the apartment Teresa's mom lived in before she passed away, way before Alonda was born. And they were lucky that the apartment was rent controlled, but even with those laws or whatever, the rent kept getting higher while Teresa's paycheck seemed to stay the same.

Everybody talked about it all the time, conversations starting with *Good morning, what's up* devolving into endless rants about their neighborhood. It always felt good to say it all out loud, but Alonda felt like they also ended the same way—helpless and frustrated, which sucked.

Teresa talked about moving sometimes, but Alonda knew she

didn't wanna. This had been her home for so long, she didn't really know where she'd wanna go. This was her home. And yeah, homes don't stay the same but, like.

It's nice to have a spot to call home.

"All right!" Michelle said, turning back to Alonda. "Sorry about the rant before—"

"Nah, everything you said is true, so may as well say it."

"Right!" Michelle said, nodding. She pulled her long black hair back into a high ponytail, getting serious. "But I guess we can't be expected to tackle gentrification on your first day of Fun-Cade duty, so we may as well get down to business."

The rest of the morning passed by in a blur of lights and sounds. Alonda found herself getting used to the noise so that it was just a dull hum in the backdrop of her mind within the first few hours. Her main job was to be helpful and answer questions and get Michelle if there was anything too confusing for her to handle. She also swept, cleaned up some spills, and put the OUT OF ORDER sign on a bunch of games until Jay the handyman could take a look at them.

"Hey, it's time for your break!" Michelle said after a few hours. "Be back in thirty."

Alonda nodded and wandered out of the Fun-Cade, the sunshine beaming down on her. Coney Island was in full motion, people waiting in long lines for the rides, frantically playing midway games, trying to win prizes. She was sure the beach was packed, but she couldn't see it from where she was at. Her stomach growled, and she figured she'd walk over to the food stands and grab a hot dog or something.

The line for Nathan's looked like it was fifty years long, so she went to one of the smaller vendors the block over that had the best hot dogs anyway and grabbed a spot on a bench. It was in the direct sun and the sun was beaming, which is probably why it had been abandoned, but Alonda loved being in the sun, even when it was scorching.

She'd have to remember sunblock tomorrow but for now, it was clutch.

Her mind started to wander away to daydreams as she ate her hot dog and let the world swirl around her.

It was so weird that none of the games in the Fun-Cade gave out paper tickets anymore. The plastic cards were more convenient but it all gave Alonda a pang of longing for the way it used to be. She remembered coming to the Fun-Cade (though she was pretty sure it was only called an arcade back then, before it got rebranded) with her mom when she was real little and her and Mami would try to get as many tickets as humanly possible. Their game of choice was the Skee-Ball—damn, Alonda used to be good at that, rolling the ball just right so it skipped right into the 100 slot each time. Or air hockey, she used to kick Mami's butt at some air hockey.

They'd play for hours, walk out with bundles of paper tickets, Alonda begging her mom to use them to get a prize right away, but Mami'd just shake her head. "Be patient, nena," she'd say with a smile—she was always smiling—"we got all summer."

And that's how they'd spend the bulk of the summer, whenever her and Mami had a spare moment, running down to the arcade, stockpiling tickets till September. There was one year when they had won five thousand tickets. Five full thousand tickets! In one summer! Like, shit.

But that's where Alonda's memory got fuzzy around the edges; she couldn't remember what it was they traded the tickets in for. Was it the portable radio? The giant teddy bear? She still had the radio, it sat broken on a shelf in her room, but she'd had to throw out the teddy bear; it had started smelling funky and Teresa opened the stitching on its back one day and saw that its graying stuffing was covered with green and black mold.

Alonda hadn't wanted to give it up, she clutched it even as its gross moldy stuffing ran out its body. "But it's just a bear! I'll get you another one! One that isn't rotting from the inside," Teresa had said, trying to be as soothing as possible, but it hadn't mattered to Alonda; that bear had reminded her of Mami and—

"Why're you dressed like a traffic cone?"

Alonda snapped out of her memory daze. Lexi stood in front of her, powdery funnel cake in one hand, sketchbook tucked under her arm.

"'Cause I didn't think they could see me from space," Alonda replied, tugging at the shirt a little bit. Damn, it really was the most obnoxious color.

"Well, you don't have to worry about that now, 'cause they can probably see you from Mars," Lexi said back, grinning.

"Nobody's on Mars to be able to see me."

"You really gonna diss Martians like that?!"

Alonda laughed.

"Mind if I join you?" Lexi asked, pointing to the bench.

"Oh yeah, sure," Alonda said, scooching over a bit. Lexi smiled and sat.

"Aren't you supposed to be at the Pride Parade or something?" Alonda asked. Lexi shrugged, powdered sugar falling all down the front of her purple shirt, dotting it like sugary snow.

"Yeah. But then my ex was gonna be there and it mighta been a mess, so . . ." She trailed off, shrugging. Alonda just nodded, not pointing out that there was probably gonna be thousands of people there, not just her ex.

"So they make you wear this?" Lexi asked, gesturing to Alonda's bright orange shirt.

Alonda pursed her lips together, nodding. "Makes us easy to spot in a crowd or something, I guess," Alonda muttered. She was suddenly super aware of her hair, how her ponytail felt like it was drooping. She took it out and started to redo it, as casually as possible.

"Yeah, they got me working the Fun-Cade, that's my main spot, I think, but they might make me go somewhere else, depends on, like, how busy they are or if they need people to sub in for people or whatever," Alonda said, trying to covertly sniff her armpit as she pulled her hair up high. She had doubled up on deodorant this morning, but she didn't trust it, not when it was so hot out. She suddenly felt silly for sitting in the sun during her break; she still had four hours of work and what if she sweat through her deodorant! She shimmied herself into a small patch of shade at the edge of the bench.

"So what're you doing out here?" Alonda asked, cringing at how grandmotherly her question sounded, "if you're not at the parade, I mean."

Lexi held up her sketchbook. "Art shit," she said.

"Like, an assignment?" Alonda asked, and Lexi snorted.

"Nah, I'm taking a break from assignments. I mean, I'm done with the school ones, but I'm kinda part of this art show in August?" Lexi said, her eyes darting back and forth. "It's kind of a big deal or whatever," she added quickly under her breath, but kept going before Alonda could ask anything about it. "Thinking about all the work I've gotta do for it hurts my brain, so I'm just people watching right now. I like to people watch. I wanna try to capture the whole neighborhood on the page," Lexi said, lighting up. Alonda noticed her fingertips and palms looked like they were stained with something black; maybe charcoal? "Like, I wanna get the energy, the emotion, I wanna make it so that if you're looking at someone's face in one'a my drawings, you can feel it in your own self. You know?"

"Can I see?" Alonda asked, reaching toward the sketchbook, but Lexi pulled it back.

"That's like asking if I could read your diary," Lexi responded, pressing her sketchbook to her chest.

"I might let you read my diary," Alonda responded. "I'm pretty boring."

"You're not boring," Lexi said. Alonda's face suddenly felt like a heat lamp just turned on inside her cheeks, and even though it was hot out, she knew it wasn't from the sun. Because she was sitting in the shade.

"I mean, I usually work with collage," Lexi said, still hugging her sketchbook to her chest. "Like, that's the medium I usually work with because it's my favorite. And it's cool and I like it a lot but like . . . my sketches? It's . . . different. More personal," she said with a shrug.

"Well, I'm one million percent not an artist," Alonda said with a laugh. "So, like, I don't get it, but also I don't have to. Being an artist seems pretty . . . intense," she finished, trying to find the right word. "Like, you're always in your emotions or whatever," she added with a shrug. Lexi laughed.

"Here, I can show you some of my collages," Lexi said, taking out her cell phone, and Alonda saw the time—shit, she was almost late getting back from break!

"Oh shit, I'm sorry, I—I gotta go," she said, bouncing up from the bench and throwing away her paper hot-dog scraps.

"Hold up," Lexi said, "I don't think I got your number."

Alonda's heart fluttered. "Oh, I, uh, why do you want my number?"

"Uh, to communicate? Because we're friends?"

"Communicate?"

"Well, I dunno, you're the one over there asking for explanations!"

Alonda laughed and instinctively went to grab her phone.

Oh shit, it was locked in that locker thing.

"My phone's not on me," Alonda said.

Lexi feigned shock. "*What?* You have to give up your phone for that job?!"

"I'm not *giving it up*, it's just locked away— What are you doing?"

Lexi had grabbed her arm and was writing out a number in blue Sharpie.

"Just gotta do it old school, then," she said, writing across Alonda's forearm. "I've seen them do this shit in movies."

Alonda laughed, but her heart was pounding in her chest. Lexi's hand on her skin had that effect on her.

"What're you doing—now anybody can see your number!" Alonda said, but Lexi just shook her head and doodled a smiling person on the bottom of the number.

"Please, nobody's gonna look at this number and be like, *Oh snap, I wonder who's gonna be on the other side of that*—if they even really notice at all. You ever notice people really don't pay attention to nothing except what's right in front of them? And sometimes not even then."

Alonda nodded, studying Lexi's hands. Yeah, she had noticed that.

"Just zombie walking through life most the time," Lexi muttered, and started making some adjustments to the face, giving it a gaping wide mouth and a stick figure body with its arms out in front of it.

"That a zombie?" Alonda asked, and Lexi shook her head.

"Nah, it's your customers."

"Okay, this is getting intricate," Alonda laughed. She didn't wanna tug her arm away, though.

"All right, all right, I'm done! See," Lexi said, letting go of Alonda's arm and gesturing toward her work of art. "So now you can text me after you're done with work and we can talk wrestling and stuff," Lexi said.

Alonda smiled hard and nodded. "Yeah, yeah, that would be cool, I think!"

"See you around," Lexi said. She tucked her sketchbook under her arm and wandered away, weaving through people until she was out of Alonda's sight.

"Ah, so you do have some ink." Michelle's voice startled Alonda. She turned around to look at her.

"I hope—it's okay—my friend—" Alonda sputtered, but Michelle just held up a hand and laughed.

"It's so fine. Just gotta make sure it don't smudge before your shift's over. I bet whoever he is would be upset," Michelle said with a wink. Alonda opened her mouth to correct her, a flush coming to her face, but she couldn't get the words to come out.

"It's just a friend," she said, but Michelle laughed a little.

"Anybody who needs to get you his number that fast definitely wants to be more than that," she said. "Besides, he coulda asked for *your* number and just texted you and you woulda gotten it when you finished work. Right?"

Oh shit. She hadn't even thought of that. Part of her had wanted Lexi to draw on her arm. The part that belonged in the locked box in her chest. She felt it shaking inside her now, trying to break open, rattling against its chains.

She walked toward the back of the Fun-Cade, Michelle's words echoing in her brain along with the bings and bangs of the machines. She picked up a rag and started dusting down the pinball machines, but her mind wasn't on getting them clean, it was on other things.

She wasn't sure when she was first aware of the box's existence. Sometimes she thought about it like she thought about breathing; she usually went about her days, not consciously thinking about how her body was breathing in and out, but somehow knew that her body was breathing in and out. She just didn't think about it all the time, didn't obsessively think about how her ability to breathe in and then out again was keeping her alive, but unlike with breathing, Alonda knew that box existed inside her, but whenever she thought about it, she tried to forget it. Because it was too hard to think about things she didn't understand.

She remembered her first crush when she was twelve was on a guy named Steve Wilson, and she remembered talking about that with her friends, they were all girls, but she remembered alongside that crush, there was Carolina Flores. And the way she felt when she thought about Steve, she felt the same way when she thought about her.

How could she like both Steve and Carolina? Everywhere she looked, it seemed like that wasn't possible, that she was weird for feeling that way.

Alonda didn't know what to do with any of that information except lock it away inside her. The box hadn't always been there, she realized, dragging her rag along the same spot. She had built it herself. Because she needed somewhere to place all the feelings she didn't understand. And now it felt like it was gonna open. And that scared her.

But she didn't know why.

Alonda was showered, had eaten a peanut butter sandwich, and had successfully dodged Teresa, who wanted to know everything about her first day, including all the boring parts, and was trying to think of something to text Lexi. She went through every greeting in the entire universe, rolling them around like marbles before she finally just sighed and settled on:

ALONDA: Hi! It's me.

She quickly added

ALONDA: I mean, it's Alonda. Hi.

She started to put her phone down, but it buzzed right away.

LEXI: Hey! =) Thought you lost my number.
ALONDA: lol, nope, I think it may be permanently a part of
my skin now.
LEXI: Ha, sorry about that.

She sent a bunch of zombie emojis back-to-back. Alonda laughed.

LEXI: Hey, you see UWW is gonna be doing live shows
around BK all summer?

Universal Wrestling Warriors, or UWW as it was more commonly known, was an independent wrestling troupe, aka Alonda's *favorite* indie wrestling troupe.

ALONDA: Yeah! You like UWW??

Lexi sent back a GIF of a wrestler flexing his arms, the words OH YEAH! blinking across the bottom brightly. Alonda laughed a little, trying to find the most perfect one to send in return.

They spent the rest of the night sending each other wrestling GIFs back and forth, and even though it wasn't really talking, Alonda knew it totally was.

☆ **6** ☆

"YOUTUBE."

King threw his arms down and looked at the four of them expectantly, as though he had just told them all the secret of life instead of just saying the words *You* and *Tube* smashed together. Alonda squinted her eyes a little. Was she missing something? She shot a glance out at the rest of the group, but they looked as lost as she felt. Spider scrunched his forehead and went back to his phone. He'd been texting nonstop since they'd gathered. Apparently he'd met someone at the parade.

"Riiiight. YouTube," Lexi said, nodding her head a little. "I . . . have . . . heard of it?" Her sketchbook was in her lap, and she was carefully outlining something with a thin black Sharpie, concentration more reserved for that than for this entire conversation.

King's face fell a little bit.

"You serious right now?" he said, looking at the group. Alonda had no idea what she was supposed to say. He was in the middle of a conversation only he was a part of.

"Facebook? Twitter?" Pretzel said in response.

"What?"

"I dunno, I thought maybe we was just saying the names of things that exist," he said with a shrug.

"No, YouTube. YouTUBE!"

"You can keep on saying it, not gonna make it make any more sense," Spider replied calmly.

"Oh come on, we only been talking about it for the last year!" King said, kicking the padding with the toe of his sneaker. A glimmer of understanding seemed to flicker through the group, though Alonda was still woefully in the dark.

"Ooooh," Pretzel said, "we have been talking about it."

"But . . . no, we can't," Spider said, looking up from his phone.

"I thought we had decided that was a bad idea," Lexi said, flipping her sketchbook open to a fresh page, "because it is a bad idea!"

"We didn't decide nothing! And it is so not a bad idea, it's the opposite of a bad idea, it's actually a—a—" King searched for a word.

"*Very* bad idea," Spider finished for him.

"*Very* bad ain't the opposite of bad, Spider, God!"

"Yeah," Pretzel said helpfully, "the opposite of bad is good—"

"My point is that it's a bad idea!" Spider said, his words exploding out a little. Seemed like everyone had strong feelings about this—whatever it was.

"Can somebody tell me," Alonda said, her voice wavering with nerves as it exited her body. The others looked at her. "What's the idea?"

King opened his mouth to speak, but Lexi jumped over him. "King thinks that we should succumb to a capitalist structure and monetize our fun for the masses."

Pretzel groaned. "God, Lexi, can you please stop it with that gibberish."

"It's not gibberish, it's the truth and the truth is not gibberish!"

"Basically," Spider said, talking over the two, "King wants us to start a troupe officially by setting up a YouTube channel where we put our shit up and try to get views and then do real shows for real, with an audience and everything."

"Yeah, and it would be dope as hell!" King said. He was talking to the whole group but was looking directly at Alonda, and realization slowly dawned on her. Damn. Oh damn, this was one of those million times an argument that had no end. She looked around. It was clear where everyone stood on the issue. Lexi was dead set against it, but Spider didn't seem too excited about it, either. Pretzel was so excited that he was hopping from foot to foot a little bit, and King was obviously the mastermind behind it.

Which meant that Alonda was the swing vote.

Got it.

Damn.

"Now that we have four of us and we can make the matches more even," King continued, carefully explaining right to Alonda, "we can really start it up and do live shows all summer and air them for everyone's eyes online."

"Yeah, but we're supposed to be doing this for fun, right?" Spider responded to King but was also really talking to Alonda, looking her right in the eye.

"And it'll be even *more* fun to turn it into a *real thing*," King jabbed back.

"Doing more *work* don't sound like *more fun*," Lexi lobbed back.

"Come on, Alonda, what do you think?" Pretzel asked her.

She took in a deep breath. What did she think?

"Yeah, what do you think?" Lexi asked. She was looking at Alonda like she already knew she'd agree with her.

But what did she think?

Yeah, it would be a lot of work, but when it came down to it, Alonda wanted to do it. It did sound like fun. And she could see how it could work. The whole thing unfurled in front of her eyes like a map with all the steps clearly defined. They could take turns using their phones to record, upload the videos, they even had stuff you could record and edit and add effects to in real time.

And they could put together a show, a whole show. They'd perform in front of a crowd. They could throw together costumes, do promos, it would be sick. And fun. Alonda could feel her heart start pounding with excitement, thinking about it, in front of people, hearing them, feeling their energy. It's what she'd daydreamed about her whole life, and sure, it wouldn't be for real, not for a professional arena or whatever, but it would still be real because they'd all be doing it together. In front of a crowd. She'd get to create a character, and she wanted that character to be seen as far as the internet could go.

It would be a lot of work.

It wouldn't be impossible, though.

"Well?"

Pretzel's voice snapped her back to reality. They were all looking at her.

"Yeah, it's all up to you," Spider said, a little too seriously.

Lexi looked at him. "I thought you didn't wanna do this shit, either!"

Spider shrugged. "Majority rules. I'll go with the group."

Alonda took a deep breath in. She felt the pressure of being the deciding vote, could feel Lexi's stare begging her to say no, could feel the hope radiating from Pretzel and King to say yes.

She looked at King, a smile creeping to her lips.

"Yeah, okay. Let's do it."

King smiled wide at her, and Lexi didn't do anything.

"This sucks," she mumbled. Spider looked at her.

"You gonna leave?"

"Never," she said, sketching something out.

"Great, then let's get to work."

Alonda was working with Lexi, trying to get some basic moves down, but they were getting distracted by King and Spider.

"And Spider throws out a web slinger—*thwt, thwt*!"

"Okay, and then after—"

"*Thwt, thwt!*" Spider said again, pretending to throw out some more web.

"Okay, but then—"

"Gotcha, you're going down!" he shouted.

"Can you take this serious?!" King snapped.

"Hey, Alonda," Lexi whispered to her. Alonda looked at her, eyebrow raised. She was talking weird. Like, the tone of her voice was soft, and if Alonda didn't know any better she coulda swore she almost sound . . . nervous?

Lexi licked her lips. They were a little chapped. She wasn't wearing any makeup. Would probably only melt off in the heat anyway.

"Yeah, I was just wondering if maybe you wanted to . . . maybe we could . . . it might be cool if we . . ." Alonda just looked at Lexi. What was she trying to ask?

"Esteban! ESTEBAN!"

A voice cut through the air. Alonda ignored it—people called from the windows all the time.

"Oh damn," Spider mumbled under his breath. "Not my moms . . ."

Pretzel snorted. "Can your web-slinging powers get you outta that?" he asked. Lexi giggled a little, and even King smirked. Most of them, it seemed, had experience being called from windows. Definitely not a random occurrence.

"Quick, maybe she can't see me," Spider said, trying to hide behind King.

King shook his head. "Nah, man, I ain't playing accomplice to your shit," he said.

"¡Yo te veo, muchacho!" Spider's mom yelled from the window. Spider groaned a loud, long groan and turned to face the window.

"What do you want?!" he shouted back, defeated. His mom answered in Spanish, and while Alonda could make out some words like *leche*, most of it was too fast for Alonda's ears to keep up.

Learning Spanish at school was so different from actually hearing it and speaking it for real. There were rules, sure, but depending on the dialect, those rules changed. And they didn't teach any of that in school. Like, Mami was Nuyorican, and the way she used to speak it, man, it was like an event. She'd jump from Spanish to English in the middle of the same sentence, sometimes in the middle of the same word. And she talked a lot. She was always talking, and when she wasn't talking, she was laughing. Alonda smiled as the memory crept inside her head, the timbre of Mami's voice, dancing almost as much as how she'd dance for real. But her smile faded. She couldn't remember a lot of the sentences or the words. She tried to chase them sometimes in her memory, but they always outran her.

"Yeah, I'll go get the milk!" Spider yelled back. He turned to the rest of them. "I gotta go get milk," he reported back. King snorted.

"Yeah, we know. The whole neighborhood knows," King said. Spider punched his arm and started clearing up his speakers.

"Yeah, I bet Javier'll be waiting for you at the corner store, already with all your mom's groceries ready," Pretzel teased, dodging outta the way of another punch from Spider.

"Damn, I gotta go, too," Lexi said, looking at her cell phone. "You going anywhere, Alonda? I can walk you."

King didn't seem like he was planning on leaving anytime soon, and Alonda kinda wanted to talk to him. She looked at Lexi's face and shook her head.

"Oh, uh, I'm actually gonna hang out here for a bit. Cooler to be outside than in my apartment, ya know?"

"Sure," said Lexi. Her voice was level, but a flash of something darted across her eyes. She had turned her head, but Alonda saw it there.

"Lexi, damn! You coming or what?!" Pretzel called from the sidewalk.

"Gotta go. Text me later," Lexi said, and she ran to meet Pretzel and Spider. Alonda watched them leave.

King was looking at the space his friends had occupied, frustration on his face. He kicked the Astroturf a little. "Man! Nobody takes this shit as serious as I do."

Alonda shrugged, searching for some words of comfort that wouldn't be lame. She landed on "I dunno, I think all of us take it serious." She cringed to herself. It wasn't as cool or deep as she wanted to sound.

Luckily, King didn't seem to hear her, lost in his own world.

Maybe he was imagining the playground to be a wrestling ring like Alonda sometimes did. It was kinda busted up. Superstorm Sandy'd been years ago, but they was slow to fix shit around here (the shit that didn't affect the tourists directly, anyway), and the playground was still messed up.

But her imagination could stretch out before her, fix what the city deemed unimportant. The park wasn't on the path the tourists took to get to the amusement park or the beach, so it was mostly ignored. Yeah, they cared more about making sure the tourists were doing okay than about the people who lived here. But she looked at it now, replacing the busted-up swings with flashing lights, the scuffed-up Astroturf with a huge wrestling ring, turning the jungle gym into its own kinda sideways ladder match. She looked around the perimeters, imagining a crowd of people watching them, cheering them on. How cool would that be?

"Hey, Alonda," King said, snapping her back to the present. She looked at him, curious. There was a lightness to his voice, and his eyes were darting all over the place, not looking her in her eyes. "It's been cool getting to know you."

Alonda nodded, a smile dancing to the corners of her lips. "Yeah," she said, "it's been cool getting to know you all, too."

King bit his bottom lip and rubbed his nose with his hand. "Yeah, yeah, about that, I was uh. I was wondering if maybe you wanted to like. Hang out. Like. One-on-one."

Alonda felt her ears start to burn.

"Tonight or something. If you ain't busy."

What?

King continued, "I mean, I figured we could like. Walk on the boardwalk, you know? See the whole thing lit up. I can try to win you a stuffed rabbit or plastic squid or water bottle or . . . something."

"You . . . wanna hang out with me?" Alonda squeaked out.

"I mean, it's cool if you don't wanna or whatever," he started, but she stopped him.

"Nah, I do, totally, yes. I just, I need to ask—I mean, I need to make sure I can, but yeah. Yeah, sure, let's do it."

King's face broke into a big smile. He nodded happily.

"Lemme get your phone?"

Alonda nodded and handed it over. King punched his number in and gave it back to her, a huge smile on his face.

"All right, cool. Just text me at like six and we'll work out the details. Cool?"

Alonda smiled so hard, she could barely get the words out. "Yeah, cool! Cool."

It was totally, totally cool.

☆ **7** ☆

"NO."

"Come on, Teresa!"

"Absolutely not."

"You cannot be serious—"

"I'm as serious as death right now, Alonda—"

"It's not that big a deal—"

Teresa leaned back on her legs, wiping her forehead with the back of her hand. She'd been scrubbing the linoleum kitchen floor. She was wearing those dorky rubber yellow gloves that went up to her elbows, still holding a spray can of some kinda toxic-lemon-smelling cleaning stuff in one hand.

"If it ain't that big a deal, then it shouldn't be a big deal that I'm saying no, so no," she said, jabbing the floor with a fresh spray on the word *no*.

"What the hell, Teresa!" Alonda said, the words exploding from her throat.

Teresa shot her a glare. "You wanna try asking that again?"

"I just." Alonda breathed in slowly, trying to collect herself. Okay. She hadn't expected this reaction. At all. Maybe she shouldn't have asked when Teresa was elbow deep into a deep clean. Like, sure, Teresa was overprotective. But this was just hanging out in the neighborhood. Sometimes Alonda felt like Teresa would be happier if she could Bubble Wrap her and put her in a glass box, where nothing could touch her.

Which is why Teresa could never find out about the wrestling. She'd throw a fit big enough to put the whole universe inside.

"Why're you even cleaning for, it's fine!" she said, sneezing. The lemon scent of clean was burning her nostrils. Teresa was in deep-clean frenzy mode and ain't nothing was stopping her. She got that way sometimes. Like, everything would be whatever, and then *bam*, she'd snap into a deep-ass clean. It's not like they kept the place a mess, but every few months it was like Teresa would spot some invisible dirt that bothered her more than a piece of sand getting stuck to the inside of an eyelid.

Teresa sat back up on her heels and sighed, stretching her arms, rolling her shoulders to get the knots out of her back. She looked at Alonda, her eyes softening a little. It was a special look she had reserved just for Alonda. It normally made her feel like she was getting a hug, but right now Alonda wanted to be as far away from Teresa as she could possibly get.

"Your hair looks all tangled," Teresa said, snapping her back to attention.

Alonda shrugged. "So what, not like nobody's gonna see it. Especially if I'm not allowed out."

"Stop acting like I'm keeping you prisoner, you're allowed *out*—"

"Just not with a *boy*," Alonda finished as obnoxiously as she could.

"Just not that *late*," Teresa said, trying to match Alonda's obnoxious tone.

"It's not that late, *and* I'll be surrounded by people, we won't leave the boardwalk. Come on, Teresa, I never ask to go out! Please?"

Teresa sighed and bit her bottom lip. Alarm bells started going off in Alonda's head. Oh shit, Teresa was doing that thing she did, when she wanted to talk to Alonda about something but didn't know how to talk to her, like *Afterschool Special* type shit. Alonda felt her stomach clench and started to back outta the kitchen. Nah uh, no way. She did not want a dumbass birds-and-bees conversation with Teresa right now.

Teresa saw her shuffling backward. "Go get your hairbrush, I'm gonna brush your hair."

Trapped.

Alonda sighed heavily and went to get her hairbrush. She glanced at herself in the mirror. Damn, she was looking a frizzy, sweaty mess.

She walked back into the kitchen. Teresa had removed her gloves and washed her hands, her sleeves still rolled up to the elbows. She'd pulled one of the kitchen chairs out from the table and was sitting in it. She'd placed a short stool in front of the chair. That was Alonda's seat. She shoved the brush in Teresa's hand without looking and sat down in front of the chair, pulling her knees up to her chin.

This was their spot, the way they sat. They'd been sitting this way for years, Alonda in front of Teresa and Teresa behind her, brushing her hair. Teresa started dragging the brush through her thick hair, tugging it through tangles. She wasn't gentle, but Alonda didn't need her to be gentle. It felt good, to know that the knots in her hair were getting undone and that Teresa was the one doing it.

"Dunno how you managed to do this to your hair," Teresa

muttered, trying to unsnarl a particularly big knot. Alonda shrugged one of her shoulders. Like she was gonna tell.

"So," Teresa said, doing that thing with her voice where she was trying to keep it light but Alonda knew it was about to get pretty deep. "Been thinking about giving in. Getting an AC."

Alonda jerked her head back so fast, she felt some of her hair get pulled out by the root. "Really?!" she shouted, but Teresa grabbed her head and kept it straight.

"Keep your head still!"

"Yeah, okay, but are you serious?" Alonda couldn't believe it. She'd been waiting for this moment her whole life.

"Yeah. Never used to need one growing up. Just used a fan," she sighed, her breath tickling the back of Alonda's neck. "And even then, Ma wouldn't let us keep it on all night or nothing. Fan's not cutting this heat, though, just pushing around more hot air."

"I love the sound the AC make from the outside of the building. Like, how a building can have a whole bunch of ACs going in the summer, it makes them sound like they're buzzing, like the building is alive. And now we'll be part of that buzzing, too. Thanks, Teresa."

Teresa grunted, still pulling the brush through her hair. Alonda crinkled her forehead. Nah, there was something else to this nonsense, she wouldn't be brushing her hair just to tell her they was getting an air conditioner.

"Wait. And?" Alonda asked, trying to keep her voice as light as Teresa's.

"And nothing," Teresa said. She started to braid Alonda's hair in a big loose braid, but her hand got caught on another knot. "You got so many knots in your hair, it's like a spiderweb," Teresa muttered.

Alonda rolled her eyes. "I'm pretty sure spiders don't make knots in webs, Teresa," she said.

"I'm sure neither of us know as much about spiders as we should," Teresa shot back.

She kept brushing.

Alonda sat and waited. She knew something else was coming.

"So hey," Teresa continued. There it was. "Things've been getting real with Jim."

Alonda rolled her eyes again, this time harder. "Yeah, I noticed." She tried not to make her words too snappy. "Been spending so much time here, he should be paying rent."

"Yeah, I thought so, too. So . . . that's actually what we think he'll be doing," Teresa said quickly.

"Oh," Alonda whispered, Teresa's words sinking into her like water. She was glad Teresa couldn't see her face, but she had a good feeling she could tell how she felt about the whole situation. Well, that explained the cleaning at least. Damn, *and* the AC! Jim probably influenced that shit, too.

Alonda scanned the apartment, her eyes lingering over all the details she had stopped noticing. She'd never had to share this space with nobody but Teresa. Teresa'd been living here for decades, and Alonda was the only other person she'd ever lived with. This place was theirs. Every inch of it was theirs, drenched in memories no amount of scrubbing could erase, and now someone else would be leaving his shoes on the doormat and shit.

"Yeah," Teresa said again. "So . . . I hope that's okay with you."

Alonda snorted. "Do I have a choice?" she asked. The words tasted bitter coming out of her mouth.

"You do, actually," Teresa said. She was unbraiding and rebraiding

Alonda's hair gently now that all the knots was out. Almost felt like a hug when Teresa did it like that. "You absolutely got a choice. I won't force you if you don't wanna."

Alonda chewed the inside of her cheek. Damn. It would be so much easier if Teresa hadn't given her a choice, if she could just brood about it without it being her choice. She wanted to say no, to keep their place their own. But Jim made Teresa happy. Anyone could see that.

"Do you like . . . love him, though?" Alonda asked quietly. The question felt weird coming out her mouth, almost like the words were in danger of getting stuck to her tongue. It was such a weird question to ask. Mostly because she'd never asked her anything like it before. Talking about love before they talked about sex felt weird. But maybe that was a thing that should be talked about.

Teresa's hands stopped what they was doing. "Yeah," she said softly. "Yeah, I do."

"How do you know?" Alonda asked, and quickly added, "I mean, not how do you know you love Jim, you don't gotta list his traits or whatever, but it's just like—how do you know when you love someone?"

"Why? Are you in love with The Boy?" Teresa asked, playing with the end of Alonda's braid.

Alonda swatted her hand away. It tickled Alonda's neck when she did it like that. "I'm obviously not," she snapped, jerking her head to the side. "No, but like . . . you can't see it, right? So how do you know it? When it happens?"

Teresa was quiet. She started playing with the end of Alonda's braid again. Alonda didn't stop her. Maybe Teresa would never say nothing ever again and they'd just sit there in silence like this forever.

Wouldn't be the worst thing.

"It's hard," Teresa started slowly. Alonda waited, holding her breath. "Because . . . there ain't no words for it. Love. No real words. Like, we say words to try to describe it, but you can't. If you can, then I dunno, I don't think it ain't love, not really. But it might be. It's tricky that way," she laughed to herself. "But . . . you know it when you feel it. It'll hit you deep, and suddenly, you'll know. You will."

"Wow," Alonda said softly. Then because shit was feeling too real, she teased, "I didn't realize you was a poet."

"Be quiet, you," Teresa said, swatting her gently on her shoulder. "Sometimes when things are true, they come out a different way. You got time, though, Alonda, to figure it out for yourself." Her voice almost begging. "You got time."

Alonda nodded, but she didn't know why. Agreeing to a thought that made sense but one she didn't quite understand.

"And it's not just one great love in a lifetime. I don't think so. The movies got that shit wrong," she muttered. "You can't just look for your one big Happily Ever After, we don't gotta mate for life, you know, we're not lobsters." Alonda choked back a laugh.

"Ava used to love, deep, you know," Teresa said in that faraway voice that meant she was remembering. Alonda closed her eyes, tried to pull Mami up close. "Used to fall in love with someone weekly. And I believed it, too. I think you can fall in love so fast and deep and that be real. And Ava, well, she had that infinite capacity to love." She breathed in, that breath of air that meant she was trying to wrap a memory around her like a blanket. Alonda opened her eyes and her mom was gone, but she was still there, sitting there with Teresa.

Alonda wasn't sure when she stopped calling Teresa Tía Teresa. That's what she used to call her, or just Tía or sometimes Titi. Teresa wasn't a second mother, but she was more than an aunt, a category that didn't exist before her and wouldn't exist after her, either, something all her own, a thing that Alonda couldn't quite put words to except for Teresa.

"Just . . . tell Jim to smoke his cigars *out* the window," she said, shrugging Teresa's hands away and standing, brushing the smell of bleach off her ass.

"You sure?" Teresa asked. Alonda looked at her. She had this look on her face, like she was the young one and Alonda was the adult. That was the way it went sometimes, they passed that baton back and forth. Alonda set her mouth in a line and nodded.

"I will not tolerate the smell of cigar in this house," Alonda said resolutely.

"Okay, then," Teresa said, sitting up. She started putting her rubber gloves on again. Alonda grabbed a banana off the fruit bowl Teresa sometimes kept full on the counter and began to leave, a full night of nothing ahead of her.

"You gotta be home tonight by ten," Teresa said, not looking up from where she was scrubbing the floor. Alonda froze in her tracks. Did she hear that right? She turned to look at her.

"Really?" she asked, trying to keep her voice nice and even.

"Nine-forty-five P.M., Eastern Standard Time," Teresa shot back, scrubbing a spot on the floor with new vigor.

"Okay, ten is great!" Alonda said, and she ran out of the kitchen. She had to figure out what the hell she was gonna wear to a board-walk date.

Coney Island in summer is like a whole different land from Coney Island in the winter if you don't know how to look at it. Alonda had deep feelings about it. Yeah, it's a beach place and a tourist spot, but it's also home. It's weird how people don't really think about all the people who live here all the time. For people who even live in different parts of Brooklyn, the City, wherever, it's like they think about Coney Island as if it's only a place that comes to life in the summer.

But really, it's alive all the time.

Alonda had undone her braid and pulled her thick hair up in a ponytail, as high as it would go. She'd just changed out of the sweaty T-shirt she'd been wearing into a loose-fitting tank top. She watched the boardwalk slowly don its evening wear, lights flickering on the rides, some of them flickering on and off like fireflies. The lights didn't come up during the winter, not like this. Coney Island was darker in the winter. To the untrained eye, people'd probably think it was asleep, but Alonda knew it was never asleep. That's what pissed her off the most about how people talked about this place, as though it shut off during the winter months and there wasn't thousands of people living there, breathing life into this place twenty-four seven. People said it was dangerous. That always got under her skin, too, that people could call a whole place dangerous without even knowing it, only reading the shit they published in the news.

Because, yeah, anywhere in the whole world could be dangerous. Even places that are supposed to be safe are dangerous sometimes.

Those stories usually disappeared for the summertime, though. Can't scare away the tourists. Let them feel safe and throw their coins in the economy. But where was that money going? Alonda didn't know if it was always back to them.

People called it magic in the summer. Except Alonda knew, this place was always magic. It's just in the summer, more people could see it. But it was always magic. There was always something special in its bones. Just because people didn't know how to look for it didn't mean the magic went anywhere.

It was alive. Always alive.

And that was magic.

"Yo, Alonda!"

Alonda's heart jabbed at her chest. King's voice carried across the boardwalk, more powerful than the murmur of the crowd or the whirl of the rides. This was it. Her first sorta date. No big deal. She took a deep breath and turned around. She turned her head in time to see his hand shoot up, waving at her almost frantically. A nervous giggle bubbled up from her stomach and came out her nose like a giggly snot bubble. Maybe he was as nervous as she was. Was that possible? Did King get nervous? Maybe excited.

She was excited. Maybe nerves and excitement were the same thing.

Maybe she was definitely babbling.

Alonda watched his head bobbing and weaving through the crowd, moving closer and closer to her. Her stomach pulled at her, and she couldn't help but notice how handsome he was, his face all happy and so open when he smiled.

"Hey!" he said, giving her a quick hug. He had changed into a white polo shirt. She could smell some sorta spicy cologne clinging to his clothes.

"Hi." She smiled back.

They kinda looked at each other for a minute, their pause hanging in the air for an eternity before King finally saved them from the silence.

"You wanna walk?" he asked, and Alonda nodded, smiling big.

"Cool! Let's go, then," he said, and they wandered down the boardwalk together, side by side but very much not touching. It was a little awkward at first. Neither of them really knew what to say to each other; their words kept squeezing out of their mouths and losing steam when they hit the air. Alonda kept glancing over at King but didn't want him to think she was looking at him, so she kept looking back at the boardwalk, letting the sights and sound overwhelm them both.

"You wanna get on a ride or something?" King asked after about ten minutes of awkward nothing. Alonda shrugged. The rides kinda scared her. She never really liked that feeling of free-falling. King nudged his arm against her. "Come on, you ever been on the Cyclone?"

"Once," Alonda said. "I threw up."

King laughed, "Nah, for real?"

"It's mad rickety, made my whole stomach feel like it was gonna fall out!"

King nudged her again. "I don't care if you throw up. Wanna get on with me?"

"I'm scared," she admitted.

"Of what?" King asked. He seemed genuinely curious, like he couldn't believe someone would actually be afraid of a roller coaster. "It's just a ride, it won't, like, bite you or nothing."

"I dunno," Alonda said, eyeing it. It was a huge wooden roller coaster—maybe the oldest wooden roller coaster of its kind?—and it'd been at Coney Island for . . . ever maybe, Alonda wasn't sure.

"Don't be scared, shit's been around for a hundred years, not like it's gonna break when we get on it! Those odds ain't good," King said, laughing a little more.

"We technically don't know that; it could fall apart at any moment," Alonda retorted, eyeing the ride suspiciously. The sound of the ride whooshing along those rickety planks almost tuned out the sounds of the screams from the riders.

"Come on," King said gently. "I got you."

Alonda swallowed her fear. She didn't wanna be afraid of anything, least of all a roller coaster. "Yeah, okay, let's do it," she said.

The wait in line was actually worse than the ride itself. Waiting, anxiety had crept into every cell in her body, jangling it with nerves. She felt like her stomach was gonna spill out of her and onto the sidewalk.

But as soon as they got in and the safety bar came down across their laps and the ride took its first dive, damn, did she feel alive. She screamed so loud, it was like all her anxiety was in that scream and her screaming it took it all away and suddenly, she could be in love with the ride. It helped that King had his arm around her shoulder the whole time. She screamed and pushed herself deeper into the crook of his arm as he laughed, holding her while the whole world shook and swayed.

They got off the ride, Alonda and King laughing hard, laughing laughs that were more than their awkward words.

"Let's go again!" Alonda yelled.

King looked at her. "Yeah?"

"Yeah!" she said, and darted to the end of the line, King chasing after her.

They stayed out on the boardwalk for another hour. King was true to his word and won her a couple of stuffed toys—an elephant and a tie-dye pony unicorn thing. She gave the elephant to a kid but decided she was gonna keep that weird-ass-looking pony, give it a home in her room.

"I gotta get back, soon," Alonda said. It was almost ten, and she was sure Teresa would be up and waiting and wanting to hear all about how it went and everything.

"Yeah, no problem. Feels like it's gonna rain soon," King said, looking up at the sky. Even though it was dark, she could see there were mountains of clouds forming. "I'll walk you back to your building." The two of them meandered along the sidewalk, back toward home.

Alonda could feel her heart starting to pick up the pace as they got closer to saying good night. She felt like she had when she was waiting on line to get on the Cyclone; her stomach was spinning again. Only this time she would look real weird if she just started screaming in King's face.

King had gotten even quieter than usual, and he kept fidgeting. Was he thinking about the same thing? Alonda opened her mouth to ask, but then

it started to rain.

"Run!" she screamed, and they dashed over to some scaffolding.

It came on quick, the rain, and it poured. The rain was falling so hard, it was splashing up the puddles in the gutter, the water nipping at their feet. It would be impossible to walk in without getting drenched, but it was one of those storms that would pass, it would be over as soon as it began.

They were breathless, a little bit from laughter and a little bit from the run to the shelter of the scaffolding. Alonda could hear the sounds of people from the boardwalk who were not at all prepared for rain yelling and laughing. It was funny to see some of them resist it, holding their arms over their heads as though their limbs would shield them from the sky. Even better to see those of them who embraced it, raise their arms like they was trying to give the rain a hug, open their mouths and let the droplets fill their whole faces.

There was nobody standing near them, where they had run, though. It was just the two of them.

King pulled her close. The rain had washed away some of his cologne. He smelled like laundry detergent and air.

Alonda's laughs drifted a smile onto her face. She looked up at King, leaning backward a bit.

Damn, he was tall.

His hands were rough but held her gently.

"Hey," he said softly.

"Hi," she said.

He brushed a finger across her cheek, cupped her face in his warm palm.

"Is it okay if I kiss you?" he asked gently.

Alonda nodded, her heart pounding fast.

He lowered his head a little.

Without even thinking, Alonda leaned forward on her tippy-toes, lifted her head to his, bridging the gap between them as their mouths found each other, and they kissed.

In the movies, kisses look perfect, but in real life, they're a wet and sloppy mess. Not that she was complaining. It was good. It was mad good. He tasted like the gum he was chewing, something tangy and sweet and something else, maybe it was something that was just him?

She could feel her body lose her bones, turning into a jellyfish as their kisses got more and more deep.

They stopped at the same time, a little breathless, just looking at each other.

"Hey," he said softly, his breath filling her face.

"Hey," she returned.

"You wanna go somewhere?" he asked.

"Oh, uh, nah," she said without thinking too hard about it. Kissing was nice, it was great but out on the sidewalk, she was safe, she didn't know what she'd do if there was only a couch or a bed between them.

"I'm sorry," she said quickly, but King shook his head.

"Nah, I'm sorry."

"You're sorry?" she asked hesitantly.

King nodded, a little sheepishly. "Yeah, of course. You don't gotta apologize, I shouldn't've asked. We're just getting to know each other, and I want you to be comfortable. All the time, not just sometimes."

His words settled into Alonda, filled her up. She smiled at him.

He had the kindest eyes.

"We can keep making out, though," Alonda said, pulling his hand closer to her again. His face broke into a huge smile.

"Okay!" he said, and they started kissing again, the rain still pounding against the scaffolding, and Alonda had to believe that this was the most romantic moment that'd ever happened in the entire world.

It was late, and Alonda couldn't sleep because her entire body felt like it was on fire, and it was still raining on and off so she couldn't go up to the roof, so she had fallen deep into an Instagram hole and she couldn't get out. She'd somehow wandered over to King's Insta page and was casually scrolling through all the posts he had posted . . . from a few years back.

She really, really liked him. He made her laugh, and she liked how gently he touched her. She wanted to get to know him from before she showed up. As she waded through all the reposted memes (man, there were *a lot* of memes) she found pictures he took or someone took with him in them, and she liked seeing all the different sides of him.

Scroll, scroll. Picture of a burger. Picture of a pigeon. Selfie with Pretzel and Spider. Picture of some graffiti on the side of a building. Picture of a pot of rice and black-eyed peas. She paused at a picture that looked like a family portrait. Not like a mall one, but one where they were all standing together, a Christmas tree in the background. A Black man who looked like an older version of King stood behind him, midlaugh, somehow even taller than King, a white woman with dark hair and his eyes exactly at his right. King was directly in the center, wearing a button-down shirt and smiling. He looked so happy.

Scroll, scroll. Picture of a bacon, egg, and cheese on a bagel. Picture of the D train as it came into the station. Selfie with Lexi.

Alonda paused, her finger hovering over the photo. Tapped the picture. A little bubble popped up, showing that Lexi was tagged in the photo. She clicked it and went to her page.

It was mostly pictures of Lexi's art, her collages. They were bright, purples and yellows mixed together, bright blues and greens, each one telling a whole different story even though there was no words. They were so good.

She scrolled back, checking out her older pieces.

It was cool seeing the progression, or the backward progression, maybe? Alonda really didn't know how to talk about art.

She noticed that there was a person commenting on a bunch, exclusively on the older stuff. Nobody really seemed to comment on the newer pieces, but there was always at least one comment per older piece of art. Alonda's curiosity got the better of her, and she clicked it. A smiling girl. Cass. "Great job, babe!" "I love this!"

Alonda noticed she'd stopped commenting a few months ago. She couldn't help herself, the person was right there—she clicked on her name and went to her page. Her bio said, "Cass. BK all day. Just living," and had the little Colombian flag emoji next to an LGBT flag emoji.

Cass seemed to be in a warm embrace in her first photo, with someone who looked as into her as she did. Alonda scrolled down a little bit more, to what seemed like a few months before and stopped.

A picture of Cass and Lexi in a similar embrace.

Cass must be the ex that Lexi was so pressed about. Alonda felt like a real detective. The locked box inside her chest started to shake a little bit.

She put her phone to the side, letting darkness fill the room.

Maybe it was time for her to go to sleep.

☆ 8 ☆

ALONDA HAD NEVER BEEN HIT BY A BUS BEFORE, BUT SHE WAS
pretty sure this is what it felt like. Teresa would tell her she was
being dramatic, but damn! Right now she felt like she had been
run over by one. Her muscles were screaming so loud she was sure
they'd wake up the neighbors if they had a voice to scream with.
Her legs felt like lead, she could barely lift her arms, but damn, if she
didn't feel the most alive she had ever felt for real.

King had started them all on an intense exercise regimen to
build their stamina and make sure they could do everything as safe
as possible, which was smart and made sense and everything, but
it was the most Alonda had ever moved in her whole life. It's not
like she was out of shape before; she always did good in gym class
and had to walk up the stairs to their apartment with a backpack
full of books slamming against her back 'cause they didn't have the
luxury of an elevator in their building (it was way too old school
for that), but King had them using muscles she had ever only seen
in her biology textbook. She could name most of them, could tell
you their functions in the body—to be honest, she was a geek for
stuff like that—but knowing about them and using them were completely different things, damn. And if her muscles could talk right
now, they'd be cursing her out.

But Alonda liked how it felt. Yeah, it hurt, but it was a good hurt, one that was all hers. It was all muscles she always had, they was just getting activated now, almost like all these muscles that had been sleeping were waking up, like the kiss that the prince gives to the princess in *Sleeping Beauty*.

Did that make any sense? Probably not, she was still sleeping.

Her alarm hadn't gone off yet, but the morning had woke her up. She'd forgotten to shut the shade the night before, and the sun was blasting into her closed eyelids, and everything seemed tinted red. She tried to sink back into sleep, but it wasn't happening. All the aches and pains were yelling at her to wake up, and it was like she could feel her body buzzing beneath her sheets. And she had to pee. Like, really bad.

She sat up, her bones groaning, and threw the sheets off her bed, swinging her sore legs to the floor in the same swoop. She glanced at her phone. Six fifteen. Ugh. Only two more days of getting up this early before school was out. She fully planned on sleeping until past ten at least four days a week, for as many days as she could get away with, depending on whatever schedule they gave her at the park. She was only working there part-time, though, so some days would be hers.

All hers.

She sighed deeply and lifted her body off the bed, stretching. Ah, yeah, that felt good, getting all the cricks out.

Alonda walked toward her bedroom door and opened it quickly before slamming it shut again. Damn. Jim was out there, sitting at the kitchen table eating cereal like he lived here. Which he technically did, right, damn. He'd officially moved in a few days ago with a couple of beat-up duffels and a suitcase. Shit. She kept forgetting. She was gonna have to start wearing actual clothes to bed instead of the boxers and tank top she normally wore, which would be fine any other season but it was summer and her room was the hottest in the house.

She pulled a pair of shorts on, fuming. Ugh, Jim. He was like a fly she couldn't swat, always buzzing around, trying too hard to be chill with her or whatever. He and Teresa would stay up late, watching TV or listening to music or laughing their asses off in the living room, long after she went to bed. And he was out there eating Alonda's cereal!

"Jim won't be a stranger if you get to know him," Teresa had said when Alonda complained. "So if you make the effort he won't be a stranger no more!"

Alonda sighed and tiptoed to the bathroom as casually as possible before shutting the door behind her. She didn't wanna make an effort. She was too tired to make an effort.

But Teresa wouldn't ask if it wasn't important.

And worst of all, Jim *was* trying. He was trying so hard it was borderline embarrassing. He asked her about school. Talked about the weather. Sometimes he even dipped his toe into conversations about pop culture. It was like the man had googled Conversation Topics for Teens 101, but Alonda did have to begrudgingly admit, he was trying.

"Guess today's as good a day as any to start trying," Alonda muttered to her reflection as she washed her hands. Time for another awkward conversation.

She stood in the doorway of the kitchen for a minute, waiting for Jim to notice her. He was deep into his phone. Probably reading the news or tweets or something. She coughed what she hoped sounded like a real cough and not the fake one she was actually doing.

"Alonda!" Jim said, sounding surprised, as though it was a shock that she lived here, in her own home.

"Hey, hi, good morning!" Alonda grunted, and moved into the kitchen.

"Was just checking the weather—supposed to be a beautiful day out today," he continued, pointing to his phone. "Not too hot or nothing."

Alonda's eyes twitched in the effort of not rolling them. He was already checking off the Weather Talk box, right out the gate. "That's cool," she said, pulling a bowl down from the cabinet, making as much noise as possible so the dreaded awkward silence wouldn't descend upon them. But the bowls were made of plastic, so they could only make so much noise.

Jim cleared his throat. "So, uh . . . How'd ya sleep?"

"Oh, you know," Alonda said, opening the fridge for the milk, "fine." She busied herself with the spoons, aggressively not making eye contact.

"Me, too!" Jim said. He was too cheerful. "I slept fine, too."

Alonda snorted. "Great!" she said, pulling over the box of cereal on the table.

"Oh, uh, that one's empty," Jim said, glancing up from his phone. A bolt of heat rushed through Alonda. Empty?! He'd eaten all her cereal?! What the hell was she supposed to have for breakfast, toast? Freakin' ew!

"There's a new one in the cabinet," Jim said, breaking her thoughts in half. He nodded toward one of the cabinets. "I picked one up on my way over last night. Figured you'd wanna fresh one. It's always better fresh outta the box, you know?"

That was . . . actually nice. "Thanks," Alonda muttered as she reached for the cabinet. He'd put the cereal on the top shelf, so Alonda had to stand on her toes and reach as far as her arms would take her.

"Holy shit, where'd you get that bruise?!" Jim asked, his rough voice jolting her to reality. Bruise? What bruise? She looked quickly at her arm. Oh, that bruise, the one that Lexi must have given her yesterday when she slammed her into the padding. She knew it would leave a mark. It was dark purple and yellow and billowed out like a cloud on her forearm. Alonda thought it was honestly kinda cool.

"Here, lemme see it—" Alonda pulled her sleeve down, keeping it from him.

"It's nothing," she said quickly, pouring cereal into the bowl.

Jim's eyes narrowed. "Don't look like nothing—lemme see."

"I already told you, it's nothing!" Alonda insisted, grabbing the milk and pouring it.

"If it's nothing, then there ain't no reason you shouldn't show it to me. Right?"

Damn. Caught.

She pulled her sleeve up a little and heard Jim suck air in through his teeth. She studied it. Yeah, okay, it looked pretty bad. But also, it was pretty impressive.

"Who did this to you?" Jim asked, his voice urgent.

Alonda shook her head. "No, I swear, it's nothing, not like that at least—"

"Again with the nothing— All right, then if it's nothing you should tell me."

Alonda looked nervously toward Teresa's bedroom door.

"She ain't here. Had to go in early, she said."

Alonda shrugged her shoulder. "News to me," she muttered, shoveling mushy cereal into her mouth.

"So. You gonna tell me how you got that bruise or what?"

Alonda smashed her lips together, considering. "You'll tell Teresa."

Jim shook his head. "Nah, I won't."

She rolled her eyes, "Yes, you will. It's, like, your duty or whatever. Especially now that you live here."

Jim shook his head, a little more emphatically than before. "Nah, I won't. Really, I won't. Teresa treats you too much like a kid sometimes, I swear, with the curfew and the whole hair thing. I mean, who cares what color your hair is, right?" Alonda listened. She liked the points he was making. He went on, "And when I was your age, nobody had me tied to nothing. I could go wherever I wanted, when I wanted, do what I wanted. It's your business what you wanna do with your time, you know?"

Alonda nodded, but she wasn't really convinced. Adults said whatever the hell they had to in order to get shit outta them.

"You can trust me," he said, but Alonda snorted.

"I barely even know you," she said, smooshing her cereal around in her bowl. It was starting to dissolve, which was good, the way she liked it.

Jim shrugged his shoulder. "Hey, fair point. We don't really know each other. I only started coming around like six months ago, right?" Alonda shrugged out a yes. Jim nodded. "Yeah, and it's not like we been on any field trips together, or had any heart-to-hearts or any of that shit. So all I got is my word, and I'm telling you, you can trust me, for real. That's part of being an adult, too, right? Like, sometimes you just gotta trust a person." Alonda turned the logic over in her head. He wasn't wrong.

He continued, "And the thing about trust, it's something you can't see. Like, trust don't exist, don't got a physical form, right?" Alonda stared at him, unblinking. Where the hell was he going with this. "So one of the tricky things about it," Jim said, looking back at her, just as unblinkingly, "the tricky thing about trust is that it's not something you can see with your eyes. It's not something concrete you can point to and know; it's a feeling that you gotta see with your gut." That made sense.

Jim went on, "So yeah, you gotta wait and see. Sometimes you know you can trust a person without saying as much. And sometimes, you gotta put them to the test. See if they keep your secret. And if they do, then you know. But you gotta trust."

Alonda licked her spoon and kept turning his words over in her head. She hated to admit it, but he did have a point. Like, why did she trust the group before she started hanging out with them? There was just a feeling, and the feeling turned out to be true.

And Teresa did want her to get along with Jim.

He looked her right in the eye. "I'll keep your secret. You just gotta trust me."

Alonda let out a big whoosh of air and matched his gaze steadily. What he said made sense. And Teresa did want them to grow a relationship or whatever. "Fine. Me and my friends . . . we wrestle."

Jim practically choked on his coffee. "Wrestle?"

"Yeah. Like, for real wrestle. Out on the playground."

"Oh!" he said, his eyes widening with relief. He seemed to have thought Alonda had meant some other kinda wrestling, which was a gross assumption to make. "You mean like . . . backyard wrestling? Like how The Hardys started out?" he asked.

"Yeah! That, exactly that," Alonda said, surprised. She didn't realize he'd know about The Hardys. They were a couple of brothers who got their start kind of the way they were, by wrestling outside and gaining a crowd. They didn't have YouTube, though.

She raised her eyebrow at Jim. "You know about wrestling?"

Jim laughed. "Yeah, what d'you think, I live under a rock? 'Course I know it. Wrestling's even older than me—my grandma used to watch it."

"Nah, it's not that—honestly, I didn't think you was cool enough to know it," Alonda said, smirking. Jim laughed again. He could have a good sense of humor sometimes.

"Yeah, I guess I'm not that cool, haven't watched it in a while. But I used to watch it all the time," Jim said. He got that faraway look that he got sometimes, when he was remembering something nice. Almost like he wasn't in the same room as her no more. "Me and my friends, we used to do that shit, too, used to wrestle outside all the time."

"Really?" Alonda asked, a little surprised.

"Yeah, really! What do you think, youse all invented wrestling on the playground? Nah, used to be a good way to pass the time. Came up with names and characters and everything." Jim's eyes glazed a little as a cloud of nostalgia seemed to wander through them. He was a sentimental guy sometimes. "'Course back then," he continued, "we didn't have no girls doing the wrestling with us, they was all too wimpy."

"Yeah, well, I'm not wimpy," Alonda said, setting her mouth in a straight line. She was bristling, ready for a fight, but Jim just nodded back at her, agreeing.

"Yeah, I can see that. If you got a bruise like that and you ain't whining about it."

Alonda smirked to herself and rubbed the bruise again. She flinched. It was still tender. "At least not out loud," she admitted.

"Hey, uh, just . . . you just stay safe, kid. Stay as safe as you can," Jim said quickly. "It's impossible to live and be safe, ya know? You can only do the best you can." Alonda nodded and took it as her cue to leave. She had to get ready for her shift at the Fun-Cade. She gathered up her bowl and spoon and brought them to the sink, cleaning them out. She looked over at Jim. His eyes had that cloud glaze over them again. She started to leave the kitchen and stopped herself, turning back to him.

"Hey, uh . . . You promise you won't tell?"

Jim nodded, his blue eyes holding her gaze steady.

"Yeah, kid. You can trust me."

The day passed by in a blur of neon, loud customers, and a little bit of vomit in the corner that Alonda mopped up. She was starting to fall into the rhythm of the job, particularly bolstered by Michelle, who was really patient and helpful, but also just generally fun to be around. She had a way of making the time pass quickly, creating games like customer bingo and teaching Alonda how to best the pinball machines.

Even though Alonda had spent the day looking forward to going to sleep, now that it was time she couldn't figure out a way to turn her mind off. Part of it probably had to do with her scrolling through YouTube. She'd fallen down a rabbit hole of Top Tens: Top Ten Wrestlers of the Eighties, Top Ten Matches of All Time. She figured she'd watch them until she fell asleep, but instead of dulling her senses, they were igniting them.

Buzz.

The shock of her phone buzzing caused her to drop it onto her lap. As it went down she saw Lexi's name flash across the screen.

She checked the time. 1:00 A.M. What was Lexi doing texting her?

LEXI: Hey, this is a weird ask, but do you think you could find a couple of extra plastic card thingies from the Fun-Cade I could use for a project?

Alonda squinted at the message. What the hell was she talking about?

ALONDA: uh, maybe?
ALONDA: Not sure what you mean . . .
LEXI: Oh, I didn't realize you'd be awake.
LEXI: figured you'd answer in the morning
LEXI: hope I didn't wake you!
ALONDA: nah, I'm up

ALONDA: been tired all day lol
ALONDA: Can't sleep though.

Alonda stretched and looked out her window. Even this late at night, the world was alive out there.

ALONDA: Hey . . . so what plastic card thingies?
LEXI: Those things you put the tickets on instead of the
    real tickets?

"Oooh," Alonda breathed out. Right, those.

ALONDA: Oh, I'm not sure . . . I can check though.
LEXI: What're you doing?
ALONDA: Nothing. Sleep-texting.
LEXI: one of your many talents
ALONDA: for sure
LEXI: lol

Alonda smiled at her phone, looked back up out her window, and breathed in deep. The air was stale with the heat, but she could still smell the freshness of the ocean clinging to it. It was more gray than black tonight, the lights from Coney Island all reflecting against the clouds that blanketed the sky. The noise carried from the boardwalk all the way to her window. Quieter than it would be if she was really down there, in the middle of everything, but still, she could hear people screaming on the rides, could hear the music playing from the rides.

Alonda looked at her phone again. She didn't want the conversation to be over.

> ALONDA: Wild how everything's still so wide awake right
>   now, yeah?
> LEXI: What, besides you?
> ALONDA: And you! Lol.
> LEXI: I dunno, pretty quiet here. Can't really hear anything
>   except my dad snoring his ass off all the way from
>   his bedroom.
> ALONDA: so . . . why do you need a plastic card thing?
> LEXI: I'm working on a new art piece.
> ALONDA: Yeah? Can I see it?

Alonda looked up at the sky while she waited for her response.

A few seconds later her phone buzzed. Alonda looked at the image. It wasn't done yet, but it already made the breath catch in Alonda's throat. It was the Coney Island skyline but made out of things people usually discarded and stuff from the beach, looked like seashells and seaweed and sand. The boardwalk was made out of Popsicle sticks, the Nathan's was a Nathan's napkin. It looked like the Parachute Jump was gonna be a mosaic collage of the glossy maps they gave out from Luna Park. The more Alonda looked, the more stuff she could see.

> ALONDA: Shit, that's . . . really great

She grimaced to herself. Really great? But she couldn't come up with a stronger word that described how Lexi's art made her feel.

LEXI: Thanks. Putting it together for that gallery thing.
Show's only like 6 weeks away. Which is a lot of
time and not a lot of time.

LEXI: all at the same time lol

LEXI: but I figure a lot of what I'm making for the gallery'll
be good for art school apps so . . .

ALONDA: o, yea, for sure!

ALONDA: You gonna apply with that?

LEXI: Yeah . . . I mean, my mom wants me to go to
Spelman College 'cause that's where my sister's at
and that's where my mom went and a bunch of my
aunts and cousins but . . .

ALONDA: but what?

LEXI: I know it's like one of the longest shots in the whole
world, I mean, at least according to my mom it is,
but like . . .

ALONDA: You gonna tell me or . . .

LEXI: Cooper Union

Alonda nodded at her phone. She knew about Cooper Union. It
was one of the best colleges for art in New York City. Which probably meant it was also one of the hardest to get in.

But she also knew Lexi's work was some of the best she'd ever
seen, so it didn't feel like it was too far a reach of a dream.

ALONDA: you're gonna apply at least, right?

LEXI: yeah, for sure. It's funny, my dad is more the
dreamer, like, he wants me to go wherever I wanna
go . . . though I guess my mom's dreaming in her

own way, that she's got her two daughters carrying on her legacy. Wherever I go's gotta have financial aid, so like.

She sent a shrug emoji.

Alonda sucked the inside of her cheek at that. Teresa was dead set on Alonda going to college, and her guidance counselor was pushing her to apply to a bunch of Ivy Leagues, the ones that cost twice Teresa's entire salary a semester, and Teresa kept telling her not to worry about it, but she knew Teresa was over there worrying about it, so how wasn't Alonda supposed to worry, too?

The soft buzz of her phone drew her eyes back down.

LEXI: anyway, Cooper Union's a huge long shot, so who knows.

ALONDA: Yeah but what's that saying? You miss 100% of the shots you don't take?

Lexi sent a string of laughing emojis.

LEXI: You sound like a cat poster right now!

Alonda laughed.

LEXI: All right, well, lemme know about the cards when you have a chance. I'm gonna get back to it—ride the wave of inspiration before I crash.

LEXI: Good night!

ALONDA: night!

Alonda sent the text out and clicked play on the paused video, but suddenly her mind couldn't seem to stay in one place. It was jumping around, from thought to thought, even though those thoughts weren't fully formed. Talking to Lexi didn't make her more tired. Just fired her up. But instead of watching YouTube videos, she watched the night sky as it slowly shed its skin, turning into a new day.

"HAVE YOU LOOKED THROUGH THE BOXES IN THE FRONT HALL closet?"

Teresa's voice jarred Alonda out of her daydream.

"Huh?" Alonda asked lightly, trying to keep her voice as bright and airy as possible.

She'd been thinking about King, but she didn't want Teresa to know anything about it. She and King had been on another kinda date, complete with some major kissing, and she really hoped that Teresa couldn't x-ray vision into her thoughts right now because they'd both be pretty embarrassed.

"The boxes, Alonda," Teresa said. She was sitting at the kitchen table, applying her "face" as she called putting on her makeup. "In the Front. Hall. Closet. Only been asking you to look through them for the week—"

"Oh yeah, the boxes, yeah, I'm, uh . . . I'll do it later."

"Or maybe you can do it, uh, now?" Teresa asked, her lips barely moving as she applied her mascara. Alonda wasn't sure why applying mascara meant you had to keep the rest of your face stock-still, but she wasn't about to ask now.

"Come on, Teresa," Alonda said, but Teresa shot her a look over the mascara wand.

"In the time it'll take to argue with me to not do it, you coulda already done it."

Alonda opened her mouth to argue again, but Teresa shot her another look and she felt her mouth zip shut. Since Jim'd moved in, the apartment felt like it'd gotten smaller and Teresa was in Get Rid of Everything mode, mostly to make room for Jim's crap. She was really acting like he was gonna be living here forever, damn.

Alonda went to grab the box outta the closet. She saw all the sweaters Teresa was talking about and was going to just tell her to give it away when she saw, tucked in between some of the sleeves, a small pink book.

Alonda picked it up, turning it over in her hands before opening it to the first page, and her heart skipped inside her chest.

It said PROPERTY OF AVA RIVERA.

Her mom's diary.

Dated a year before she died.

Alonda stared at the book in her hand, the worn-out plastic veneer with its yellowing pages turning into a jewel encrusted with gold before her eyes.

A piece of her mother that she never knew.

Mami.

She heard Teresa moving from the kitchen into the hall. Alonda quickly shoved the book into her back pocket and kicked the box toward Teresa.

"Do whatever you want with it, I'm good!" Alonda said as she ran into her room.

She opened the book.

Began to read.

Music filled the air.

A throbbing drumbeat. Music you can feel in your bones. Music so loud, you could almost see it moving in the air.

From the darkness, the silhouette of a guy. Tall. Muscular. Cool.

He enters the ring, his arms raised high to the sky.

The sound of cheers getting louder and louder as they mix with the music.

Some boos mix in with the cheers, but they just bounce right off him, those boos? They make him smile. Those boos strengthen him, give him power. And in this moment, he's untouchable, in this moment, as long as they're making noise, this crowd is his.

They're all his.

He picks up a mic.

He opens his mouth to speak.

"They say—"

And the obnoxious chimes of like ten rapid-fire text messages cut him off.

"Oh shit, my bad!" Spider said, running to his phone.

Alonda swallowed a groan and hit stop on her recording. "Cut," she said feebly, rubbing the frizz out of her bangs. Damn, it was at least ninety degrees out and the sun burning hotter with no shade or wind in sight.

King threw the fake mic down. It bounced a little. They had

attached a tennis ball they Sharpie-d black on top of a hairbrush and Lexi had written RIZE WRESTLING (their official wrestling troupe name) on the side in a glittery red.

"Spider, what the hell, man! That's like the tenth time!"

It was technically only like the fourth time, but yeah, it definitely felt like more. King, Alonda was learning, could turn from a powerful entity to a whining baby in fifteen seconds flat.

"The hell keeps texting you?!"

"Is it that guy you met at Pride?" Pretzel asked, trying to peek over his shoulder.

"Yo, it's none of your business! And nah," said Spider, texting.

"You sure about that?" Pretzel said, laughing, trying to grab his phone, but Spider just held it over his head, texting with one hand.

"Nah!" said Spider, still not looking away from his phone.

Turned out, filming promos was a lot more annoying than Alonda thought. Every time they went to film, something interrupted them. Like the pigeon that came from outta nowhere and scared the crap outta King. Or the ambulance siren that got so loud, nobody could hear themselves talk, let alone the music that was supposed to be scoring his promo.

And in between those catastrophes, someone was texting Spider and interrupting the music. They was using his speakers to play King's promo music and had to use his phone because his speakers were only compatible with his phone.

Turned out trying to put on a show had a lot more logistics than any of them had realized.

"Turn the ringer off, man!" King said. "Come on, we gotta get this filmed!"

"Or else what? Will the world stop turning?" Lexi said lazily from her post underneath the bench.

"Helpful, Lexi," King said.

"Not trying to be helpful," Lexi said, turning onto her stomach and pretending to fall asleep.

It was a lot to keep track of, and all of it, if Alonda was being serious with herself, was pretty annoying.

"I can't turn the phone sound off, though," Spider said belatedly. "If I turn that off, then the music won't play!"

"Great," King muttered, kicking at the ground a little.

It was June 28, the first official day of Summer—yeah, summer technically started eight days ago, but today was the first day without school, which made it Real Summer. The days stretched in front of her like a horizon she couldn't see the end to, and for the first time in a while, she was actually excited about them.

Or at least she had been before trying to get this shit filmed.

"You know, you can film it without the music—" Pretzel started to say, but King cut him off, "Right, but I need the music."

"No, I know—" Pretzel started again, but King wasn't listening. He'd been trying this whole time to tell King not to film with music because they could add it later, but he wasn't listening. King could be really stubborn when he wanted.

"Maybe we should work on, oh I dunno, actually wrestling." Lexi's voice was muffled because she was speaking into her arms, still pretending to be asleep. Her small frame fit perfectly under the length of the bench. She refused to participate in the filming, which meant she refused to make herself be useful in any way, shape, or form and had planted herself under the bench like the world's most ornery daisy.

"But—my promo—"

"We can film it another day!" Spider said, putting his phone down. "Come on, I wanna wrestle, I never get to."

"Fine, whatever," King said, clearly annoyed but refusing to be defeated by the setback. King nudged the mic out of the way and turned to face Spider.

"Let's go, then, the sequence we practiced."

The two of them fell into a sequence—started with a couple of fake-out strikes. Alonda watched them, impressed. It almost looked like Spider really was attacking King for real, but really he was making most of the noise.

It was pretty cool to watch.

Alonda turned to Lexi, who was aggressively not watching. She was just staring up at the planks of the bench.

"Come on, let's practice something," she said, nudging Lexi with her foot.

"It's too hot," Lexi said.

"Oh what, you can't take the heat?" Alonda asked, making her voice kinda corny sounding, wiggling her eyebrows. Lexi laughed and swatted at her but didn't move. Like, at all.

"Come on, let's do *something*, I'm bored," Alonda said, nudging her some more. Lexi groaned but started to get up. Before they could do anything, they were cut off by Pretzel's enthusiastic shouting.

"Here, I did it," Pretzel said, interrupting the sparring practice.

"Did what?" Lexi asked, but Pretzel just held out his hand in response, his phone playing something.

"Here, just watch," he said, holding his phone out in front of him. The four of them gathered around as he hit play on a video. A kinda deep bass techno beat started playing, and Pretzel's face filled the screen. He was wearing dark sunglasses and a striped shirt, his blond hair carefully gelled.

"You are watching the RIZE WRESTLING YouTube channel, coming at you straight from Coney Island.

"If you're not watching Rize, you're not watching WRESTLING.

"WE ARE THE **FUTURE.**

"School may be done, but we're just getting started, we will be coming at you with the FRESHEST content that you will EVER see on YouTube or Facebook Live or on any network television ALL SUMMER!

"If you wanna be in the know, don't forget to hit like and subscribe for the latest rivalries, biggest matches, and dopest action you'll find this side of the Atlantic.

"And if you wanna see us in the flesh, you'll get your chance on July 8. Bring a friend! Bring your cousin. Just don't bring your mom. We'll be back with more soon, stay tuned."

"Well?" Pretzel asked. He was looking at them all and shifting from side to side, blue eyes gleaming from the sun.

Alonda was impressed. He musta somehow figured out how to set up a green screen in his room so the background was a still of a professional wrestling ring, complete with lights and empty folding chairs and stuff.

"How'd you get it to sound so good?" Alonda asked, curious. The sound was almost legit; it definitely didn't have a weird tinny ringing to it.

"I recorded it in a closet," Pretzel said eagerly. "I just took all my mom's shoes out of her bedroom closet and set up this clip light and my makeshift green screen, and then when I was editing it, I duplicated the track and placed it directly underneath the other one to give it more depth, and then I added an echo effect," he said, his words leaping out of his mouth, looking at King pointedly.

"See, so you don't need my speakers at all!" Spider said.

"We still need them for the show—" King started to say, but Pretzel cut him off.

"Right, see," Pretzel continued, his words racing over one another the way they did when he was excited about something, "I added a track for music so I didn't have to play it to capture it, which helps, too, I think."

Spider was looking at him, nodding. Alonda kinda understood what he was talking about, but Spider was more the tech guy, him and Pretzel. It sounded legit, though. And it obviously worked—the video looked legit.

King and Lexi didn't say anything; they had immediately pressed play and were watching again from the beginning, which seemed to make Pretzel antsy.

"It took me like fifteen tries to get it right," Pretzel continued, "and I know the sound kinda cuts off a little at the end of the second sentence, but I don't think it's too noticeable, almost gives that kinda authentic vibe, I thought, and—"

"This looks sick," King said, interrupting him.

Pretzel's whole face lit up. "Yeah? It's okay?"

"It's better than okay," Lexi said. "It's great, it looks almost like we know what we're doing."

"That's because we *do* know what we're doing," King said.

"I mean, you didn't know about the music—" Pretzel muttered before King cut him off.

"Yeah, I mean, with the important stuff."

"But . . . this is part of the important stuff—"

"All right," Spider said, nodding. "So we got at least one video that we can put up online. We gotta work on getting people to subscribe, and hopefully we can get some people around to have some sorta real crowd, which won't only look good for the videos, but'll be good for us."

"Yeah," Lexi said, "no point in doing this shit if there's not at least some of a crowd."

King looked surprised. "Thought you was against this shit," he said.

Lexi shrugged. "I'm allowed to change my mind."

"We could go old school with marketing and put up some flyers around," Alonda said. "Don't gotta be fancy, can just say our name and when the first show's gonna be."

"Yeah," Lexi agreed, "we can put them up on the bulletin boards in the lobbies of the buildings and in the library and shit."

"Boardwalk, too," King said. "There's mad people that'll see that."

"Yeah, but we don't want tourists to come over here," Alonda said quickly. Not only was she already sick of needing to be surrounded by them all the time, but the more outsiders they let in, the more trouble could follow them. "This shit's not for tourists," she said, "it's for us. Like, the people who live here, first and foremost. Tourists be coming from places like Iowa and Manhattan, let them be entertained by the boardwalk, by the beach, the amusement park, but this? This is for us, for the neighborhood." The others nodded, though King did look a little disappointed. Alonda could tell that he wanted to fast-track his way to the WWE, but this was a playground in Coney Island.

"Besides," she added more kindly, "we're putting it up on the internet, right? And the internet's got no boundaries."

"Fair point," King said, slipping his hand into Alonda's. Her cheeks went warm at his touch, but she tightened her grip on his hand, holding it back.

She felt Lexi's stare burrowing into their hands, felt her energy shift.

"Okay," Alonda said, pulling her hand out of King's. "Should we start trying to promote it?"

"For sure. Summer ain't that long," Spider said.

Alonda nodded, glancing between King and Lexi.

They were both looking at her, the same kinda look on each of their faces.

Alonda had to agree.

For once, summer didn't feel like it was gonna be long.

She was worried that it was actually gonna go by too fast.

July

☆ **10** ☆

"WHAT DO YOU THINK THEY'RE THINKING ABOUT?"

Alonda snapped out of her reverie.

The dim blue lights of the aquarium reflected off King's eyes.

She'd been lost in thought, staring at the stingrays as they swam through the water. They were as elegant as ballerinas, the way they moved, slowly and quickly all at once.

Alonda secretly loved the aquarium. King had surprised her by taking her. Which was nice not only because she loved it, but because there was AC. It was only the first day of July and it was humid as hell outside.

She knew that there were other exhibits to see, but she found herself lingering here. She could watch the one tank all day. What was happening inside was always changing, stingrays swimming by, huge fish with lumpy, grumpy faces, small schools that twittered through the water together, leaving a trail of tiny bubbles in their wake. She'd gotten lost in the quiet stories of the tank, had almost lost sight of the fact she was on a date.

"Who's thinking what?" she asked.

King pointed at the tank, his finger following a stingray as it danced across the water. "Them," he said.

"The stingrays?" she asked, trying to keep disbelief from her voice. King nodded. "Yeah, you think they're, like, daydreaming of being outta there and hanging with us?"

He put on a silly high-pitched voice, pretending to be the stingray. "Hey, I hear your weather ain't as wet as this!"

Alonda let a giggle escape her mouth. "Uh, yeah, I'm sure they're all begging to be out here."

"What do you mean, of course they might wanna come and chill with us on land, isn't that what Ariel wanted?" King asked.

"Ariel was a fictional character; stingrays are real creatures!"

"Wait, hold up, you think that mermaids are fiction?" King asked. Alonda looked at his eyes to see if he was joking, but he looked super serious.

"You . . . think that they're . . . real?" she asked carefully. She didn't wanna be judgmental, but also, was he serious?

King hesitated. "I didn't mean to say . . . You're gonna make fun of me."

Alonda shook her head. "Nah, what are you . . . what do you mean?" she asked lightly, trying to erase any judgment from her voice.

King took a deep breath, his eyes doing a sweep of the small space. There was a couple of kids with their adults tottering around, a couple of adults on their cell phones, not even paying attention to the blue tanks in front of them. He stepped closer to Alonda, his voice low so only she could hear.

"Well, okay, it's not that I think that mermaids might be real or whatever, it's just that I don't think that we know for sure that they ain't. Like, look at all this," he said, gesturing at the tanks in front of them. "They're always finding out about more and more creatures they didn't know existed, right? And there's so many stories about them—you're telling me that all just came from outta nowhere?"

Alonda shrugged a little. "I mean, I read that the myth got started because of manatees."

King nodded. "Yeah and that might be true, too. But like. We dunno."

Alonda opened her mouth to argue facts but closed it. She didn't feel like getting into a whole debate about something she knew was true. She was more interested in those creatures that haven't been discovered, not half humans, half fish that would never be found because they simply don't exist.

She slipped her hand in his instead. The palm of his hand was rough and nice. She looked up at him and caught a shy smile flickering across his face.

"Be careful, people're gonna think you're happy," she said, poking him lightly in the stomach.

He laughed a little and pulled her close. "Yeah?" he asked, his breath smelling like cinnamon from the mint he had popped into his mouth.

Alonda nodded. "Yeah."

She saw his eyes dart around, checking to see the status of the humans nearby.

"Don't worry, nobody's paying attention. Only the stingrays could be watching us," she said playfully. "And they might get jealous."

"Oh well," he said with a small smile, and he gently kissed her.

It was the Fourth of July, which was technically a national holiday, but that didn't apply to workers at the amusement park. When most of the country had off to celebrate not having to go to work, they went out to play games and eat food, which meant that a lot of people had to work. The irony wasn't lost on Alonda as she helped with inquiry after inquiry, customers rushing to her to complain about a game that wasn't giving out as many credits as they felt they deserved, or that stopped working midplay, or to complain that the prizes were priced too high.

Alonda yawned, silently cursing herself for staying up so late last night. She and Lexi had stayed up until, like, 3:00 A.M. texting. What had started as a quick check-in about wrestling characters had evolved into a conversation about future plans, which had evolved into a conversation about relationships. Alonda still wasn't completely sure how it had happened, it had felt so natural. One minute they were talking about archetypes; the next, Lexi was sharing about Cass.

LEXI: I feel like when people break up or whatever, the person they were with is supposed to turn into a villain or something. But we just weren't working out and I dunno, couldn't keep trying?

ALONDA: What about it wasn't working?

LEXI: Cass is more of an extrovert than me.

LEXI: Always wanting to go to parties and stuff.

LEXI: Which, sure, it's great to be pushed outside my comfort zone, but it's also important to just be me. You know?

ALONDA: For sure.

LEXI: we were better friends. But now we're not really
friends and that sucks.

LEXI: I do miss her, though

ALONDA: Yeah, makes sense. Especially if you were
friends.

LEXI: Thanks for listening =)

Even though they were texting, Alonda felt like they were talking for real. Which, just because it's text on a screen doesn't make communication any less real. But Alonda felt like they were right next to each other, talking side by side throughout their entire conversation. She didn't even feel the minutes slipping into deep night; if anything, she was energized by Lexi's texts.

Alonda stifled another huge yawn, trying to swallow it down before it exploded out her mouth. Too bad that energy didn't lend itself to today.

At least she got to work in a place with shade and some semblance of a cooling system.

"All right, let's see how many tickets you've got—" she said, running the card and looking at the number of tickets.

"It's one hundred whole tickets, I swear!"

Alonda looked at the number and smiled a little. "Actually, looks like you've got one hundred and ten tickets."

The kid's face lit up so much, his joy filled her heart. Sometimes it was really cool getting to work here.

She yawned again.

"Hey, there's free hot dogs and hamburgers and stuff by the

employee lounge," Michelle said, poking Alonda. "You can go get some if you want."

Alonda's stomach rumbled in response, though nobody could hear it over the roar of the games. "Sure, that sounds goooo—" Alonda cut herself off with an epic yawn. Michelle laughed a little.

"Hey, and why don't you go take a walk or something?" Michelle asked. "Maybe the fresh air'll give you a second wind."

"I'm good." Alonda was able to get the whole word out before she yawned again.

"Maybe grab a coffee! With extra caffeine!" Michelle called after her as Alonda walked out of the Fun-Cade and into the fresh air of Coney Island.

The sky was overcast with clouds, and it was so windy out that the wind was making little mini sand tornadoes on the beach, but that didn't deter any of the people on the boardwalk. Fourth of July was always crowded as hell, which is why Alonda usually avoided heading down to the beach on that day, preferring to spend the Fourth at home with Teresa in front of a whirling fan in her living room, watching old black-and-white episodes of *The Twilight Zone* on TV.

The boardwalk was packed. People bumped into one another, walked in groups, laughing and smiling, sunglasses on their faces, heads, carrying chairs or umbrellas, huge beach bags, most people only wearing their swimsuits as they meandered along the boardwalk, tripping over uneven planks every other step. Some people rode their bikes (which they weren't supposed to do), others tried to get by on skateboards or scooters, parents tried to maneuver huge strollers that carried oblivious sleeping (often slightly sun-burned) children through the crowds of legs while others let their dogs lead (or plop down midwalk, refusing to move another step, a move Alonda respected). She walked by, moving slowly through the chaos, breathing it all in.

A group of people were playing salsa, their Puerto Rican flags flying behind them, stretched out in the wind that blew. They had music blasting from a beat-up-looking radio but were play-ing along with instruments for real. A few of them were playing different kinds of drums—looked like they had bongos and even a conga—someone was playing a güiro, another the claves. Some others were sitting next to them, on folding chairs they'd obviously brought, sipping on drinks and swaying their bodies to the beats, singing loud whenever they knew the words. A crowd of people had stopped in front of them, most of them with their phones out, recording or singing with the songs, clapping, looking, cre-ating a semicircle so those who wanted to dance for real could be in the center—and they were dancing hard, moving their bodies to the music, raising their arms high, shouting or clapping along themselves.

Alonda stopped to watch the musicians, a smile stretching across her face. She loved salsa. Especially that old-school salsa. Mami would always have it playing. All the memories of her childhood when she was still alive were scored with the music of Héctor Lavoe and Celia Cruz and Ismael Rivera, the brass of trumpets, thumping of drums, she felt it in her own heartbeat.

It was music that didn't make its way on any of her playlists; those were mostly full of pop music, she always forgot about those old songs for some reason, but whenever she heard them, she could always remember all the notes.

She watched two people really letting loose, dancing hard, and felt a twinge inside her. Damn, if Mami was here, she'd be dancing right in the center of everything. Reading her mom's diary was harder and less cathartic than she thought it would be. She wrote mostly about mundane things, the sentences dashing back and forth between Spanish and English in some of the hardest-to-read handwriting Alonda'd ever tried to decipher. More often than not she'd put the book down in a puff of frustration.

Well, what the hell'd she expect from reading it, though? A heartwarming Hallmark TV moment like those corny movies Teresa watched at Christmas? Did she wish Mami's ghost would float out from the pages and stand before her, glowing with a gleaming light and speaking in an echoey whisper, like "Nena, now you have found me." Nah, Alonda knew none of that would happen. Her brain knew it anyway.

Her heart was less convinced. Every page she turned, she knew she was hoping for a secret to waft from its pages and fill a hole Alonda was sure she'd stitched up. She wasn't Mami on those pages; she was Ava, a stranger, or a thin reflection that Alonda had never gotten to know.

Alonda felt her foot tapping to the beat, felt her body starting to sway, but she stopped herself. She couldn't bring herself to join the group, all dancing and laughing. "You gotta dance like nobody's watching, nena, 'cause nobody is watching!" Mami'd say, but she still couldn't bring herself to move, watching the bodies swaying, her foot tapping against the wood of the boardwalk but somehow unable to join.

She took a deep breath in and turned around, toward the Fun-Cade.

She had to get back to work anyway.

She walked away, the music following her way past the point where she could hear it.

☆ **11** ☆

"Welcome to the Rize YouTube Wrestling channel. Stay up-to-date on our latest matches, get to know the wrestlers, and don't forget to like and subscribe.

"If you're not watching Rize, you're not watching wrestling.

"Rize Wrestling, promo number one."

A blank screen dissolves into the bright sunlight of the outside world. The words THE INCREDIBLE LEXI flash across the screen. The camera goes all shaky, almost like it's flying, and suddenly bam.

The Incredible Lexi jumps into view, having just landed from flying, her hands on her hips. She wears a green cape draped over her shoulders, long braids cascading down her back.

She winks at the camera, pulling a mic out from her back pocket.

She lifts the mic to her lips and begins to speak.

"What is a belt?" she asks the camera directly, as though it can respond.

"No, really, what is a belt?" she asks again, but doesn't wait for an answer this time.

"Usually it's just something that helps keep your pants up, right? Is that the first thing that comes to your mind? First thing that used to come to my mind. That was before I got this."

She holds up the Rize belt, a thick, round belt, covered with glitter that has RIZE written in the center.

"THIS is our belt. Definitely not something you'd be able to keep your pants up with, right?" She smirks and tosses it over her shoulder, holding it with pride.

"And this belt? It's not just some random little thing, to me it's EVERYTHING."

She holds it up again, high over her head with one hand, the other still grasping the mic.

"It's honor, it's glory, it's prestige! I know, I know there's some out there who think they can just cheat their way to glory, lie their way to victory, but I know, I know it's not about all that. I'm here to show you that I can be the best by being the best.

"This belt?

"It belongs to me because it IS ME.

"And I got a message here for King.

"King, if you think that belt is built for you, you in for a rude surprise.

"Because I'm coming for you, King.

"I know, I know we go way back, but guess what.

"I ain't looking nowhere but forward.

"Long live the King?

"The King is dead!"

She says this and drops the mic to the ground before she raises her arms to the sky, holding the belt in both hands, because she means business, serious business. She starts to walk away but stops, grabs the fallen mic, and speaks into it again.

"And remember, if you wanna see us live, you gonna get your chance on July eighth, one o'clock Eastern Standard Time!"

She gives the camera one big smile before she drops the mic again and—

"Okay, cut!"

"We got it?" Lexi asked.

Alonda nodded, looking at the video. "Yeah, looks good!" she shouted.

"Okay, great," Lexi said, squirming, her fluffed-up veneer completely dissolved. "These pants are really riding up my butt." Along with the green cape she'd tied around her shoulders, she'd insisted on wearing a white pleather tube top and a matching pair of pleather pants, and while the costume looked really cool, it did, indeed, kinda look like it was giving her an intense wedgie. "I'm so sweaty, they're like sticking to my butt crack!" she said, wiggling around.

"You can just wear shorts, you know," Spider said. He was at his spot by the bench, sewing something.

"I don't know any superheroes who wear shorts," Lexi said, still pulling at the fabric around her crotch. "I mean, I know they wear jeans on their downtime, but I dunno any who wear them when they're out superhero-ing around," she said. "It'd be a pretty inaccurate costume, that's all."

"Right, but jeans can be a costume; they're my costume," King said, pacing a little. As was becoming their norm, it had been their fifth or sixth take at a promo and the sun was moving the shadows around, messing up their shots.

"Okay, but," Spider asked, "how're you gonna wrestle in something if you can't even stand still comfortable?"

"Oh, I'm not gonna wear this specific outfit to wrestle in," Lexi said. "This is just my promo gear. I got a different costume to wrestle in."

"What do you mean different?!" King shouted. He sounded flabbergasted. "This is what you said you was gonna wear! How different's the costume? When're you gonna practice in it?"

"Oh my God, calm down! I'll figure it out!" she tossed back with a yawn. The more tense King got, the more chill Lexi became, which only made King more tense and Lexi more flippant.

"You don't got time to figure it out—it's almost time for the first show!" King snapped back.

"It's not that serious," Lexi said, rolling her eyes a little. "Not like WWE is coming to judge us or whatever."

"Hey, where's Pretzel?" Alonda asked, cutting off King before he could respond.

Spider shrugged, happy to tag team with her to try to dilute the dispute. "I dunno, he said he'd be here. Something came up, probably."

"He should be here by now," King said, looking at his phone. "We're already running behind."

"Running behind what?" Lexi muttered. "Time is a societal construct," she started to say, but Spider talked over her.

"It's cool, we don't need him for the filming. We got time to get Alonda's promo done," Spider said, smiling at Alonda. His words made Alonda's heart tighten in her chest a bit; she felt it trying to climb out of her throat.

"Oh, uh, that's okay, we don't gotta," she said, busying herself with the phone.

"We've already filmed everyone else's," Spider said. "Yours is the only one we got left."

"I still . . . I don't—"

"Don't tell me you still don't know what you're doing," King said, annoyance coloring his every word. "I mean"—his words came out quickly, trying to cover up the annoyance with something else—"that's cool, that's cool, do you, uh, do you happen to know when you might know what you'll be doing?"

Alonda tried to play it cool.

"No, I, of course, I know what I'm doing," Alonda said, "I just . . . I'm still practicing, I haven't memorized it fully yet, I need to get my costume together, not exactly camera ready or whatever."

"Those are a lot of reasons," Lexi said with a snort.

"Can you at least tell us your name?" Spider asked.

"I . . . uh," she said, her words drifting off.

No, she couldn't tell them her wrestling name 'cause she didn't know it yet.

Alonda knew that this was ironic. And annoying. She wanted to wrestle more than anything in the world but still hadn't come up with the most basic shit. Like, she had routines down with everyone, and sequences, but she didn't know who it was she wanted to be. Wrestlers chose personalities that were exaggerations of themselves, mostly, but she sometimes, deep down inside her, felt like she didn't even know if there was anything there to exaggerate. She felt like she was a boring person living out a boring life most of the time. Teresa would tell her not to be silly, but she also would tell her not to wrestle if she knew about it. So she couldn't even talk about wrestling to the person who knew her best.

Not that she was even around to talk to her. Lately Teresa was like a ghost in the house, never around, and even when she was around, she wasn't really 'cause she was always busy with Jim.

But then again, Alonda wasn't really at home; she was either at work, hanging out with King, or here. She didn't realize she could miss someone she lived with.

Her heart pulled, thinking about it.

"It's cool," King said, as though he could read her mind. "You still got time to come up with it."

Lexi scoffed loudly, "Yeah, okay!"

"What, it's true!" King shot back, but Lexi kept talking over him.

"You JUST said that I didn't have time to change my outfit, but she's got time to not even know what the hell her wrestling name is? You're just giving her special treatment 'cause she's your girlfriend."

Girlfriend? That was a little much. Alonda opened her mouth to correct Lexi, but King got ahead of her.

"Yeah, and so what, perks of being my girlfriend," King snapped back.

"Wait, am I . . . ?" Alonda asked, unable to finish the question.

King looked at her, surprise softening his eyes. "Well, yeah," he said, "I mean, I thought . . ."

"Oh, I—I just didn't know," Alonda said. It's not like they had talked about it—but maybe that's not how these things worked?

"Yo, Pretzel!" Spider said suddenly, and Alonda's heart breathed a sigh of relief. Thank goodness for Pretzel. "Where you been, man?!" Spider continued. "We been here for an hour."

Pretzel was walking toward the group slowly. Alonda squinted a little. Something was off. He was more disheveled than usual; his hair wasn't in its hard-gelled perfection, it was sticking up on the side, and his shorts seemed baggier—it looked like he was clutching them at his waist. And his shirt looked weird, was it—it was backward. And inside out, she could see the seams sticking out on the sleeves.

"Hey, guys," he said, looking at the ground. "Sorry I'm late."

Lexi narrowed her eyes. "What's wrong?" she demanded.

Pretzel shook his head. "Nothing," he said. "I'm just late. And for that, I am sorry." He shrugged nonchalantly, but the movement made his shorts slip. He grabbed them to keep them from hitting the ground.

"Where's your belt, man?" King asked.

"Nowhere," Pretzel said.

Alonda watched as the three of them exchanged a silent look over Pretzel's head before staring back at Pretzel again. After a moment, Spider walked over to him and punched him in the arm. "Tell us what's wrong!" he demanded.

Alonda pursed her lips; she felt like if he didn't feel like telling them what was wrong, then they shouldn't push it, but she also recognized that this seemed like a group dynamic she didn't get yet.

"Nothing, nowhere, damn! I was just hanging out with Tania!" Pretzel said. The three of them exchanged another look. Alonda felt a pang of jealousy. They were doing that thing again, where they could all talk to one another without saying a single word out loud.

"And . . . what happened?" Lexi asked tentatively.

"We . . . lost track of time," Pretzel said.

All right, there's the answer, Alonda thought, but the three others kept staring at him.

"And?" King prompted.

"And we didn't hear her mom come home, but she came home . . . ," he said, his voice trailing off.

"She caught you?" Spider asked. Pretzel just nodded, and a collective cringe rippled through the group.

Alonda was piecing the clues together. Okay, Tania was Pretzel's girlfriend. He'd talked about her enough. And her mom must have come home while they was . . .

Alonda flinched, too. She couldn't imagine Teresa finding her just kissing a guy, let alone anyone watching them have sex together, damn.

"She saw your . . . It?" Lexi asked.

Pretzel sighed deeply. "I mean . . . it technically wasn't *out* at that point, but . . . ," he said. King and Spider groaned deep, and Lexi flinched so hard, Alonda wasn't sure if a bug had flown into her eye.

Another silence descended on the group. Seemed like nobody really knew what to say or how to say it.

"Well, Tania's mom sucks," Lexi said. She stated it as solidly as an indisputable fact.

"Yeah, for sure," King agreed, nodding enthusiastically.

"Right," Alonda said, even though she didn't know Tania or her mom. But it seemed like it didn't really matter who she knew because that's not what Pretzel seemed to need in this moment.

Looked like he just needed them.

"You want some water, man?" Spider asked, shoving his water bottle in Pretzel's hand before he could respond.

"You want my belt?" King asked, unbuckling his own.

"Dude, no, keep your belt on," Pretzel muttered, but his face fluttered as though a smile that was trapped inside was trying to break its way through.

"What, it's mostly just for show anyway!"

"Stop, you don't have to give me your belt, man," Pretzel said. "I left so fast, I didn't have time to look for it. Barely had time to put my shorts back on. Grabbed my shoes, didn't have time to put those on, either, threw them under my arm, running around in my socks. And her mom was blocking the door to her bedroom and screaming, throwing Tania's shit at me, like books and makeup and stuff, so there was no way to get past her, and so I had to jump out her window and run down the fire escapes. Everyone could hear her screaming, I could hear her the whole way down. And she lives on the tenth floor. There were . . . so many fire escapes."

Lexi stifled a cough that sounded a lot like a laugh. They all looked at her.

"It's not funny," she said defensively. "I'm not laughing, I'm . . . choking."

"Choking on what," Pretzel asked, a smile threatening to flicker across his lips.

"The air," she said, her face stoic and her voice calm, but a peal of high-pitched giggles escaped Spider's lips. Alonda looked at him, biting her own lips to keep from smiling.

"I'm not laughing, either," he said, getting the giggles under control, "I just, I think the sun's tickling me. I hear if you get hot enough, it makes you laugh."

But Pretzel's sad face kept cracking. "It's really not funny," Pretzel said, smiling a little bit. "But also, her mom was screaming so loud, I heard the neighbors start to pound on the floor for her to be quiet and she started yelling at them worse than she was yelling at me, and that was pretty funny."

"Tania's mom yelled at me once," Lexi said. "I was walking from the train, and she was walking their dog and talking on the phone, and that little scraggly rat dog—"

"Cupcake," Pretzel said.

"Cupcake," Lexi continued with disgust, "totally peed on my leg! And she yelled at me for getting in the way of his pee."

"Tania's mom yelled at me once, too!" Spider said. "She said I should have helped her with her groceries. I was like, ma'am, are your groceries invisible? 'Cause I don't see any groceries, and she goes, 'No, the other day, I needed help and you was crossing the street and went the other direction!' I was like, ma'am, I have no idea what you're talking about, and she was like 'You gotta be more observant!' and then she walked off the curb 'cause she was looking at her phone."

The five of them burst out laughing even harder than before. Alonda hadn't realized how uncomfortable she'd felt, just because there was a lot of tension in the story and because she felt second-hand embarrassed at what happened to Pretzel. But it was like that laughter was popping a bubble: It was healing, it was medicine, it was balm for the moment, somehow, and Alonda didn't really know what any of them was laughing at, but she felt that laughter bubble up inside herself, too, she felt that joy that was being passed around to each of them, she felt that healing, too, and she wished that the laughter could last forever, could last longer than this one moment.

She probably wouldn't remember this moment in ten years, in a year, but she knew she was living it and felt every inch of it, and that was something that she hadn't felt before, and that was something she could get used to.

It was like those moments she had seen from her window, where they'd all been busy doing nothing. Well, no, Alonda had *thought* they were doing nothing, but it turned out this, laughing, being together in a moment, turning a moment of pain into something else, that was doing a lot more than she had realized.

A lot more.

"Hey, would you guys wanna, like, . . . come over my house and watch the Friday night fireworks tonight?" Alonda hadn't planned on saying anything, but it felt right.

"Yeah?" Pretzel asked.

"Yeah, like, bring Tania and whoever, and we can all watch from my roof. You can see everything from up there," she said, gesturing toward the general direction of her building. "Like, they do the fireworks over the ocean and you can see them good from my roof, got a clear shot and everything," she said. "Plus, I really do wanna meet Tania. She seems cool."

"Yeah, that'd be awesome," Pretzel said, a huge smile crossing his face.

King slung his arm over Alonda's shoulders and reached down for a quick kiss. "Sounds great," he said.

"Yeah, I'll be there," Spider said.

"What about you, Lexi?" Alonda asked. "If you're not too busy working on your art stuff," she added quickly. She knew that they were texting more and more late at night because Lexi's deadline was looming ever closer and she didn't wanna stress her out.

"Yeah, why not," Lexi said. "I could use a night off." Alonda smiled.

"Okay, then. See you all there."

☆ **12** ☆

"If you're not watching Rize, you're not watching wrestling.

"Rize Wrestling, promo number two."

A drumbeat thumps as text appears on the screen.

KING.

The letters fade away, and the picture focuses on a well-worn sneaker. The camera pans up, up, up to reveal King's face. He holds the mic and looks directly at the camera, unflinching. He makes a motion off-screen, and the music fades away. He takes a moment before he begins to speak.

"They say that Brooklyn is the hottest place to live,

not outta the five boroughs, not outta the state, not outta the country,

nah,

they say that Brooklyn is the hottest place to live in the whole entire WORLD!"

He holds his arms up for a moment as the tinny sound of a crowd roars. The crowd cuts off suddenly as he puts the mic back to his mouth and says,

"And I say, yeah. I know.

"I know that Brooklyn is the greatest place to live in the entire world, in the universe, but you really wanna know why that is?"

He puts a hand up to his ear, pretending to listen.

"Well, it's not because Brooklyn is full'a cute little fancy coffee shops.

"It's not because Brooklyn has commissioned artsy walls or because it's a hot place for artists to come to make a name for themselves.

"It's because Brooklyn is made of the people who live here, who have lived here, who are here, it's because we been here!

"This is a county for Kings, baby! And I'm the King!

"All hail the King!"

The fake crowd sound comes on again, louder than before.

"And I got a message for the Incredible Lexi. Lexi, I know you think that belt is yours, and I'm sorry to disappoint you, but . . ."

He raises the Rize belt and shows it to the camera; he's written his name on it.

"As you can see, it's actually got my name written all over it. You wanna take it back? I'll see you in the ring." He almost drops the mic but stops himself, puts it back up to his mouth, and says, "Here, live on the playground, July eighth, one o'clock Eastern Standard Time. See you there."

"Whoa, this view's sick!" Pretzel said, poking his head out the door.

Alonda smiled wide, proud of the space. "I know, right?" she said. She'd taken them through the door that led directly out onto the roof, not Alonda's secret way out her window and up the fire escape. Technically nobody was ever supposed to be on the roof, but it was one of those rules that everybody kinda nodded away, and everyone in the building had set it up so it was pretty nice; there was lanterns strung along the perimeter and a bunch of folding chairs that were up for grabs, for whoever's asses wanted to sit in them. There was no real rule as to who was gonna replace them or when or whatever, but whenever a chair was super moldy or broken through with wear and tear, a new one would usually pop up in its place. Besides, there was always plastic crates to sit on or lean against. The magic was in the view.

Alonda could just barely make out the ocean from the living room window, but the roof had Coney Island all spread out in front of it, almost like a postcard. To the left, the Parachute Jump stood proudly, already lighting up with lights as the sun sank on the horizon line, shading everything in a pinkish-sepia tone.

"Oh, sorry, I'm being rude, Alonda, this is Tania Gonzalez, my girlfriend," Pretzel said, introducing a really pretty girl with dark brown skin and dyed red hair.

"Hi!" Tania said, the word bursting out of her mouth, opening her arms but hesitating. "I'm sorry, I'm a hugger, can I hug you?"

Alonda smiled harder. Tania had such a warm and loving energy. Alonda immediately wanted to be friends with her. "Yeah, okay," she said, and Tania grabbed her in a huge hug.

"Oh, and this is my little sister, Kimmie," she said, pointing to a girl who looked like Tania's duplicate but smaller, about twelve or so and with black curly hair and big dark eyes that shone under the lanterns.

"Hi, thanks for letting me crash your party, Mamá thinks we're at the beach and wouldn't be happy if she found out that Tania was hanging out with Pretzel since they're banned from seeing each other, just like Romeo and Juliet—isn't it so romantic!" she said, all her words tumbling out on top of one another in one breath.

Tania rolled her eyes. "Kimmie, shush, nobody wants to hear about none of that."

Pretzel looked stricken. "She's still upset?"

"Nah, she's fine," Tania responded at the same time Kimmie said, "Oh yeah, she hates you."

"Why don't you help me set out the brownies," Tania said to Kimmie, picking up a bunch of Tupperwares and shoving them into her sister's arms.

"Um, wow, ouch??" Kimmie said pointedly, but Tania just rolled her eyes. "You're fine and you know it," she said.

"Here, I got a table. I'll help you set it up," Alonda said.

"It's only been three hours—you gotta give her a chance to calm down!" Alonda heard Tania saying to Pretzel as Alonda helped Kimmie with the table.

Alonda was struggling with the table, trying to set it up, when strong arms helped straighten it. "Thanks," she said, turning to see Lexi standing there, straightening the table.

"This is not the sturdiest contraption I've ever seen," she said.

"Can't argue with you there," Alonda said. "Not even sure how old it is. Might be ancient."

"Would probably be a really great table to, like, fake a fall through," Lexi said, her eyes lighting up with excitement.

Alonda laughed. Wrestlers were throwing themselves through inanimate objects all the time. "Yeah, but I don't think we're at that level yet."

The two passed a smile back and forth between each other,

but neither said anything else. "Well, I'm just gonna go . . . sit over there," Lexi said, wandering over to Pretzel and Tania.

Why was it so much easier to text with Lexi than it was to talk to her face-to-face?

"Hey!" a soft, low voice said. Alonda turned to see King's smiling face.

"Hi," she said, and leaned into his hug.

"Hey, you got something we can play some music off of?" Lexi called over.

Alonda pulled away from the hug. "Yeah, is this a party or a fart-y?" Pretzel asked. Everyone collectively rolled their eyes. "Save me from myself," Pretzel said, and Tania shoved a brownie in his mouth.

"Yeah, for sure, let's get it set up!"

Alonda was sitting next to King on the blanket they'd set down on the roof. She was cradled inside the nook of his arm. It felt nice. Safe.

The fireworks started, pops of color lighting up the whole night sky. They'd been going like this every Friday since May, but Alonda hadn't really been paying attention. Like, they'd start up every Friday night and she'd clock it in her head like, *Oh, is it Friday again*, and then would mostly ignore them, losing track of their noise until they started up again the next Friday and the Friday after that.

The booms weren't in sync with the color explosions that painted the air; they echoed later, after the bright lights were already dissolving into the night sky. She loved watching them streak across the sky. Looked like paint on a canvas almost.

She glanced at her friends. Tania and Pretzel were making out toward the darkest end of the roof, trying to be discreet but also being kinda obvious. Kimmie was sitting in front of them, watching the fireworks, her eyes so big, it looked like a star could fall into them. Spider was on his phone, probably texting his new boyfriend, and Lexi—

She was staring up at the sky, too, but not at the fireworks in front of them. She was staring at the sky directly above them. Alonda followed her gaze, looking up, edging her head away from King's arm a little bit to get a better view of the sky. It was as unremarkable as usual. A clear night but no stars. There were never any stars in Brooklyn—too much light.

So what was Lexi looking at?

"Oh shit, that's sick!" King shouted, his voice bringing her back to her present moment with him, with the stars, on the roof with him. He was pointing to the lights, but the firework that had made him shout with excitement was already dripping back down into light dust, falling gently into nothing.

"How do you think they did that?" he asked, awe in his voice. Alonda just shrugged.

"Come on, you gotta know, you know everything! You're like an evil genius with that brain of yours," King said, tapping the side of her forehead. She swatted it away.

"Why do I gotta be an evil genius, why not just a regular genius?!" she said, and he shrugged.

"I guess I never really heard of a genius who wasn't evil. All the brains, it corrupts people."

"Nah, that's capitalism," Lexi said from her spot over by the brownies.

"You're not wrong," Alonda said.

"I know," Lexi said, snorting slightly.

It was just something she didn't know. The fireworks, she meant the fireworks. She settled back into King's arm and looked up.

That was the thing she just didn't have an answer to.

☆ **13** ☆

"IS ANYBODY LISTENING TO ME?"

Alonda popped her head up. She'd been scrolling through a wrestling hashtag on Twitter, kinda mindlessly getting sucked into lots of different dramas. She was still tired from the night before; after the fireworks, they'd all stayed up talking till, like, 4:00 A.M. and her brain still felt like sleepy mush from it and all she wanted to do was scroll. She could usually get away with it because Jim and Teresa would marathon talk about their day and boring stuff like what groceries they were gonna buy and whose job sucked the most.

But now that Alonda had looked up from her phone, she could see that Teresa was giving Jim a kinda death glare. It looked like he was sucked into his phone, too, his stubby fingers flying across the screen.

"Sorry," Alonda said, "I was just—"

"You know better than to be on your phone at the table, Alonda," Teresa snapped at her.

Alonda gave Teresa her own death glare right back. She looked down at her phone and then swiveled her whole head toward the phone in Jim's hand.

Talk about a double standard.

"I'm not the only one on my phone—"

"Don't get fresh with me tonight, I'm tired—"

"Hey, I'm gonna have to go in, gonna have to work a late shift," Jim said, pushing his chair away from the table.

"Not everybody's done eating," Alonda said mockingly.

"Where are you going?" Teresa asked, ignoring Alonda, her eyes staring steadily at Jim.

"That was just the foreman—Bobby can't make his shift tonight, some sorta family emergency."

"And you're the only guy who can fill in?"

"No, but I'm the guy they asked to fill in."

Alonda tried to focus on the mac and cheese in front of her. She mushed it up with the broccoli Teresa insisted on making with it, willing it to turn into bacon instead. Ever since Jim moved in, he and Teresa had been less lovey-dovey and more terse. It was weird. And she could usually ignore it but right now it was happening right in front of her.

"Ah," Teresa said, jabbing one of her broccolis with a fork. "If duty calls, guess you got no choice but to respond."

"What're you implying?" Jim asked, his voice low.

"Not implying nothing, just asking a question."

"I dunno, sounds like you're trying to ask a different question," Jim said.

"Can I leave?" Alonda asked.

"You're not done eating. Finish," Teresa snapped at her.

"Hey, if she wants to go to her room and eat, she should be able to do that!"

"I don't want her eating in her room. That's how we get bugs."

"What the hell, Teresa, I'm not a gross mess. I clean up after myself!" Alonda said, defensive.

"Fine! You do what you want," Teresa said. Her words sounded like they were meant for Alonda, but when she looked at her, Teresa was looking at Jim. Jim was buried deep in his phone again, his lips stretched up in a smile.

"Happy to be getting called into work?" Teresa asked sarcastically.

"Sure, happy for the overtime. Who wouldn't be?" Jim said, dropping his phone in his back pocket. "Just gonna get cleaned up."

Alonda grabbed her plate and went to her room, shutting out the mess with a click of the door. She could hear the water running in the bathroom. Her nose wrinkled involuntarily. The aggressive smell of Jim's cologne wafted into her room.

She furrowed her face, a question she didn't wanna ask buzzing around her mind like a fly.

Why would he need so much cologne if he was just going to work?

She could hear Teresa and Jim murmuring to each other. She couldn't make out anything specific, just listened to the buzzing of their tone as it got louder and softer, louder and then softer again until all she could hear was the front door slamming shut and the door to Teresa's bedroom closing with a softer click right after.

The heat was making the air kinda hazy. Alonda hated mornings like that, when it was so hot she could physically see the heat. It was too hot to think, too hot to stay inside, too hot to be outside; days like today made her a wanderer, just a person trying to figure out where she could be most human.

It was an odd day, not having anything to do, not having any plans. She wasn't scheduled to work, the group wasn't meeting up, and King was busy today doing errands for his mom, which was fine by Alonda—at least it took some of the pressure off feeling like she was supposed to be doing girlfriend-y things with him.

She still didn't know how she felt about being King's girlfriend. It was weird that he had called her that and she wasn't sure if she liked it, or if she even agreed. In order to be a girlfriend, shouldn't people at least have been friends for like . . . at least a minute? Furthermore, she didn't know if she wanted to be known as King's Girlfriend; she had just started hanging out with the group and she wanted to be Alonda, no apostrophe *s* about it.

She checked her phone for the hundredth time. Nothing since their last exchange. She reread it for the fifty-seven-millionth time:

ALONDA: What're you up to?
LEXI: My sister's in town!

Followed by a photo, a selfie. Lexi's face, smiling big and cheesy next to a girl who had to be Lexi's sister. Her skin was a little lighter brown than Lexi's, her face a little rounder, and her hair was braided into a bunch of smaller braids, twirled up in a cool-looking updo. They both had paper plates of food in their laps, hamburgers, hot dogs, homemade mac and cheese. Alonda's mouth watered at the sight.

LEXI: Allie says hi

Alonda smiled back at the phone. Must be nice to have a sister.

ALONDA: Hi, back
LEXI: we're in Queens for the day. Allie flew in from
       Spelman College a few days ago, and she's now
       doing the Great Summer Vacation Family Tour.
ALONDA: sounds intense!
LEXI: It's cool tho my aunt's gonna rebraid my hair. Gonna
       look sick for the show
ALONDA: I bet

Lexi hadn't responded to her last text 'cause really, what the hell else was there to say? Alonda chewed her bottom lip and tried to push any worries out of her mind. She didn't wanna think about Lexi. She was hanging out with King. But she just liked talking to Lexi so much.

Alonda found herself wandering toward the playground. There was something nice about it, now that it was theirs. And yeah, sure, they couldn't own a public playground, but also . . . they kinda did. Nobody ever really played on it anyway, not with the beach and everything yards away.

We brought new life to it, Alonda thought a little bit proudly. Giving it a new flair.

"Spider?" she asked, seeing him in his familiar spot by the benches. She wasn't super surprised to see him there. The playground almost felt like a clubhouse, but one without walls, a place for them all to go whenever they wanted, not just when they had to for practice and stuff.

It took a second for him to notice her; he was wearing his huge headphones and his forehead was twisted up in concentration as he worked on the sewing project that was in his lap, but when he finally looked up, his face broke out into a huge smile. "Oh, hey!" he said, taking his headphones off. "What's going on?" he asked, though his eyes went immediately back down to the needle and thread in his hands.

"Nothing much," Alonda responded.

"That's cool," Spider said. He brought the needle and thread up to his eyes, trying to thread the needle, but his sweat was making the thread stick to the needle.

"You need help?" Alonda asked. "I'm oddly good at threading needles."

Spider made a surprised face but handed it over without a word. "I hate threading this shit," he said.

Alonda nodded. "Yeah, it's a pain, but it gets easier the more you do it."

Spider rolled his eyes. "I dunno, it feels like I've done it like a thousand times and threading this shit don't get any easier. Thanks," he added, taking the freshly threaded needle from her. He immediately started sewing again.

"Hey, what're you like . . . working on?" Alonda asked. She perched herself on the end of the bench. It felt weird to just be chilling with Spider, she was so used to them always being together in a group. "I didn't even know you could sew."

Spider laughed, a little bit bitter. "That's because I can't sew. I been trying to work this shit out for the past three weeks, and I keep messing up." He held up the piece of cloth, and Alonda could see it clearly for the first time—it was a luchador mask but in the design of a Spider-Man mask.

"Oh shit, that's hot!" Alonda said.

Spider's face lit up. "Yeah?" he asked, looking at the mask in his hands.

Alonda nodded. "Oh yeah, for sure, it actually fits your whole vibe perfectly. Like . . . damn."

Spider looked back at the mask and shrugged, but he was still smiling. "Yeah, I thought so. I mean, I definitely wanted to do a mask 'cause of my whole Spider-Man thing, but also, like, Rey Mysterio's one of my ultimate, all-time favorite wrestlers, so I wanted to be like a shout-out to him," he said. Alonda nodded. Rey Mysterio was awesome, one of the greatest masked wrestlers ever known for his high-flying moves, almost like he was a Spider-Man of wrestling. "So I figured this would be the perfect way to combine my Mexican culture and my geek culture all rolled into one," Spider continued. "And I know it'll look really dope when it's finished, but I dunno if I'll be able to finish it in time for the show. I keep pricking myself, and I bled all over the last two, and the first one didn't even fit my head, like damn. Peter Parker makes sewing look easy, but shit, this shit is not easy."

"Yeah, but, like, don't he also make leaping from tall buildings, spitting out spiderweb from his wrists look easy, too?" Alonda asked.

Spider sighed heavily. "Yeah, and that is shit I know I can't do. Sewing? Should be easy."

Alonda snorted at the logic but could tell he was in his feelings so didn't harp on it. It's not like amateur wrestling is any easier, but Spider'd been getting really good at it. Anything's hard until it becomes easy, right?

Alonda started to play with the ends of her hair. "At least you got all that figured out. I'm still figuring out my costume and . . .

everything," she said. "I feel like, if I could just like . . . dye my hair pink, my whole thing'll come to me."

"So dye your hair!" Spider said.

Alonda snorted. "Yeah, easier said than done," she muttered.

"Why?" Spider asked. "Your moms won't let you?"

Alonda shrugged. "Yeah, something like that," she said.

"Well, it's your hair! So you should do whatever you want," Spider said.

"Sure," Alonda said, sarcasm clinging to her every word, "like I haven't thought of that before."

"I mean, I don't know your mom, but how long can she be mad for? I bet you're like perfect at home." Alonda shrugged. She didn't like being read like that. "And honestly," Spider continued, "it's not that hard to do. I bet my sister would do it—she works at a salon on Surf Avenue and loves to do that shit, especially if you tell her you're not supposed to. She's a rebel that way."

"I dunno . . . ," Alonda said, looking at her hair again. She didn't wanna face Teresa's wrath, but Spider was probably right; Teresa probably wouldn't be that mad. Especially since her report card boasted some grades that were beyond Teresa's wildest expectations.

"I didn't even know grades go this high!" Teresa had exclaimed when she saw her report card. It had come in the mail a week after the last day of school, and Teresa had practically attacked Alonda with a hug when she came home. Some of the grades were weighted, which meant Alonda's overall average was way over 100. "Your guidance counselor called me, Ms. Vasquez? She said that you could probably go Ivy League next year!" She'd even put it on the fridge, which Alonda protested, but Teresa was too excited to listen.

Yeah, Alonda could probably get away with dyeing her hair.

"Well, come on, you do really need to figure your shit out," Spider said. "Our first show is in days. How's Pretzel even supposed to announce you if you don't got a name? What's he supposed to say"—Spider cleared his throat as he did a pretty spot-on impersonation of Pretzel—"'Introducing, for the first time on the Playground of Coney Island, please welcome, the Nameless One'?"

Alonda shrugged. "I know, I know! I been thinking about it non-stop, but nothing feels right. All you all figured out your shit so fast."

Spider stopped sewing and looked right at Alonda. "Look, it's not that serious. And you're not gonna be, like, glued to it, so if it don't feel right, then you can always change it. But, like, what is it you wanna do? Or, who do you wanna be? Come on, you can be anyone in the whole world, so who you gonna be?"

Alonda snorted. "It ain't that easy," she said.

"It is so," Spider said.

"So what, you wanna be Peter Parker?"

"Nah, man," Spider said, shaking his head. "Nah, it's not that I wanna be Peter Parker. More like Miles Morales—he's a different Spider-Man, from Brooklyn. So that's who I wanna be, my own version." Alonda didn't realize there could be more than one of the same superhero. That was pretty cool, though. Spider continued, "I mean, no denying, I do love Peter Parker 'cause he's the original. And he's not from Brooklyn, but he is from Queens. From the boroughs. I feel like a lotta people dunno what that's like. 'Cause you don't really see it in the world. And I mean, Queens ain't Brooklyn, but it still ain't like . . . Milwaukee or some shit."

Alonda knew what he meant. Sometimes, the way the world talked about Brooklyn, it was weird. It seemed to focus on one area of Brooklyn and then made it into all of Brooklyn, but shit, Brooklyn was big. It was huge. And on top of that, every single neighborhood was different, and the way all those people in them lived and interacted, that was different, too. And nobody really got that, not unless they were from here.

"Yeah, I get that," she said softly. "People think a lot of stuff about us, but they don't really know us."

She was always searching for her Brooklyn out there.

"I like to take the train at night," Spider said softly. "Like, I'll ride the D train out, down to Ninth Avenue just so I can ride it back at night. On nights when I can't sleep. I got mad nights where I can't sleep, and . . ." He paused, letting the words get stuck in his throat. Alonda just listened. Spider didn't really talk much in the group, but now that they was one-on-one, she could see he had a whole tidal wave's worth of words that were looking to crash from him.

"I ride the train at night because it's something I like to think Spider-Man would do. Not Peter Parker, but Spider-Man.

"I like that the trains are all empty except for, like, someone who's making it their bed for the night or a couple, eyes shut tight and holding on to each other for dear life, and I like it when the train comes in so I can watch the lights in the windows of the projects pulsing. I like the fact that they're all still on, and that the buildings are like night-lights, lighting the way. Makes me less lonely. Because sometimes I get lonely? Ain't that weird? What do I gotta be lonely for? But I do, I get lonely. It creeps on me and latches onto my blood like Venom, becomes a part of me that I can't shake."

Alonda never rode the train out by herself that late at night, but she'd watch trains coming in and leaving from her bedroom window on nights where sleep wouldn't come. She could see the tracks from their side of the building, and sometimes seeing the trains coming back in made her feel less lonely. Because she was like Spider. There was some nights when she was lonelier than others, and it just always felt nice to know that there was other people living their lives, coming in and out, existing.

The streets were noisy with traffic and people all laughing and talking, a hundred boom boxes playing different music in the distant but all at the same time, crashing over them all like waves of sound, but between Alonda and Spider in that moment, it was quiet. One of those quiets that's full of unspoken words saying I get you, I see you.

Alonda suddenly jumped to her feet. "Come on," she said.

Spider furrowed his brow. "What?" he asked.

"Let's go dye my hair."

His face exploded into a huge smile. "Oh hell yes, okay!" he said, jumping up, shoving his mask in his backpack as he grabbed her hand and they raced away from the playground.

"If you're not watching Rize, you're not watching wrestling.

"Rize Wrestling, promo number three."

Some tinny music sounds; the old-school Spider-Man remix over a shot of the empty playground. Suddenly, a masked person jumps into frame and a word flashes across the screen. It says:

SPIDER.

Spider throws out some web-slinger moves before raising his arms to signal the music to be cut off completely. He grabs the mic from behind his back and raises it to his mouth.

"You all know I'm doing Rize a favor by being here, right?" he asks, his words muffled by the mask he wears.

"I'm the greatest, most undefeated-est person who's ever stepped into a ring, ever," he continues, scoffing a little bit with a swagger. "Nobody has ever been able to match my skill level, not on a technical scope necessarily, but just when it comes to raw, unparalleled talent."

He does a series of movements with his arms, making comic book noises along with each gesture.

"I hear that they got me wrestling the New Girl come Saturday," he continues, boredom filling his voice, "and I told 'em, yeah, I guess if I've got the time! And then the Incredible Lexi asked me if I was scared and I just laughed and laughed!"

He lets out some laughter, letting it come from the bottom of his toes and out his mouth before abruptly stopping and speaking quickly but menacingly into the mic,

"Nothing scares me. Not when I am fear itself!"

He stares for a couple of more seconds before he drops the act and says,

"And that's why you ain't gonna wanna miss our first match of the season, July eighth at one o'clock P.M. Eastern Standard Time. Unless . . . you're too afraid?"

He lets the question linger in the air for a second too long before he drops the mic and leaps out of view, like he was never there to begin with.

14

"ALL RIGHT, EVERYONE, HOW'S IT GOING, THIS IS DONNY DRAGO
giving you all the pro-est of tips on how to give a good promo—"

Alonda blew on her nails, letting her breath dry the bright pink polish she'd just applied. She had her laptop on the kitchen table, taking care of her biweekly manicure and hoping that the color she'd chosen this week wouldn't clash too bad with the neon orange of her work shirt, while she listened to how-to after how-to of how to create a compelling wrestling promo.

"First up, you're gonna wanna make sure you got your character down—what're your wants, needs, what are you gonna be in the ring fighting for—"

"Yeah, but how," Alonda muttered as Donny Drago went droning on, giving all the advice that Alonda knew by heart but she couldn't quite access. King had suggested Donny, calling him "the Best!" but she wasn't really feeling him; he was pale with huge muscles, kinda squat with a shaved head and a huge, loud personality, but she was definitely not resonating with anything he said.

Like, she knew the *what*, but *how, how* was she supposed to know what her character's wants and needs were gonna be? She knew so many of the mechanics of being a wrestler, the technical needs of creating a character, but when she sat down to write it out, or even to just imagine it, her mind went as blank as the page. There were too many options, which made none of them feel feasible. Like, did she wanna be someone built on vengeance? Or like someone who felt like the world was hers to own and everyone else was just getting in her way?

Nothing felt right.

"Then, you're gonna wanna amplify it—remember, wrestling is about being larger than life at all times, and the stakes are always the most important in the whole world, so make it big!"

Alonda liked doing her nails out in the kitchen because the table out there didn't wobble like her desk, and besides, she didn't wanna stink up her room with that nail polish smell. Teresa had taught her how to do her nails way back when. Mami had never really cared about painting her nails or wearing a full face of makeup; it was always Teresa who'd come over, blond hair big and smelling more like hair spray than shampoo, the same uniform of makeup on her face, the one she'd taught Alonda how to do, too: powder, liquid base, blush, eye shadow, eyeliner, lip liner, gloss. Alonda didn't really do a full face of makeup every day—she couldn't find a good base that matched her skin tone, everything was too dark a brown or too light and it wasn't really her style anyway—but she liked wing tipping her eyeliner (she could do both of them super even on each side) and couldn't break the habit of doing her nails. There was something about it, the methodical routine that never changed, never altered in its steps.

It was nice.

She blew gently on her nails again. Teresa usually helped her. While she was doing her nails. But she wasn't home. Again.

Alonda didn't realize how much she missed it until it wasn't happening.

"And that's how you make a great promo! If you liked what you saw, don't forget to subscribe—"

Alonda sighed. Shit. Maybe there was some stuff she couldn't learn from YouTube. An ad for something annoying started playing.

Her nails were still a little gummy, but she really liked the rosy pink color. They'd definitely match her highlights even if they didn't go with her work shirt.

Spider had been right. His sister, Sandra, had happily worked on her hair for a few hours in the salon she worked at, bleaching and dyeing and even trimming off some of her dead ends, the whole time talking over the whirl of hair dryers, the chatter from the other ladies in the shop, and the radio. Just like Spider said, Sandra was excited to work on Alonda's hair. "Pero," she had said over the sound of the hair dryer. "It's your hair, though! So, like, you gotta do what you wanna do with it, you know?"

Alonda had decided to not go full pink and go with pink highlights instead; apparently a full hair dye would've taken a lot longer than a few hours because her hair was black and so it would've needed to be fully bleached and then rest for a day before Sandra could finish the job. She wasn't sure how she felt about her hair getting fully bleached and also figured having highlights would ease Teresa into the shock and that she wouldn't be quite as pissed with her decision. And she'd been kinda right! Teresa had just looked at her and sighed and initially said nothing, but later on in the day she had said, "I have to admit, pink does suit you," which Alonda took as a win. It probably helped that Jim was super enthusiastic about it, too. "I ain't never seen hair like that!" he'd said, talking over Teresa before she had barely opened her mouth. Teresa had shot him an annoyed look but didn't say nothing to him, and Alonda would be lying if she wasn't grateful for the assist, though she hated seeing Teresa looking annoyed like that. She had never kept her mouth shut before but seemed to be doing it more with Jim around, like she was acting on her best behavior instead of being her at-home self. Alonda'd noticed that, even though she didn't think Teresa realized it.

But Alonda had thought that her awesome hair would be like a light bulb going off in her heart about what kinda wrestler she'd be, that the dye would be some sorta magic wand waving its way into her mind, but she was like six videos deep and no closer to any answers about her character.

"What are you good at?"

Alonda looked up at the video that had started playing. A woman wearing a neon-green crop top was talking. She had light brown skin and a shock of short bright blue hair and wore enormous sunglasses with the word LOVE spelled out across where the shades would be, a Puerto Rican flag proudly displayed on her wall.

Alonda felt her eyebrows rise on their own accord. Who was this spectacular human?

"Hey, I'm Lovely Loveless, and I'm gonna tell YOU how to make a killer promo.

"All right, so there's a lot of advice out there for how to make good promos and I'm just one more voice adding to the pile," she said. She had a great smile. *"The best characters are ones that are true to yourself. They're taking a bit of your truth and blowing it up like a balloon. They're not You-You, but they are a part of you."*

Alonda's head started nodding, her heart thumping. Shit. She wanted to take notes, but her nails were still drying! She sat and listened, waving her hands frantically to try to let them harden.

"So what part of yourself do you wanna amplify? What part of your-self do you wanna make larger than life, that you wanna poke fun at, that you want people to see?"

Alonda felt a smile creeping to her face.

She suddenly knew exactly who she was gonna be.

"You think anyone's gonna show?" King asked. He was hopping back and forth on his heels a little bit. True to his word, he was just dressed in jeans and a T-shirt, but it fit his character.

"It don't matter if anyone comes or not," Lexi said for the hun-dredth time, straining her neck to try to look around the corner to see. The four had agreed to meet up by the dumpster in back of the swings to group up and make their entrances. "We're doing this shit for fun," Lexi said again, stretching her neck as far as she could go.

"Can you see anyone?" Alonda asked.

Lexi snapped her head back. "I dunno!" she said. "How should I know? I'm not looking."

"Sure," Alonda said sarcastically, adjusting the strap on her costume.

Lexi looked over at Alonda again, her eyes lingering on Alonda's hair, and she shot her a smile. "I really do like your hair," she said.

Alonda felt her face flush. "Thanks," she said, running her hand through her hair a little self-consciously. "I like yours."

Lexi flashed her a big smile and tossed her freshly braided hair over her shoulder. Her aunt'd braided in a bunch of green strands, and they matched her cape perfectly. She had traded in the pleather for baggy jean shorts and a cropped T-shirt, her green cape in her hands, ready to be thrown for her grand entrance into the ring.

"Yo, there's people here!" Pretzel's voice snapped her back to the present. He'd run from the playground around the side of the building to deliver them the news. He was wearing an oversized plain white T-shirt, but he'd slicked back his hair for the occasion.

"How many?" King demanded.

"Like more than ten, almost fifteen!" Pretzel said. King's face fell a little, but Lexi and Spider looked surprised.

"Fifteen whole people?" Spider asked. "Anyone we know?"

"Well, Tania and Kimmie," Pretzel admitted, and everyone kinda nodded; Tania was really supportive and excited about the whole venture so she'd volunteered to be their videographer, the plan being for her to capture the matches on her phone, then give them to Pretzel to edit and upload to their channel for later viewing. Kimmie had also been super into the whole thing and told them she'd be there. Alonda peeked over and could see Kimmie bouncing from foot to foot, looking excited. "And she brought her friend, Taylor, and, like, your brother's here," he said, nodding toward Spider, "but the rest I don't even recognize! Word's getting out!"

"Word's getting out when there's nothing to get out yet," Lexi said, but Alonda noticed that she started bouncing on the toes of her sneakers.

"Yo, our last upload had like twenty views! People are watching!" King said back, cracking his knuckles.

"Sure that wasn't just you watching twelve times?" Lexi muttered, so that only Alonda could hear. Alonda suppressed a smile. It was funny but she felt like maybe she shouldn't be laughing at her boyfriend's expense, even if it was Lexi.

Alonda felt good about the outfit she'd put together for herself. Once she'd listened to what Lovely Loveless had to say, something inside her just clicked and she decided to go with what she was—the New Girl. Like, kinda playing up her newness and freshness to the group, trying to prove herself to the characters she'd wrestle.

So she dressed like it was her first day of school, a backpack slung over one shoulder, a T-shirt tucked into some jean shorts, but also with some cute pink suspenders that matched her highlights perfectly. Her sunglasses kept slipping down the edge of her sweaty nose (she had worn them as a tribute to Lovely Loveless and had some plans for how to work them in the ring, but right now, they were mad annoying). She was one million percent ready to go out there, talk trash, and do it!

"You ready for this?" Pretzel asked.

"Born ready," King said.

"Yeah, we know *you* are, I was asking Spider and Alonda," Pretzel said, rolling his eyes a little. Alonda versus Spider were up first—they'd be warming up the crowd for the main event, which was King versus Lexi. Alonda didn't really mind not being the main event; both she and Spider were much chiller about the whole thing, but now she wished that someone was gonna go before her so she could watch them.

"Yeah, of course," Spider said, putting his luchador-spider mask on. It looked sick, though Alonda was sure he was gonna get hot, especially since he had insisted on wearing leggings, too.

"Yeah, let's do this," Alonda said, trying to keep the nerves out of her voice. She pulled her ponytail higher, adjusted her suspenders, and yeah, she was ready to go.

After she had come up with her gimmick, her name had come to her, too. And just like what she felt when she had talked to Spider, she felt like she had always known her name.

She was just nervous to say it out loud.

"So you got a name I can announce or what?" Pretzel asked.

Because saying it out loud would make it real.

Alonda took a deep breath in, and on the exhale she said,

"Yeah. Alondra."

She felt their eyes on her. Pretzel raised an eyebrow.

"Ain't that just your name?" Pretzel asked, and Alonda shook her head. "Nah, Alond-*ra*, *ra*, with an *r*," she said, stretching out the *r* sound as far as it could go, which wasn't very far to be fair.

"OH! Got it, okay, great," Pretzel said, and he ran away toward the crowd.

"Cool name," Lexi whispered to her. Alonda turned, shot her a smile, and felt her stomach twirl, though it was a different kinda nerves.

"Hello, hello, hello, everyone! Thank you all for coming by and watching Rize Wrestling's first-ever show!"

Some weak applause and a couple of quiet "Woos!" rippled through the crowd.

"Wow, they sound riveted," Lexi muttered, her sarcastic words making Alonda's mouth threaten to twitch into a smile.

"Who's ready for some wrestling?!"

Alonda could hear some coughs from the crowd, but that didn't deter Pretzel.

"Hey, now, come on, maybe you can't hear me, I asked a question and a question deserves the respect of an answer. Now tell me! Who here is ready for some wrestling?!"

A little bit more applause.

"All right, that's more like it! Hey, we're out here in public, this is the middle of the day, and it ain't a show if we don't hear from you, so don't be afraid to show us some love!"

"Yeah, use your outdoor voices!" King yelled. His words seemed to pump up the crowd a little more.

"All right, first up, we wanna introduce you to Rize's heavyweight champion of the summer, blink and you might miss him, I need you to give it up for Spider!" Pretzel's voice rang out as he pressed play on the speakers that cued Spider's intro music, a remixed version of the old-school Spider-Man theme song.

Spider ran into the center of their agreed-upon "ring"—they couldn't get ropes or anything but taped out an outline for where the action'd take place. He jumped up quickly and squatted low, pointing out his wrists in the iconic web-slinger move, milking his entrance.

"And innnntroducing, new to Rize, school may be out for the summer but class is in session today, I'm gonna need you all to give it up for the New Kid on the Block, new to Rize, lemme hear you scream for ALONDRA!"

Her intro music blasted from Spider's speakers, and Alonda felt her nerves threaten to freeze her in place. She took the world's deepest breath and threw a smile onto her face as she left the safety of the dumpster and cartwheeled her way right onto the padding. It was definitely sloppier than what she'd been practicing, her nerves making her wrists all tingly, but she could hear someone say, "Oh dope," which must mean she did something cool.

She raised her hand to the air, jerkily waving to the crowd.

God, she felt like an awkward disaster.

Her music finally stopped.

Good. Time for the easy part.

She faced Spider.

"Who the hell're you?" Spider growled out, making his voice low and deep and menacing. He was the heel, the idea being that Alonda was the new girl who was trying to take over his spot in Rize. "I never seen you here before."

Her adrenaline was pumping. She felt the stares of the crowd but refused to look at them. She wasn't gonna imagine them naked, she was just gonna pretend like they wasn't there, like they didn't exist at all. "Oh no, I mean, yeah, that's right, it's because I'm new! To you. And this!" she said, throwing her arm out stiffly. "But here is where I have lived!" What was she saying?? *Come on, Alonda, get it together*, she thought to herself. She took a deep breath. "But if you've never seen me, I guess it's just that you haven't been look-ing hard enough. And here I thought spiders had good vision, what with your eight eyes and all. But I guess I musta been mistaken."

"I dunno," Spider said, "you look like a tourist to me." He turned to the crowd. "In fact, this looks like a crowd full've tourists."

He was looking to get some boos outta the crowd since no self-respecting Coney Islander would wanna be called a tourist, but they didn't take the bait. They was just standing, watching. Alonda couldn't see Spider's face because of the mask, but she decided to keep going—as long as they didn't act like something wasn't going right, nobody would notice, right?

"Yeah, so, I'm new!" Alonda continued, gaining strength as she went, "and I'm here to prove to you, to all of you, that I belong here! 'Cause I am the best!" She raised her arm to the air and brought it back down quick, pointing at Spider. "Not afraid to fight, are you, Spider-Man?" she asked, taunting.

"Hey, I'm not Spider-Man, don't get it twisted, I don't need no radioactive spider powers, I'm all natural, baby!"

"So am I!" she said, and tightened her ponytail, making it go as high as it could go.

"So let's do this."

The sound of their fake-ass bell rang through the air, and Alonda ran at Spider, but he moved to the side, holding out an arm that Alonda pretended to run right into, headfirst, clapping her hands together to make a thwacking sound. She held her head and moaned, pretending to be in pain.

"Be careful, you don't wanna break your glasses," Spider taunted her.

"What, these?" she asked, taking her glasses off her face and cracking them in half. She had rigged them to do that the night before; she'd be able to put them back together easily for the next show.

"I don't need to see you to kick your ass," she said. She ran at him again, but this time he dodged out of the way, so she ran into nothing but air. She did it again; he moved out of the way again. And again.

It was like a dance they had choreographed together, but each time Alonda had to pretend like she didn't see it coming.

She kicked high, and he grabbed her leg. She stood a little shakily, getting her balance. She could hear the crowd start to clap a little. She nodded at Spider, and he pulled her forward, knocking her down.

She landed with a loud bang as her body made contact with the ground, the padding breaking her fall a little, but damn, it stung. She moaned and made her body go limp, so Spider grabbed her body easily and put her into a submission hold, holding her arms behind her back while she pretended to writhe in pain.

"Come on, give up!" Spider shouted as Alonda wiggled against him. "Give up!"

"Never!" Alonda yelled, continuing to fight against him.

"I can do this all day," Spider said. He pretended to yawn, moving his hand to cover his mouth, leaving Alonda with the perfect opening.

"And Alondra fights her way out of Spider's submission, knocking her foe to the ground." Damn, Pretzel's commentary was on *point!* He sounded for real.

It was Spider's turn to land with a thud, Alonda taking the opportunity to grab Spider's arm and pull it back, putting him into a submission now.

"Now who's ready to tap out?!" she yelled, pulling his arm as far back as it would go. Spider was double jointed, so the move looked particularly gruesome and cool.

"You're gonna rip my arm right outta its socket!" Spider yelled, twisting his body back and forth as Alonda laughed.

"Why're you worried about your one arm—don't you got eight?" Alonda snapped back, but Spider kept wiggling.

"Hey, let me go!" he said.

"So tap out!" she shouted. "Just tap out!"

She could hear some voices in the crowd echo the advice before—

Spider fought his way out and knocked Alonda to the ground. This time, he rolled her up in a pinning maneuver, throwing his body over hers, pinning her to the ground. Alonda struggled against him, trying to force her way out of the pin.

"One, two—"

But before Pretzel could get to three, Alonda kicked out, knocking Spider to the side. She could hear the crowd's noises of surprise; they really didn't see that coming.

Spider rolled over, holding his side and feigning pain while Alonda stood to face him. She was sweating hard; the sun was beaming down, and she was sweating so much she was sure she had damp stains everywhere, but damn, was she ready.

"That all you got?" she demanded, standing over him.

"Never," Spider choked out, and rolled himself up. His recovery was a little too fast to be believable. They'd work on it.

"You sure that's all YOU got?" he threw back at her, crouching low in his web-slinger pose.

"Me? I wouldn't ever hurt a fly," Alonda said innocently. Spider pretended to let down his guard, standing and turning to the crowd.

"I didn't think so," he said. While his back was turned, Alonda started climbing the jungle gym, right across from where Spider stood, next to their barrier.

"But," she said, prompting him to turn around, "I didn't say nothing about not hurting a spider." She knew it was kinda corny, but that was part of the fun of wrestling, the puns, the quips, reminding people that even though it was serious, even though what they was doing was dangerous, it was still fun, it was athletic, not violent, it was consensual.

But it didn't matter if it was corny or not, the crowd seemed to respond to it. She heard a few laughs and even more enthusiastic "WOOs!"

Alonda clocked the noise from the crowd, but all her focus was on Spider. They had practiced this move so many times, both of their bodies had bruises from it, but she was ready. He gave her a quick nod, letting her know that he was ready.

"I'm gonna squash you like the bug you are!" she said, and without letting herself think too hard about it, she leaped forward, feetfirst and fell next to Spider, quickly taking him down with her, pinning him to the ground.

In the movies, falls like that happened in an artsy kinda slow motion, scored to dramatic and suspenseful music, but in real life, they're fast and loud. Her body landed right next to Spider's, and he fell to the ground, with her on top of him, the slam of their bodies colliding only made louder by the sound of Spider's body hitting the ground. He had actually caught her before they both went down, but from the crowd's perspective, it looked like she had knocked him to the ground. She felt a smile crawl to her lips. It did look like she had squashed him!

It took a minute for both of them to get their breath back, to recover from the fall. Because even though they were doing these moves as safe as they could, they still hurt. The recovery was part of the move, making sure they felt safe enough to go on. She looked at Spider, and he gave her a slight nod. The signal. Good.

With a flash, Alonda grabbed Spider's legs and, throwing the full weight of her body on top of him, pinned him to the ground.

"Spider's struggling, he's struggling!" Pretzel said, crouching low and doing his double duty as commentator and referee. "Now for the count—can he stay down for the count of three: ONE, TWO—"

The sound of the bell cut through the air, indicating the end of the match, and before she could fully catch her breath, Alonda stood up as Pretzel raised her arm in victory.

"Winner of Rize's inaugural match, I need to hear you make some noise for the New Kid on the Block, ALONDRA!"

Alonda looked around, surprised as more cheers than before rang through the air. While they had been wrestling, more people had joined. There was a larger group than before, people standing around cheering for the match that had just taken place. Like, she could see Becky from B3 standing, her bedazzled cell phone now out and recording, and Big Ricky was there clapping, his big hands carrying the claps to her ears loud. It even looked like Michelle had wandered by and had stopped to watch the show! And sure, it wasn't like WWE level, but there was definitely people.

Cheering for her.

Alonda smiled hard at the crowd, raising her arms in victory.

Spider stood up slowly and pointed at Alonda, hushing the crowd with his gesture. "Everyone's cheering for you now," he said, his growl back and even more menacing than before, "but will they be cheering for you next time, when you lose?!" Alonda cringed a little. They was gonna have to work on their verbal jabs just as much as they practiced the physical ones. "If you think this is the last you'll see of me," he continued, crouching low, "you better think again! This ain't the last!"

"Why don't you just crawl outta here like the bug you are?" Alonda asked, and the crowd responded with cheers for her, boos for Spider. He turned to them, opening his arms wide toward them.

"Keep your boos coming! I eat your hate for lunch!" he said. They booed louder and longer than before.

"You're wasting my damn time. Why don't you get outta here before the sun goes down?" Alonda asked, making a shooing motion with her hands.

"This ain't the last!" Spider said again, and he walked out of the crowd, all their boos following him.

Alonda raised her arms to the sky again, and the boos transformed into cheers. She waved as her music came on, blasting its poppy beat. She ran into a cartwheel again, and then skipped the rest of the way to the back of the building.

Spider had already taken off his mask and was pouring water all over his head, but his face broke into a huge smile when he saw Alonda. They jumped up and down a little bit when squealing to King and Lexi, who had watched the match from the back of the building. "Oh my God, that was perfect, it was awesome, did you see us, ahhh!"

King nodded. "Not bad," he said.

"Not bad?" Alonda shot back. "You kidding, we were great!"

"Definitely a strong start—we've got some work to do, though," King said. Before Alonda could open her mouth to refute his claims, Pretzel was announcing his name and his attention was drawn to the center of the playground. He gave Alonda a quick peck of a kiss on top of her head before leaving the alleyway and heading toward the center of the ring.

Alonda resented that kiss. It felt like a kiss that an uncle would give his niece, not a boyfriend to his girlfriend, ew.

Lexi looked at her, eyebrow raised. It's almost like she could hear what Alonda was thinking. Alonda played it off.

"I dunno if my deodorant held out," Alonda said, nervous babbling rising to her lips. "I think I might stink right now."

"So what if you do? Nothing wrong with smelling like your body's supposed to," Lexi said. She was fumbling with her cape, trying to get it on.

"Here, lemme help you with that," Alonda said, unfurling the fabric.

"Thanks," Lexi said, shooting her a small smile.

"We warmed up the crowd good for you guys," she said, gesturing toward them with her head.

Lexi smirked. "Yeah, it looked like fun," she said, snapping her cape in place. "Man, I wish I could, like, fly in. Like a real superhero. How dope would that be?"

"Yeah, that'd be pretty cool," Alonda said softly.

They could hear Pretzel pressing play on her intro music.

"Good luck out there," Alonda said.

Lexi just looked at her and shook her head. "I don't need luck. I got skill," she said in her goofy character voice, flinging her cape around.

And with that she walked out to her music.

"That was so dope," Spider said. His eyes were dancing with excitement. "I think we really got them."

"For sure," Alonda said, trying to return his enthusiasm but distracted by the playground. She couldn't make out what Lexi and King were saying to each other, but she knew that their match would be even better than hers and Spider's. Lexi and King acted like the crowd was and wasn't there at the same time. Like, they interacted with the crowd a lot more than she and Spider had. But when they was focused on each other, it seemed like the crowd disappeared for them. It was as if they wasn't wrestling for them even though they were standing right in front of them.

"Hello? Earth to Alonda?" Spider asked, snapping her back to the present.

"Oh, what?" she asked, distracted.

"I said, do you think Tania got the whole thing?"

"Oh yeah, for sure," she said, looking back at the match. She could hear Spider snort a little bit.

"You gonna tell him or should I?" he asked.

Alonda looked at him. "What're you talking about?"

He nodded toward the match. Lexi had knocked King to the ground. Alonda looked back at Spider.

"Nothing to tell," Alonda said. Spider gave her a little smirk.

"Right," he said, and started walking away.

"No, really!" she called after him. "There's really nothing!"

"Then why're you trying so hard to convince me otherwise?" Spider asked. Shit.

As Alonda searched for words, he walked away.

The noise of the crowd pulled her back to the match. They was still in the middle of it.

She watched the match from the back of the building, rooting for King but knowing that it would be Lexi who would really be the winner.

15

ALONDA STIFLED A YAWN, TRYING TO SHOVE IT DOWN INSIDE HER throat.

It was so early out, the sun was only just waking up, as sleepy as Alonda was and trying to crack the slate gray of dawn into the blue of the day. The wind blew gently, the early morning ocean breeze still cool, making her skin prickle into goose bumps.

"Cold?"

Alonda looked up at King and smiled sleepily. "Yeah, a little," she said, and without a word, he pulled her into his arm.

It was King's idea to take a dawn morning walk on the beach because it was supposed to be quiet and whatever. And it was quiet, only the occasional jogger jogging past, more seagulls screaming than people. It had sounded like a good idea at the time, but now Alonda was cold and tired and hungry and somehow damp from the air.

It was nice, burrowing into King's arm, though.

"You wanna sit?" he asked, pointing to the ground. Alonda nodded. She was having trouble coming up with words this early in the morning. Her thoughts were sludge in her brain, still thick with sleep, and she couldn't quite fit them through her mouth.

They sat, the water rolling in and out.

"What do you think it's saying?"

Alonda started, surprised, turned to King. "What're you talking about, who?"

He pointed at the water.

"I still dunno . . . ," Alonda said, trailing off.

"The ocean! What d'you think it's saying?"

"Oh, I . . . can't speak ocean," she finished weakly. King gave her a small smile.

"I bet the ocean talks to the birds," he said. "Maybe the ocean tells them stories about when they used to be dinosaurs."

Alonda laughed a little. King glanced down, giving her a small look, and kept going.

"Yeah, 'cause I bet the gulls, I'm sure they got stories among themselves, right, like, they know they used to be something else and became this, but the ocean? The ocean was there for it all, right. Like, the ocean's been around as long as there's been Earth. So the ocean knows."

He smiled at her a little wider and looked back out, almost like he was getting caught up in the waves of his own story himself. "I don't think the ocean forgets. I think it remembers everything that's ever happened, just out there, rising, coming in and out."

"Yeah, but, like, the ocean's more than just here," Alonda said, waving her arms at the water. "Like, it's everywhere else. So . . ."

King shook his head. "Nah, you're thinking too literal! It's a story. Stories don't gotta be literal to be true, you know?"

"I guess," she said, trying not to shrug away his comment. She didn't really know what to say when King got like this, making stuff up. She wanted to try to play along, but her brain just didn't work that way.

"Here," he said, his voice gently bringing her back. He held a seashell in his hands, one that wasn't all cracked like a chip at the bottom of a bag the way most of them were. It was big, full, white with streaks of coral.

"I've never seen one so perfect," Alonda said, taking the shell.

"Yeah, I bet you can hear the ocean in it. Like, not just when we're right next to it," he said teasingly.

Alonda opened her mouth to explain that nobody could hear the ocean in seashells, not really, it was just sound echoes, but she caught sight of his eager face and swallowed her words down, changing them to "Thank you," and giving him a quick kiss before she looked back at the water, watching the waves creep ever closer.

"So what you're gonna wanna do is grab right above the shoulder . . ."

Alonda was spending her evening camped out in her room going down another Lovely Loveless rabbit hole of YouTube videos. She'd watched a lot of wrestling videos in her time, but there was something about Lovely Loveless that Alonda really, really loved.

". . . which means you're gonna need to—"

"You dunno what you're talking about!"

Alonda made a face at her door. Jim was being loud. Again. He seemed to be getting louder and louder by the day. That was the real reason Alonda had holed herself up in her room, to avoid him and his nonsense. But now he was somehow intruding on her space, even when he wasn't physically there. Not cool.

She plugged her headphones into her computer and turned up

the volume a little bit, trying to block out the noise. Living with Jim kinda sucked. He didn't pick up after himself, and he didn't like being asked to pick up after himself. He didn't like to cook but expected Teresa to cook, and to only cook what he wanted to eat, expected her to be home when he was home.

When Alonda complained about it to Teresa, Teresa told her she was being too sensitive. But Alonda knew she wasn't being too sensitive. She wished Teresa would listen to her. She wished she'd never said it was okay for Jim to live with them. She wished—

"Hey, lovelies! So today, I wanted to make a detour away from wrestling, I hope that's okay, and just wanted to talk about something near and dear to my heart."

Hmm. This was different.

Lovely Loveless was looking directly at the camera, but she was way more toned down than usual; instead of the bright, colorful eye shadow and neon crop tops she normally wore, her face was void of makeup and she was wearing a simple gray hoodie. She even looked a little nervous, the fierce, confident expression Alonda was so used to seeing more open and vulnerable instead.

Lovely took a deep breath. "So, if you've been following me for a while, you know that I'm a, like . . ." She trailed off, looking to the side, chewing her bottom lip a bit before looking back at the camera. "Wow, I didn't think this would be so hard, but it is! But I guess that makes sense, 'cause society's made it hard for us to speak our truths. Society, actually, the way it's constructed, it actually relies on us lying about our true selves. But I know that every time you get to step into your truth, every time you share your truth, the better the world becomes. So." She took another deep breath and said, "I'm bisexual." The second she said it, her face transformed into a smile. She let out a small laugh. "Yeah, I'm bi."

Alonda's heart started to beat a little faster.

"I told my mom a few hours ago. And she was like, 'But how do you know?' Which is a really annoying question. Because the answer is, I know because I know. I don't have a big, fancy answer with a huge revelation; I know I'm bi because it's me. It's who I am, how I see the world, how I create my community, how I interact with the whole entire world. It's inside me, it is on me, it is me. So, like, I don't know when I knew or how I knew, I just knew. I know."

Alonda could barely breathe. She felt tears rising to the back of her eyes, but she couldn't explain why. Why?

"I'm gonna drop some links in the box of this video, ones that helped me discover my voice and understanding of my sexuality, so if you're questioning, I just wanna let you know you're not alone and I encourage you to check some out, do some intense googling, and to try to enjoy your journey. Because it is a journey. Like, I'm sure my understanding of my sexuality will continue to change, grow and evolve, just like my understanding of gender—it's always shifting and changing and that's okay. That's good. So . . . yeah. I know it didn't have to do with wrestling really, but it also did. Because it is me. And who I am. And so is wrestling. So yeah, I'm Lovely Loveless. Good . . . bi," she said, winking at her pun.

Alonda pressed down on her space bar, pausing the video before the next would autoplay. The box in her chest was shaking, it was opening. She had spent so long trying to keep it shut, locking it as tight as it could go, ignoring it, but Lovely, the way she'd just said it . . . Alonda tried to put words to the feeling but couldn't, it made sense in a way that it'd never made sense before because it was her.

Alonda held her breath in her stomach and replayed the video again, watching over and over again before she clicked the first link, spending the rest of the evening discovering a secret language that she somehow already understood.

16

"AND HER OPPONENT—ALONDRA!"

Alonda felt the crowd cheer—like, she heard them, but she could also feel them, in her bones, feel their energy. They were so loud, she almost couldn't hear her intro music—Spider's speakers were getting a little busted from being used all the time, so the sound quality was kinda crackly now. But the the crowd's cheers were sweeter than any song she could walk out to, anyway. It was their third show, and they were slowly getting more views on YouTube, more people coming by to watch them live.

It was pretty dope.

Alonda tried to push the crowd out of her sight, blur them along the edges of her mind as she adjusted her pigtails, pulling them high into the air. Lexi was waiting for her in the center of their ring, hands on her hips in her superhero stance, smiling her huge smile. She'd already discarded her cape, throwing it into the crowd, and it seemed that Kimmie had been the lucky one to catch it; she was standing there with it proudly draped over her shoulders.

Alonda gave Lexi a slight nod, the secret signal that she was ready for them to start, and Lexi raised her arm, the one that was holding their belt dramatically, and a hush slowly trickled over the crowd. Lexi waited for them to be quiet before she started going in on Alonda.

"I hear that you're after my belt," Lexi said. The crowd had been talking but quieted down when Lexi began to speak. Some of them had taken out their phones, recording the match along with Tania. Alonda felt her heart thump a little faster. Damn, there was more people here than ever before! She could even see Michelle standing there with a few people Alonda didn't recognize; looked like she had brought some friends!

"You've heard correctly," Alonda responded with all the confidence her body could muster. "I know you won that belt from King 'fair and square,'" she said, making quotes in the air, "but I have to say, I think our ref was distracted." The crowd clapped approvingly. Alonda smiled at them, soaked it up.

"See, that's the issue," Lexi continued, hoisting their cardboard prop over her shoulder. "I did win this belt fair and square. I faced King with honor, and he couldn't handle it. I came into this ring to—" Alonda cut off what Lexi was saying, making a huge, loud yawning motion and sound. Lexi looked at her, open mouthed and aghast, and Alonda smiled sweetly back at her. She took a dramatic pause, letting the crowd boo her and cheer Lexi, trying not to giggle for real. When the crowd finally settled down a bit, she continued, "I'm sorry, were you saying something? I thought I heard a bug buzzing around my ears . . ." The crowd laughed along with Alonda, which gave Lexi the oomph she needed to take control again.

"This!" she shouted, holding the belt up again, "is more than just a belt. This is my victory. So if you want this belt, you're gonna have to drag it from me."

"You don't scare me, Lexi!" Alonda shouted, trying to throw out the words to her as confidently as possible. "I know, you think you're the hottest shit around," Alonda said. Someone in the crowd kinda sneezed. "But you're going down."

"Kick her ass, Lexi!" someone yelled out. Alonda's ears caught on fire. Shit, she was losing them, and losing them fast. Lexi was still standing there, but her eyes was saying, *Come the hell on and get it on with!*

So Alonda took a deep breath and did just that.

"I didn't wanna be this rough on you," she said to Lexi. "You've been my hero ever since I got involved with Rize. My actual, literal hero," she continued, gesturing toward the cape. Kimmie held it up and said, "Yeah!!" Alonda went on, "I've looked up to you, because you've always claimed to not be afraid of anything."

Lexi puffed out her chest farther, raising her arm toward the crowd, who rewarded her with cheers.

"But," Alonda said, wielding the word like a dart—"and I've been thinking about this *But* a lot—but you think you're so great because you say you're not scared of nothing," Alonda stated, letting each of the words land, "and I believe that, I totally believe that you're not scared of nothing. But that's because you haven't met anything to be scared of, not yet. Because you never met me. And you're gonna be scared of me."

And with that she ran at Lexi, who only had a few seconds to toss their precious cardboard belt to the side before readying herself to receive Alonda's first blow. She pretended to hit Lexi with an arm bar, starting off with an easy move between the two of them. Lexi received it and sold the hell outta it, acting like Alonda had just dealt her the deadliest of blows when it really was just her making a lot of noise.

Lexi grabbed Alonda's fake glasses off her face and smashed them. Alonda exaggeratedly rolled her eyes. "Oh, boo-hoo, now I can't see through my rose-colored glasses," Alonda said. "Let's see how you like it!" she yelled, reaching out her hand quickly and brushing it across Lexi's face, pretending to temporarily scratch out her vision.

Lexi grabbed her eyes in fake pain, moaning while Alonda stood by and laughed. The crowd started booing her; Alonda could hear them as they called out, "That was dirty! Cheater!" and she could hear Pretzel shouting at her, "We wanna clean match, okay, none of this dirty business!" and she had to keep herself from breaking character and laughing.

She loved stuff like this.

Lexi pretended to recover her vision and used the opportunity to reach out to strike Alonda, throwing an elbow at her chest. It was the safer way to do a hit, but it was still a hit that packed a butt load of hurt.

Alonda countered by pretending to trip Lexi, who threw her body hard onto the ground. "Wanna give up?" Alonda asked tauntingly.

"Don't make me do what I'm gonna have to do if you keep cheating!" Lexi called from the ground cryptically. Alonda had to stifle a smile. The best part was about to come up. She walked over to Lexi and raised her arms, getting ready to move forward to strike when—

"It seems like Alondra's stuck!" Pretzel yelled out. "The Incredible Lexi is using her force field to keep her standing in place!" Alonda struggled against the Incredible Lexi's invisible field.

"Let me go!" she shouted out, struggling. Lexi kept her hand out in front of her and stood slowly, pretending to gather energy in her hands.

"Stop cheating!" Lexi said, and she threw the energy at Alonda, who responded by doing a backflip. She'd practiced the move for weeks, and she landed it perfectly. The crowd was screaming. "Do we got a deal?" Lexi asked.

Alonda nodded. "Yeah, stop messing with me!"

Lexi nodded. "Good," she said, and flicked her hand so that Alonda fell to the ground. The fall stung, but after weeks of throwing her body onto the ground in a fall, Alonda had gotten good at embracing the sting. But she rolled around a little bit on the ground while Lexi came over and pretended to kick her in the side a couple of times. In reality, Lexi was just kicking the ground, the sound of a kick causing the shivers of pain to crawl up the more empathetic audience members watching, but she wasn't touching Alonda at all. Alonda pretended to receive each blow, rolling around on the ground and moaning in pain.

Lexi got on top of her, pulled her arms back as far as they would go. A submission move. Alonda screamed and wiggled as she pretended to struggle to free herself from the move.

"Tap out!" Lexi yelled, pulling Alonda's arms farther back.

"Never!" Alonda yelled. She yanked her body against Lexi's, pulling herself forward with Lexi, leveraging Lexi's body over hers. They both slammed to the ground hard, the fall partially knocking the wind out of them both.

Pretzel jumped over to her and started doing his referee duties, hitting the ground and shouting "One!" If he got to ten, then the match would be over, a draw. Not what they had planned. This was both their cues to start getting up, so that's what they did while Pretzel counted, Alonda staggering to her feet like her body contained no more air.

"Continue," Pretzel said, looking from one to the other.

Lexi was smirking at her. She ran at Alonda again, and Alonda stepped to the side so Lexi ran past her. She turned to Alonda again, and again Alonda stepped out of the way.

"You too scared to fight me?!" Lexi asked.

"Guess I'm just too fast for you to fight me," Alonda said, sticking her tongue out at Lexi. Lexi ran to her and grabbed one of Alonda's pigtails and pretended to yank it, but really, Alonda just jerked her head closer to Lexi so Lexi could breathe a whisper into her ear, saying,

"The gate?"

Her breath damp and getting caught in Alonda's hair, using her hair to hide her mouth from the crowd, Alonda gave a quick "Yes" before pretending to free herself from Lexi's grasp.

"And Alondra breaks free of Lexi's grasp—what's she going to do?"

Alonda positioned herself so she was within striking distance of the gate. She caught Lexi's eye and gave her the slightest of nods.

She breathed in deep,

and Lexi stepped forward and attacked, throwing Alonda's body over the chain-link fence by the swings. It was only about three feet tall so Alonda's body went over easy, but it definitely looked dangerous.

"And Alondra is incapacitated—there's no way she can recover from that!" Pretzel shouted as the crowd shouted and yelled. Lexi ran over as fast as she could and pinned Alonda to the ground.

"One, two—"

The sound of the bell, and Alonda lost.

"Your winner and still champion—the Incredible Lexi!"

But Lexi hadn't stood up yet. She was looking at Alonda odd. Alonda felt Lexi's eyes inside her own.

"What?" Alonda asked, her voice breathless and shaky.

"Uh—" Lexi said, pointing.

Alonda looked at her arm.

Oh shit.

☆ **17** ☆

"IT WON'T STOP BLEEDING," ALONDA SAID, BURSTING INTO THE living room. Jim startled himself off the couch. It was the middle of the day so she knew he'd be home; Jim didn't usually leave for work until five on Wednesdays.

"What the f—" The words stumbled out of his mouth, his knee barely missing hitting the coffee table by inches.

She shoved her arm in his face. "My arm, my arm," she shouted impatiently, "it won't stop bleeding, I don't even know how I did it—"

Jim took her arm gently in his calloused hands and looked at it while she tried to stop shaking. She'd run outta the playground so fast, nobody'd had a chance to follow. She'd gotten bruises and scrapes before but never had anything that was actively bleeding as much as this. There was too much blood, and she couldn't see the cut, which was what was making her nervous.

"Really, you don't know how this happened?" he murmured sarcastically. "It couldn't have been because you was out there wrestling?"

"Is it okay, do you think it'll be okay?" Alonda asked, ignoring him. Jim didn't say nothing, just led her over to the kitchen and snapped on an overhead light so he could see better. He turned her arm around in his hands while she waited with bated breath, her knee bouncing with nerves and trying not to panic all at the same time. She knew it happened when she went over the fence, she hadn't even felt it happen in the moment, but now she couldn't believe she had never felt the deep ache that was throbbing through her body right now.

"Hate to be the one to break it to you," Jim said, snapping her back into being, "but looks like we're gonna have to take the whole thing."

"Oh God, Jim, not now," Alonda moaned, rolling her eyes. How was this man joking while she was bleeding all over herself?!

"Yeah, you know, like," he said, and started making a drilling sound on her arm, pretending to chop it off.

"Seriously, you're not funny!" Alonda said, trying to grab her arm out of his hand. He laughed and didn't let go, still examining the arm.

"Calm down, it ain't that bad," he said, setting her arm down.

"Then why won't it stop bleeding?!" Alonda asked, trying to mop off the blood with a paper towel.

"Because that's what cuts do sometimes. It's all right though—here, run it under the water," Jim said, gently guiding her arm to the sink. He turned on the faucet and let the cool water run over the cut, washing out the dirt and grime. It stung a little bit, but Alonda'd felt worse. He was so close, she could smell the scent of cigar that clung to his tank top. Alonda refrained from wrinkling her nose. Even when he wasn't smoking, it was like he was smoking, ew.

"Pretty brave to get this," he said.

Alonda shrugged. "It's whatever," she said. "Not sure it's brave or dumb or something in between."

"Hey, getting cuts and scrapes and shit is part of life, right?" Jim said. "That don't make you less brave because of it."

"Right," Alonda said, trying to shut down the conversation. She wasn't really in the mood to listen to Jim wax poetic about something.

"How's all that going otherwise?" Jim asked, and Alonda shrugged again.

"Good, I guess. We're starting to get people who wanna watch our shows."

Jim raised his eyebrows. "You do?" he asked, surprised.

"Yeah, we're getting a following. We got our matches and shit up online, so we been getting views there, too. It's kinda cool," she admitted, "to be known in some kinda way? The trolls are whatever, but most people've been supportive, so . . ." She gave her shoulders a shrug, and her voice trailed off.

He laughed a little bit to himself. "Who knows," he said, "you might get famous from that, I seen it happen—or like, maybe youse all can go on one of those talent shows with it."

Alonda shook her head. "I dunno," she said. "It's supposed to be for fun."

She understood what Lexi had been saying better than she had before. Adding all these elements made it feel less like playing around and almost like a job—almost like a job they weren't even getting paid to do, not that she wanted to be paid for it. King wanted to make his life as a wrestler, but Alonda wasn't sure she knew what she wanted to do with the rest of her life. Or why she had to have a plan or make a decision about it.

"We got Band-Aids in the bathroom," Alonda said, gesturing with her head, but Jim shook his head.

"Band-Aids are too weak for this," he said, and dramatically tore a strip of cloth from the bottom of his shirt.

Alonda couldn't help but laugh. "You're so extra!" she said as he started wrapping the cloth around her cut.

He stopped himself. "Oh shit, I should disinfect this," he said. "You got rubbing alcohol?"

Alonda shook her head again. "Nah, we're out." Jim scrunched up his forehead, thinking hard before walking over to the freezer and opening the door, taking out a bottle of vodka. Alonda snorted.

"What, same shit, right?" he asked, and Alonda scrunched up her eyes. "

Uh, I don't think people drink rubbing alcohol like they drink vodka?" she asked as obnoxiously as possible. Jim laughed at her and poured a little bit into a shot glass.

"This is gonna sting," he said, and poured it gently over the cut.

Alonda hissed through her teeth and tried to grab her arm away, but he kept it in place. "Goddamn!" she said. "Yeah, it stings, stings like a fire!"

"I know, I know," he said. "But it's killing the germs—gotta make sure it don't get infected. Had a buddy once, got himself a nasty cut that he covered in a Band-Aid and nothing else. It kept getting more and more itchy, but he was ignoring it, thought he was a strong guy, but that cut started seeping its infection out into his blood, and before he knew it, his whole body was infected and smelled bad, and I think he had to get the whole thing cut off for real."

Alonda felt her stomach turn a little bit at the thought of her arm getting that infected. A little sting wasn't too bad.

Jim wrapped her arm in the shirt tightly. Once the blood was washed away, it was clear the cut wasn't that big or deep, and it had stopped bleeding.

"Thanks," she said, shaking her head a little. She turned to leave to go back to her room, but Jim stopped her.

"You wanna try some?" he asked, pouring out a shot.

She turned back to him, confused. "Are you for real?" she asked, and he laughed.

"Yeah, I'm having one," he said.

"You got work in an hour," she said, but he shrugged.

"It's just a shot," he said, stating it like it was a fact, like it was no big deal.

Alonda paused. Teresa never even let her have rum raisin ice cream, she was so paranoid about Alonda drinking.

And it was kinda weird for Jim to be offering her a drink.

Wasn't it?

Although . . . he was an adult, and if he was gonna watch her while she tried it, it couldn't be that bad, right?

"Come on, you ain't scared, are you?"

That made her bristle. Nah, she wasn't scared. It was just a shot, and it's not like she was gonna go anywhere or do anything.

He handed her the shot. "Now," he said, very serious, "what you're gonna wanna do is drink it real fast, like it's medicine."

"Why do I wanna drink anything that's gonna taste like medicine?" Alonda asked, very skeptical about the whole experiment.

"Then you're gonna wanna chase it with this," he said, ignoring her question and pouring her some soda.

She held the shot glass in her hand. Damn, it looked just like water.

"Come on, on the count of three, now."

Alonda raised the shot to her lips and waited for him to count it down.

"One, two—"

Alonda did the shot. It burned her whole throat like how the water had burned her cut, but the burn barreled all the way down her throat where it felt like it exploded into a fireball in her stomach.

She coughed and coughed, and Jim laughed and passed her the soda.

"It burns!" she said through the coughs that escaped her lips.

"Yeah, I know it burns," Jim said, his laughs getting louder and louder.

"Stop laughing at me!" Alonda said. The vodka had made her blood feel warm, her head a little woozy. She didn't like how any of it felt. She sat down at the table, trying to shake the feeling out of her.

"Why do people like this?" she asked, and Jim just smiled again.

"You get used to it," he said. He poured himself another shot, but Alonda pushed herself away from the table.

"I'm gonna go to my bedroom," she said.

"You'll learn," he said, his voice a little foggy and faraway, as though he was willing himself to be somewhere else. "Your whole life is stretched before you right now. You got all of it to live. One day, you'll turn around and you'll look ahead and see the horizon growing closer. And you'll look back and see all the life you lived, all the wasted dreams paving that path, and you'll wonder, was any of it worth it?"

Alonda didn't know what to say so she said nothing.

Jim didn't seem to notice she was still standing in the kitchen. He looked to be surrounded by ghosts only he could see.

Alonda squinted at her phone. It was 2:00 A.M., and she was watching YouTube videos about the evolution of birds. She sighed, rubbing her forehead hard. Alonda had been moments away from falling into a deep sleep when she had rolled over on her injured arm, the sharpness of the pain jolting her awake. She was trying to lull herself to sleep by watching boring videos, but it was backfiring because the evolution of birds was turning out to be super interesting.

She knew she should put the phone away, but a new video caught her eye. Just as she went to click it, a text came in.

LEXI: Hey, hope your arm's okay

Alonda's thumb slipped and hit the message. Instead of opening the text, the cheerful chirp of the phone making a call filled her ears.

"What?! No, no, no," she whispered under her breath, trying to figure out how to end the call.

She saw the red phone icon, had her finger right over it when—

"Hello?"

Alonda's mouth went dry and dissolved her words.

"Alonda, that you?"

"Uh, yeah!" she squeezed out. "Yeah, sorry about—thumb dial."

"Thumb . . . dial?"

"Yeah, like a butt dial but with my thumb?"

Lexi laughed.

"Yeah, so . . . sorry about that!" Alonda said awkwardly. She never used her phone to talk. It felt weird.

"How's your arm?" Lexi asked.

"I'll live," Alonda responded. "Didn't need stitches or anything."

"Cool!" Lexi said. There was an awkward moment of silence. "So I guess . . . ," Lexi started, but Alonda jumped in. She suddenly didn't wanna hang up the phone, wanted to keep the conversation going.

"So what're you doing awake? Working?"

"Yeah, on a piece for that show."

"Cool! Can I see?" Alonda asked. She liked when Lexi sent her works in progress.

"Mmm, well, I can describe it to you."

"Okay."

"Yeah, close your eyes. They closed?"

Alonda closed her eyes, even though she felt silly doing so.

"Yup."

"Well, okay, so picture this—a big blank piece of poster board. Can your imagination handle it?"

"Oh, so it's going well, sounds like," Alonda said, trying to be as lighthearted as possible.

"Oh, for sure . . . ," Lexi said, her voice trailing off so far that Alonda could imagine the ellipses darting past the end of her sentence.

"Do you wanna . . . talk about it?" Alonda asked gently. She wasn't sure that she could be of any help, but the tone of Lexi's voice was shaky, like it wanted to crack open and say more than what she was saying.

Lexi made a small noise that sounded like the mix between a laugh and a sigh before breathing out deep.

"I'm scared," she said so quickly, the words almost got lost in Alonda's ear.

"You're ... scared?" Alonda asked, sure she'd heard her wrong. Lexi didn't get scared—at least, not of the huge, scary stuff Alonda had seen her do. She didn't even seem to get nervous before a match, or cutting a promo or anything.

"Yeah," Lexi said, her voice muffled.

"Did you stuff your face in your pillow?"

"I dunno, maybe," she responded, her voice more muffled. Alonda stifled a laugh.

"Well, there's no holes to different universes to be found at the bottom of your pillow," Alonda said, giggling.

"Yeah, well, I wanna find one instead of working on this piece," Lexi said, her voice still muffled. "Making art is scary."

"But ... it's just art." Alonda cringed as the words left her mouth. "Sorry," she quickly said, "I didn't mean it like ... the way it sounds. I honestly, I don't know anything about art or, like, doing it or anything, but all I mean is compared to wrestling?"

"Don't gotta compare it to wrestling," Lexi said. "It's its own thing. And yeah, it's scary."

"What makes it scary?" Alonda asked softly. She could hear Lexi take a sharp breath in, as though she was gathering her thoughts into words before speaking.

"Like, I know what I want the piece to be, I can almost see it in my mind, but when I go to make it for real, it looks nothing like it did. But it kinda looks better? Better than I planned it instead? And, I dunno, that's scary. Because then I wanna go deeper into that, but I'm scared 'cause I dunno what I'll find."

"Right," Alonda said. She didn't wanna interrupt because it sounded like Lexi had more to say.

"It's gonna be my heart on display. Like, most people won't even know it's my heart, they'll just look at a piece and feel their feelings about it. But it's scary to have so many people's eyes on my heart. Even if they don't know it's my heart."

Alonda felt her own heart clench. That was always a scary thing, like reading the comments on the YouTube videos.

"But," Alonda said, her heart thumping in her chest, "at least you're putting your heart out in the world. And sure, there's gonna be people who'll hate it for whatever reason, but then people are gonna love it, too. They're gonna love it a lot. And they'll see into it, into what you're trying to say, and that's really exciting. Something I definitely could never do in a million years."

"You ever think about how long a million years is?" Lexi asked with a laugh. "Like, I actually bet that if you had a million years to kill, at some point you'd do the thing that you said you'd never do."

Alonda snorted. "Yeah, okay, I guess that's true." Especially since she never thought she'd be in an amateur wrestling troupe when she was seventeen.

"But thanks," Lexi said, her voice low and soft. "Seriously, that . . . it's helpful."

Alonda felt a small smile tug. "Hey, no problem."

They lapsed into silence again, but this time it felt comfortable, like they were okay with it being quiet. Alonda felt her eyelids getting heavier. Sleep was finally coming.

"How's things going with King?"

Lexi's question snapped her eyes back open. "Oh good!" Alonda said, her voice leaping an octave. She cleared her throat, trying to sound more normal. "Yeah, it's good, he's really great."

"For sure."

The silence fell again, but this time it was more electric, fraught with words Alonda didn't know how to say.

"I guess I better go tackle the scary," Lexi said. "Hope you get some sleep."

"Yeah, yeah, you, too," Alonda responded.

"Sweet dreams!"

"Thanks—" Alonda started to say, but the call had already ended. She sighed deep, putting her phone on her nightstand, turning the face down. Maybe it was time to stop chasing sleep.

☆ 18 ☆

THE OCEAN SOUNDED LIKE IT WAS YAWNING, WAVES COMING IN
and out, in and out. It was midnight, and the beach was getting
quiet now. Party was still going strong on the boardwalk, but even
that'd be dying down in about an hour.

Alonda breathed in the wet air by the water. She could smell the
sea salt and the damp sand, could smell the bitter scent of decaying
fish and other people's garbage, could smell the sweet lotion Lexi'd
spread on her arms and King's musky deodorant as they sat on
either side of her on the beach.

She wrinkled her nose. Could also smell that joint Pretzel was
trying to light up.

"Hurry up," Spider hissed at Pretzel. He was fumbling around
with the lighter, couldn't quite seem to get the little joint lit.

"Night's feeling good, ain't it?" Lexi said. She was looking out
into the dark water.

"Yeah," Alonda responded, "good break from the sun." They'd
all spent the entire day on the beach, from early morning until now.
It'd been a sunny day, super hot, but incredible by the water.

"I like the sun, though," Lexi said, stretching her arms high.
"Would always rather have the sun than a day of clouds."

The glow from the boardwalk and some streetlights were making it so they could see one another, but the shadows were keeping them hidden from whoever else might've been looking. It wasn't illegal for them to be out on the beach this late at night in summer, but they didn't really want anyone bothering them.

Alonda had never been on the beach this late at night before. She wasn't even sure if Teresa knew she wasn't home yet. Probably assumed she was in her bedroom, locked away from the world and going to sleep. Jim was home again tonight, and things had just been getting louder and louder with him. Alonda didn't wanna be home. He didn't really make it feel good.

"You got that thing lit yet or what?" Lexi asked the boys.

Pretzel took a deep breath of it and immediately started to choke. "Got it," he said, choking out coughs and passing the joint down the line.

Spider thumped his back and laughed a little. "Man, you know you shouldn't even be smoking this shit with your asthma and everything!"

Pretzel shook his head, still coughing. "I . . . got it . . . under control," he choked out in between hits of his inhaler, which made the rest of them laugh while King passed him some water.

"Shit's strong," Lexi said. "Almost too strong for me, even."

She passed the joint to King, who took a hit, too, before passing it to Alonda.

She took it in her hand but passed it down to Spider.

"Something the matter?" King asked, and Alonda just shrugged.

"Not my scene," she said. He nodded as Spider took a huge hit.

"Yo, slow down!" King said as Spider started coughing, too.

"I am going slow!" he said. "I'm smoking Alonda's half."

"Don't hog it," King said, holding out his hand over Alonda's head for the joint and breathing it in.

Quiet descended over them once more, wrapping them all up in its arms like a blanket.

The waves. The muffled sound of music, people walking, laughing. Felt like a backdrop for a movie when really, this shit was real life.

Alonda didn't realize that real life could feel so otherworldly.

A question bubbled up in her mind, one she'd been saving for a moment they could all talk about it, and this felt like as good a moment as any in her whole life.

"Why do you think WWE doesn't let the men wrestle the women?" Alonda asked.

"'Cause that shit's dangerous. Just because we do it don't make it safe," Pretzel responded immediately.

Spider punched him in the arm. "All this shit's dangerous, man."

Pretzel punched him back. "No, I mean but extra!"

"How's it dangerous? It's just sexist and wrong," Lexi said. "They're just basing it off what body parts people've got, and that's so shortsighted, like damn. Body parts don't define nothing. Also, that's just totally heteronormative thinking, right, like, they think, 'Oh, a man and a woman can't wrestle 'cause they're attracted to each other and it might get wrong,' but, like, they don't think that automatically if a gay man is wrestling a gay man, they just erase it completely."

"Nah, man," King said, "it's not that deep. They're just, like, uncomfortable with the idea of a man putting his hands on a woman."

"Yeah, but why?!" Lexi asked. "Especially if we know it's all fake! That they're equals in the ring. I know they're trying to say that men shouldn't put their hands on women in real life, which they shouldn't, nobody should be putting hands on anybody for real, but by doing that they're also saying you shouldn't fight back to protect yourself, you know? Like, they're not saying that with words, but they're still saying it."

Lexi let out a big breath of smoke before saying, "Gender's just a social construct anyway. Thinking like that reinforces the binary, and honestly, that shit's more violent than anything we do in the ring."

Silence fell over them again. Alonda took the words and held them inside her heart. After watching Lovely Loveless's video, she'd been falling down more and more rabbit holes about sexuality, about gender. She hadn't realized that there were more than two and there seemed to be an infinite amount. And most wrestling, most sports, most everything just broke things down into a half-this, half-that fake truth, rather than embracing all the differences. No wonder Alonda didn't know till she found out.

But she wished she had known sooner.

"Yeah, I mean, like, where are the nonbinary wrestlers?" Alonda asked, softly at first but her voice growing. "And there's so few trans wrestlers because most places won't let them wrestle without them being misgendered! Wrestling's gotta get it together, damn," she finished, flicking some sand into the ocean's edge.

"So what're you gonna do about it?" King asked, his voice teasing a little. "Send WWE an email?"

Alonda playfully punched King in the arm. He grabbed his bicep, feigning pain.

"This is why they don't let women fight the men, 'cause you too strong for me!" he wailed out, falling to the sand and flopping around. Lexi got up and started tickling him, which caused King to really try to break free.

"Don't, don't!" he shouted, but Lexi kept tickling him.

"I need an assist!" he called out, and Alonda got up and picked up Lexi, carrying her off King. They both fell to the sand, laughing and rolling around.

"I bet I can do a cartwheel better than you, though!" King said, and he got up and started doing cartwheels.

"You got sand in my eye!" Spider yelled.

"You got sand in my everywhere," Pretzel grumbled, trying to dust himself off.

Suddenly, a light shone on the group and a voice rang out,

"Hey, what're you kids doing?"

"Run!" King shouted, and the five of them scampered off, their laughter chasing them as it echoed off the waves of the beach.

☆ **19** ☆

"AND THEN THE WAY SHE *FLIPPED YOU OVER*? WITH *HER MIND*?! It was just so cool!"

Alonda just kept nodding, unable to hide the smile that Michelle's excited words brought to her face. Even though the match had been days ago, Alonda hadn't worked since then and it seemed Michelle had been bursting to debrief the entirety of the match with her. She'd been going on and on about it since Alonda clocked in.

"Like, I don't even really like wrestling, but I loved that," Michelle said. She was leaning over the prize case, keeping a watchful eye on the Fun-Cade and talking to Alonda all at the same time.

"If you liked us, then you'd *love* professional wrestling," Alonda said. "We're pretty cool for sure but nowhere near as legit as real wrestling."

"I dunno, what you were all doing seemed pretty real to me," Michelle said, shaking her head. "I mean, it was so cool watching how you all just put together a show and did it out on the playground. I've passed that park a million times, but I've never seen it used like how you were all using it, like, you saw something else in it and brought it to life, and that's automatically cooler than any 'real wrestling' I can think of," she said, complete with some big air quotes. "Also, I thought that all your characters were cooler than anything I'd ever seen on TV. Usually it's all hulking guys taking themselves way too seriously."

"Well, things are changing—" Alonda started to say, but Michelle's words spilled over her, "I mean, it was like you were all *the neighborhood*, you know? And that's just so, so cool."

"Yeah, I guess that is cool," Alonda said, smiling. Michelle probably would've gone on talking, but just then a kid vomited in the corner at the same time as their most popular game went out of order and suddenly the most important thing went from discussing the match to everything right in front of them.

"Oh my God, it's the Incredible Lexi!"

Michelle's voice snapped Alonda outta her reverie. Lexi was standing at the entrance of the Fun-Cade. She had her sketchbook under her arm, probably trying to find new people to sketch, and Michelle had spotted her.

"Yeah, that's . . . me," Lexi said, a little unsure.

"You were *so* good," Michelle said.

"Oh, for real?" Lexi asked, a little surprised.

"Yeah, she's been talking about it all day, like, nonstop," Alonda said with a little laugh. "What're you doing here?"

She held up her sketchbook. "Just looking for more faces. Didn't realize you'd be working today."

Alonda nodded. "Yeah, someone called out sick."

"So Alondra came to the rescue!" Michelle said, super cornily. Alonda and Lexi both grimace smiled at her.

"So, are you going on break anytime soon?" Lexi asked.

"Uh, not for a little while," she started to say, but Michelle interrupted. "Oh no, it's totally fine, you can go on break now."

"You . . . sure?" Alonda asked, but Michelle was nodding. "Yeah, don't even worry about it—I'll see you back here in a half hour."

"You wanna walk on the boardwalk?" Alonda asked Lexi.

She smiled widely. "For sure."

They walked to the boardwalk, not really talking, just walking side by side. It was packed again—not Fourth of July level of packed but pretty busy, especially because it was a sunny day, people all walking, soaking in the sun or standing under umbrellas, trying to create a moving shade.

"You heard there's gonna be a wrestling expo here in August?" Lexi asked Alonda.

She nodded. "Yeah, they been putting up signs on the fences and shit."

"We're gonna go, right?" Lexi asked, and quickly added, "I mean, I'm definitely gonna go, I can't wait. There's gonna be like hundreds of wrestlers here, even some WWE people rumored to come."

"If you could, like, meet any wrestler in the whole world, who would it be?" Alonda asked Lexi, but before she even finished her question Lexi was already responding with "AJ Lee! AJ Lee, one million percent AJ Lee." Alonda couldn't help a laugh coming out her mouth at Lexi's excitement. When Lexi got excited about something, her eyes got all wide and her voice went into a higher pitch and she even started hopping in place.

"But she retired earlier this year—" Alonda started to say, but Lexi put her fingers in her ears and said, "No, I live in a denial that I'm very comfortable with, thanks!"

"Why AJ Lee?"

Lexi took her fingers down and just shook her head with awe. "She's, like, power. Short, like me, but when she stands in that ring, she's seven feet tall. Can't do nothing but watch her, and even when she loses, it's like she's won, you know?"

Alonda nodded, smiling a little. She knew exactly what Lexi meant by that.

"Well, you never know, she might show up to the expo!"

"Yeah, right," Lexi said, but she sounded a little hopeful.

Alonda nodded. "Yeah, if Lovely Loveless comes, man, that'd be dope," she said. "Of all the wrestlers in the whole world, she's the one I'd wanna meet."

"Really? But she ain't pro or nothing," Lexi said, sounding genuinely curious.

Alonda looked at her and bit her bottom lip. "She's just . . . really helping me. Like, without even knowing she is, you know?" Lexi nodded.

The group of musicians Alonda had seen on the Fourth of July were back and playing. They came pretty much every weekend in the summer, playing music, having a blast. There was a smaller group this time, and even though they was still blasting music on their radio, they only had a couple of drums and a cowbell this time, somebody even playing a beat with their hands on a plastic tub, but it was as lively as any other time. Their music had attracted a crowd of listeners again. The two stopped and listened, watching them all dance. The music made its way into Alonda's ears, and she felt her foot start to twitch to the music, keeping time with the tempo.

The songs all blended into one another, never really ending but always moving from one to the next to the next. Lexi started to dance, moved her way into the circle. She turned to look at Alonda, clapping her hands. "Come on!" she shouted. "Dance!"

"I can't," Alonda said.

"Come on, what're you, scared?" Lexi said, bouncing more aggressively to the beat. "Show me what you got!"

Alonda started to shake her head no, but she stopped. Why shouldn't she?

Yo vivo sin miedo.

Nobody was paying any real attention to anybody. They were watching but also bouncing, dancing with one another.

The music picked up, something faster paced that seemed to electrify the crowd, everyone replying with cheers and claps, a few sharp whistles joyfully ripping through the air.

Alonda and Lexi danced faster and faster, Alonda abandoning any semblance of knowing the "right" steps and just dancing, letting her body flow with the music and watching Lexi do the same. Lexi raised her arms and started doing a slow kinda spin and stomp to the beat, spinning her body on each stomp, and Alonda started mimicking the movements.

Lexi grabbed her hands and started dancing with her, silly. Alonda felt her body stiffen up. "Come on, get loose," Lexi said, laughing and gently waving Alonda's hand in hers. Lexi's hand felt so soft, and it was guiding her back and forth, in and out of the dance, in and out, in and out.

Alonda stopped thinking and spun Lexi around, their laughter too soft to be heard in the noise of the crowd.

Suddenly, the music slowed. Some lone dancers closed their eyes and started moving their bodies slowly to the beat. Couples that had been frantically dancing a few feet apart zipped together like they were magnets finally returning to their poles. Alonda looked at Lexi and slowly pulled her closer. Lexi put her head on Alonda's shoulder so naturally, Alonda didn't even fully realize it was happening, just swaying with Lexi.

Holding Lexi.

Lexi.

The box in her chest rattled.

Suddenly, like an invisible current racing through their bodies, they jolted apart, Alonda shoving her hands in the back pockets of her shorts and Lexi fiddling with the straps of her backpack, both of them kinda not looking at the other but at anything and everything else, trying to act like nothing had just happened.

"Good . . . the music's really good, huh?" Lexi asked a little too loudly, and Alonda nodded a little harder than she ever would, saying, "Yeah, it's great, it's good." The two passed a weird smile back and forth and turned back to watching the crowd sway to the music.

Alonda's thoughts zoomed around her head, as quickly and frantically as though they were the Cyclone itself. Why'd she do that? She hadn't meant to do that.

Then why'd it feel so right?

The two of them stood side by side until the slow song ended, the music scoring their awkward silence.

"Put your hand over here—"

"No, you gotta put yours—"

"Lexi, can you just—"

"Hold on for one second, King, God!"

Alonda let out a sigh so deep that it actually made her bangs fluff up on its exhale.

Another stifling day and King had called an "emergency" practice and Alonda was, quite frankly, a little over it. And from the looks of annoyance on Spider's, Pretzel's, and Lexi's faces, everyone else was over it, too.

"Hey, how much longer's this gonna take?" Pretzel called out. He was lying on top of the bench, his legs over the back and his head upside down.

"Till we get it right. Obviously," King said, keeping his eyes on Lexi.

Spider rolled out from under the shade of the bench. "Yeah, but why're the rest of us here? If you need to practice with Lexi, you don't need us—"

"'Cause we're a group!" King snapped, turning to face the rest of them. "What do you mean, Why? We're all in this together!"

"God, I'm just saying!" Spider said. "Maybe we don't all gotta be at every single thing, that's all."

"Okay, and what if we decide something that *does* impact the group, what then?" King asked.

Spider scrunched up his face, saying, "Maybe just text it?"

"Not the same," King muttered.

There was something that was shifting in the group. Alonda could feel it. The more they tried to make things work, the less fun it was. The more stressful. It was hard because she didn't want Rize to end. But she also wanted to go back to the way things felt before. When it was easier, and better.

She decided to push that thought as far to the corner of her mind as she could. She would push it out her ears if she could, but she knew thoughts didn't work that way. She hated that thoughts didn't work that way and knew once they were usually stuck to her mind, she wouldn't be able to get them to magically leave. Just like how she couldn't stop thinking about dancing with Lexi or why she pulled her so close or why it felt so natural or why the box in her chest wouldn't stop shaking.

Spider opened his mouth in what was sure to be something not helpful, so Alonda decided to open hers instead, cutting him off.

"Hey, while we're all h-here," she stuttered out, a little nervous, "I, uh . . . I got a catchphrase? I think I wanna try?"

"Is it a question, or do you got one?" Pretzel asked. He sounded so bored. Alonda tried to act casual.

"Anyway," she said, "I figured I needed a catchphrase. Like all the greats, you know?"

"Sure," Lexi said, nodding.

"Not every great has a catchphrase," Pretzel said.

"Well, I mean, John Cena has 'You can't see me,' and Becky Lynch's got 'I'm the Man,' and Daniel Bryan's just got 'Yes,'" Alonda said, shrugging as she made her way up the jungle gym. She'd come up with it a few days ago, rewatching Lovely Loveless's video. Gotta bring what you love into the ring, right?

She climbed to the top of the jungle gym and turned to face the group. She put her hands on her hips and called out "¡Sin Miedo!" before jumping down, landing on her feet with her arms in the air. She turned to look at the rest of the group.

"I'd do it before a finisher, you know?"

"Do you even have a finisher yet?" Spider asked. It was a fair question, but for some reason, it made Alonda bristle. Like, she asked about the catchphrase, not her un-invented finisher.

"No, but does it matter? I'm gonna get one. Besides, I can say it whenever—I just think it'll be *cool* if I *say it* before a *finisher*," Alonda said, throwing out some of her words. She knew it wasn't necessarily fair, but she was getting tired of having to talk everything through. She felt the tension rising like the heat boiling off the ground.

"Why Sin Miedo?" Lexi asked.

"Because I like that it means Without Fear. Fearless," Alonda said. Like Mami used to say. Yo vivo sin miedo. That's how she wanted to be. That's who she was becoming.

King was nodding. "Yeah, that's good. Maybe you and Lexi should try something out with that."

"Or maybe I can try something with someone?" Spider asked. "Like, damn, I thought once we had a fourth it'd make things even, that's what we all said, right, but somehow I'm still the one always getting left in the dust."

"That ain't true," King said, but Spider scoffed.

"Please, it's like either you're working with Lexi or Alonda's working with Lexi and you're watching and making pointers—"

"At least you get to do things. I just get to sit around and watch all you and your 'genius' at work," Pretzel said with huge air quotes around the word *genius*.

"Fine, if you don't wanna be here, don't be here, then!" King snapped.

"Hey, I'm more important than you give me credit for!" Pretzel said.

"Nobody said you ain't!"

"Then why're you telling me to go?!"

"I didn't say To Go, I said if you don't wanna be here—"

Alonda's head was twirling with the fight. She wasn't even sure how it started, but it was picking up steam.

"Listen, we're all important, obviously," Lexi said, cutting in. "But, Pretzel, if you feel like your time's being wasted, then you can go!"

"And what about me?!" Spider interjected before Pretzel could respond.

"It's not all about you!"

"Really? Thought that the whole reason we all gotta be practicing together is because we all 'in this shit together,'" Spider said, putting huge air quotes around his own words.

"Hey!" King said. "What the hell, man, you don't gotta go mocking this shit."

"Who's 'mocking' it?" Spider said, more air quotes.

"Screw this," Alonda said, walking to her bag and throwing it over her shoulder.

"Alonda, where you going?" King asked. He sounded genuinely confused, but she didn't care.

"I wanna wrestle, I don't wanna fight, all right?" she said, turning to face them all. "And that's all we're doing, is fighting, or if we're not fighting we're picking apart every single move we do or every word we choose to say or whatever! And I just don't wanna do it today. Too hot for this shit," she muttered.

And with that she walked away.

☆ **20** ☆

"WAIT, NO WAY," KING SAID, LOOKING AT THE LINE THAT STRETCHED around the block of the church.

Alonda's face broke out into a huge smile. "If by 'No way' you really mean 'I can totally believe that Alonda surprised me with tickets to Universal Wrestling Warriors' Indie Show,' then yeah, Nooo waaay," she said, drawing out the vowels, trying to sound as cool as possible. He picked her up and swung her around a little before putting her down and giving her a long, deep kiss. Alonda soaked in the kiss. It filled her up with warmth, and there was a smile on her face when they finally broke apart.

"Okay, enough of that now, come on, let's get on line," she said, grabbing his hand and pulling him over.

"This has got to be the greatest surprise in the history of surprises," King said as they stood on line, waiting for their turn to get in. "How'd you get tickets?"

Alonda shrugged nonchalantly. "It was no big deal," she said.

Yeah, sure, no big deal, the show had been sold out for weeks, but Alonda had kept stalking their social media pages, leaving comments, asking if people had any extras until someone finally was looking to sell a pair of tickets they couldn't use and she'd made the purchase, putting her summer job money to use. But it was all worth it seeing the smile on King's face, she thought as they made their way into the gym.

There was a ring set up in the center of the gym, surrounded by folding chairs on all four sides, about eight rows deep. It was mostly open seating, so King dashed to grab a seat as close to the front of one of the rows as possible, Alonda running to keep up with him while trying to take everything in. Like, yeah, it was just a setup in a school gym, but the energy pulsed with excitement and people all wearing wrestling shirts. She just wanted to soak it in.

Universal Wrestling Warriors was an indie promotion that was pretty well known; they usually rented out spots like this, did all their own setup, split ticket sales. Some of the wrestlers brought their own merch to sell during the show. Usually they'd be by their merch table until it was time for their match, do their whole match, and then be back by their booth, still breathless with makeup and sweat streaking down their faces but smiling as they made change for a ten.

"You excited?" Alonda asked King, shouting a little over the pregame music they had blasting. He was sitting on the literal edge of the seat of his folding chair, waiting.

"I'm so ready, haven't had a chance to see live wrestling for a minute," he said, his knee bouncing up and down so hard, the chair next to her shook a little. Alonda smiled big. Yeah, this was pretty dope.

The first three matches went by in a blur of yelling, chants, boos, and cheers. The sound system wasn't the best, so sometimes the entrance music was so loud, it felt like Alonda's brain was going to rattle right outta her ears. And other times it was too fuzzy to really make out what the song was. But when each wrestler entered, it was like it didn't matter. They brought the energy with them, the excitement, all the possibility.

King's eyes were wide with excitement, but instead of focusing on the match and getting swept up in the moment, he was dissecting each one, talking about how they could bring it back to the group. "You see that, we can do that move, we just gotta try," or "Okay, I got an idea for the next time, we gotta . . ." Alonda kinda laughed and nodded along, but really, she just wanted to watch the show. She didn't really wanna keep talking about Rize, and it felt like King was talking about it every second of every day. She was starting to kinda regret bringing him. Or at least going with him to watch the show—maybe she shoulda just given him the tickets and said "Bring a friend" or something. Which kinda sucked because she wanted to be able to do stuff like this and not watch him get all carried away with the techniques of a thing.

Before she knew it, it was intermission, but before she could ask King if he wanted to go check out some of the merch tables, the announcer was tapping on his mic, getting the attention of the crowd.

"A very special announcement: We are happy to share that a surprise guest has dropped by," the emcee was saying. A buzz of excitement zapped through the air, everyone looking around to see if they could spot who it was.

"I need you all to give it up for the great Donny Drago!"

"No way!" King said, shooting up out of his seat. Alonda strained her neck to follow where he was looking and saw him, straight from YouTube. He was wearing a camo-patterned tank top, his big muscles bulging out around the straps. He kinda waved to the crowd, his signature smirk on his face.

"I gotta go say something," King said, and he left Alonda sitting there. Annoyance welled up in her and began to rise in her bloodstream. She tried to push it down, to be more understanding. Like, yeah, of course he was excited, Donny Drago was exciting, but he didn't even ask her if she wanted to go over there, too, or anything.

It was intermission anyway, so Alonda decided to get up and check out some of the merch. She wandered through the folding tables that were set up, trying to keep her excitement at bay. She didn't recognize some of the wrestlers, but there were even more she did like Jazzica and Rebel Bells and Danny Prince and—

"Lovely Loveless?" Alonda felt her name fall out of her mouth in shock, but there she was, fully right in front of her, Lovely Loveless, sitting there wearing bright pink eye shadow and a neon-green cropped hoodie, selling merch. Her heart started to pound, holy shit, it was Lovely Loveless, sitting feet away from her! She checked the program that she had shoved into her back pocket without looking—holy shit, she was gonna be headlining the main event, she was gonna be wrestling freakin' Jazzica, and she was sitting right there and—

Alonda looked around, trying to find King to share her excitement with him, but—

It looked like King was in the middle of a conversation with Donny Drago, but he wasn't looking excited anymore. His face was kinda smiling, but his eyes definitely weren't, and his shoulders were all dejected. Alonda took a look at Lovely Loveless—there was still some time before intermission ended, she could definitely go back later—and got closer to King.

"Well, what school'd you train at?" she heard Donny asking.

"Well, uh, right now, none—" King started to say, but Donny

was talking over him. "Whoa whoa whoa you mean to tell me you're all doing that kinda stuff without any training?"

"Well, yeah—"

"That's dangerous, dude! You shouldn't be doing that!"

"Right, but—"

"What, you think that you can just watch a YouTube video and then call yourself professional?" Donny laughed, shaking his head. "Dude, you are truly delusional, bro."

Alonda rippled. She got his point, what they were doing wasn't exactly grade A careful, but also, why'd he put how-tos online if he didn't expect people to try it out? And his shit's what they mostly watched!

King's shoulders looked more and more dejected as he stood there. "I'm just saying, if you wanted to, like, come out and watch us—"

"And watch you all injure yourselves beyond recognition? No thanks," Donny said, taking out his phone and texting like there wasn't a real human standing right in front of him.

King stood there for a few more seconds before Donny turned away from him. "Hey, Joey! Great to see you, man," he said, giving some other white guy a bro hug.

Alonda came over to King, gently pulling his arm, bringing him away from them. "He's a jerk. His name should be Jerky Jerk-o."

King didn't say anything. He had his jaw clenched, his brow furrowed.

"Come on, I wanna show you—" she started to say, but he cut her off.

"I'm going."

"Like . . . now?" Alonda asked, surprised.

"Yeah," King said. He headed toward the door. Alonda ran to keep up with him.

"But . . . intermission's about to end. Don't you wanna see—"

King kept moving toward the door, not listening to her. Alonda had to walk twice as fast to keep up with his long legs.

"Come on, King, it's not that serious, just because one person—"

"He's not gonna take me serious? Okay. So I gotta do more to make him take me serious."

"It's not that big a deal—"

"Yeah, it is. To me it is, it's a big deal."

Alonda looked back inside the gym. The emcee was tapping on the mic. Intermission was about to end.

Looked back out at King, who was walking toward the train, getting farther and farther away.

She turned toward the gym again, back where Lovely Loveless had been sitting but saw she was getting up, being pulled away by somebody else, a huge smile on her face.

Sighed.

Followed King out and away.

They were silent as they walked to the train, silent as they waited for it, and silent as they boarded. King took out his phone and immediately starting texting. He was texting their group chat so her phone was buzzing and buzzing, King speaking soliloquies into her phone even though he was sitting right damn next to her! Like, shoot.

Like damn, Donny had a point, it's not like they knew what they were doing for real; they were piecing it together, and Alonda was proud of that, proud of what they put together—and it was fun. That was the most important thing, they were having fun. And who cares what he thought—he was one person! What about everyone who came to their shows, who cheered for them? They mattered so much more than Donny freakin' Drago!

Following King out had seemed like the right thing to do at the time, but that was before he started ignoring her. She shifted in her seat, trying not to let her anger rise to the top of her heart . . . It wasn't working.

King's brow was scrunched up in concentration, he was rapidly texting like he was trying to outrun the end of the world, and all Alonda could do was shake her head and close her eyes, letting the train rock her back and forth.

It definitely felt like the end of something.

August

☆ **21** ☆

THE ART GALLERY WAS ALL THE WAY OUT IN THE MIDDLE OF
Manhattan, which meant it took over an hour to get there. But the
trip wasn't that bad, mostly because the group claimed a corner of
the train and all of them together somehow made the train ride go
faster than usual, even with all the delays. Lexi had gone ahead earlier, which was probably better for her nerves, so taking the journey was just Alonda, King, Spider, Pretzel, and Tania, all hanging
out and dressed slightly nicer than they normally would be, though
nothing too extra—like, King was wearing his polo and Spider was
wearing denim shorts instead of the gym shorts he usually wore.

Alonda had decided on a purple sundress, though she still wore
sneakers instead of heels, much to Teresa's dismay. "You look so
nice, why are you ruining it with sneakers?! You can borrow a pair
of my heels, it's really no problem!" she said desperately, flinging
around a couple of different pairs of her shoes in Alonda's face.

Alonda had scrunched her nose at Teresa. "Even if I wanted
to wear heels, you know we don't wear the same size and I don't
wanna be tripping all over the place—you got giant feet."

Teresa had opened her mouth to say something, but Alonda cut
her off at the pass. "Besides, I read that sneakers are like the new heels
now." That information caused Teresa's mouth to open in a wordless

horror that Alonda tried hard not to laugh at. It was true, Alonda had read it somewhere, but she didn't really care; no matter what, she was gonna wear her sneakers, especially with a dress. It was how she felt most herself.

There was still some weirdness between her and King. It was like they couldn't get back into the ease of the rhythm they had fallen into, like they had fallen out of step and couldn't find the beat.

The gallery was big, super bright, and echoey, already packed with people. Alonda had known this was a big deal for Lexi, but seeing how crowded it was and looking at all the other art on the walls, it made her heart jump a little bit inside her.

"Art's wild, man," Spider said softly. His eyes were wide, not focusing on any specific piece but jumping from piece to piece to piece. "Like, how crazy is it that all this art was like . . . in each individual person here's head," he said, gesturing around at the crowd. "And then they reached inside their brain and pulled it out and somehow made it a part of the world?"

"Yeah . . . that's . . . something?" Alonda responded. She realized she just pieced together a few words that didn't really mean anything, but it was because she didn't know what else to say. Spider looked like he was in a trance, sucked into all the art around him, wandering over to a section that had a bunch of pieces that looked like neon goldfish escaping their tank. She'd lost sight of Pretzel and Tania. They had a couple of other friends in the show, so they'd probably gone looking for them.

"Come on, let's find Lexi," she said to King, pulling his hand through the crowd. His head was down, deep in his phone, frantically refreshing the score of the Yankees game. It was apparently a tight one, his face glued to his phone rather than the world of art around him.

Alonda's eyes darted from installation to installation, scanning over strangers when she finally caught sight of Lexi. She was standing by a display of her pieces, face fully confident but her body at an angle that Alonda knew meant she probably felt awkward. She was shifting from her left foot to her right, looking at her hands, at her art, back at her hands again, picking at her cuticles, catching herself and stopping only to do the fidgety cycle all over again. It was weird seeing Lexi twitch with nerves.

But it was also kinda endearing.

Alonda pulled King over to Lexi. He still had his face in his phone. "Hey!" Alonda called out to Lexi. She looked over at Alonda, and her face broke into a huge smile, relief lighting her eyes. "Oh, hi!" she shouted out, as though they hadn't seen each other in months rather than a day. Lexi reached out to give Alonda a hug of greeting, but before she could, Pretzel popped up in between them, diving in for his own hug.

"Damn, this is impressive! Like, this is legit, like you're a real artist!" Pretzel said excitedly, his words running over one another to get outta his mouth as fast as possible. Lexi gave him a weird look and he hurriedly backtracked a bit. "I mean, I know you've been a real artist, but it's, like, cool that there's a buncha strangers looking at your work now, too, not just us or whatever."

"Yeah, thanks," Lexi said with a grin.

King nudged Lexi in a way that seemed like a hug. "This is really cool, like, I'd say I can't believe you did all this, but I can believe it. 'Cause you're the Incredible Lexi or whatever," he said.

"Shut up," Lexi said, nudging him back, but her face was bright with a smile.

Alonda wandered away from the group, looking at the pieces Lexi had on display. Most of them were charcoal sketches, according to the little signs that were tacked against the wall next to the pieces. Alonda knew that charcoal wasn't Lexi's favorite thing to create with, that collage was really what she felt drawn to, but charcoal was the medium her teachers were always pushing her toward. She could see why; the sketches were pretty cool. It felt like they were moving, even stuck there on the page. She took her time looking at them, though she wasn't completely sure what she should be looking for.

She saw the finished collage piece of Coney Island. It had come out so cool, even cooler than the work-in-progress text Lexi had sent her earlier in the summer. And though it was made up of a bunch of different materials, it looked even more real than a photo. Up close she could see all the different textures that Lexi had included, the sand, the plastic of the ticket card, Popsicles. Her hand twitched a bit, wanting to touch it, but she knew touching art was bad, so she refrained.

Her eyes hit one piece, and she felt her breath skip a beat. Her eyes flicked to the little index card of information. It was called *Self Portrait*. The piece that Lexi had been working on the night Alonda had accidentally called, the one that had been giving her all that grief.

It was awesome.

It was a painting of Lexi's face, one that she had painted herself, but she had cut up the face part like the pieces of a jigsaw puzzle. Instead of putting the pieces back together so they fit neatly, they were a little bit apart from one another, leaving space underneath, in between the cracks. And in between those cracks, Lexi had created another collage, one with all the colors of the rainbow. The whole thing took Alonda's breath away. It somehow made her feel like she was being stared at, or like someone was holding her hand or giving her a long hug. Alonda had always prided herself on her logical mind, on the fact that she understood facts that were right in front of her, found comfort in the fact that there was a solution to every math problem. But somehow, even though there wasn't any formula to this piece, somehow Alonda felt like she understood it.

"Well?" Lexi asked, her voice bringing Alonda back. "What do you think? And if you hate it, definitely lie," she said with a weird laugh that told Alonda she was totally joking–not joking. "I'm too fragile for the truth right now."

"I really love this piece," Alonda said, pointing to the self-portrait.

"Yeah, that one's a really pretty one," King said. Alonda could barely not make a face at him, and she could see Lexi's face kinda fall, too. Really pretty? Sure, it wasn't a bad thing to say, but it definitely wasn't the right thing to say, either. King could tell he said something off. "I mean, it's all really pretty. Your art is so pretty, Lexi."

Alonda cringed. He was making it worse. "It's all great," she said, hurrying over King's awkward words. "Your self-portrait looks . . . it somehow feels like a mirror. Even though it's not," she finished softly. Lexi caught her eye. She opened her mouth to say something, but Spider appeared with a hug and glowing words, and Lexi was pulled away by some patrons who wanted to talk to the artist, and whatever it was that she was gonna say was lost to the crowd.

ALONDA WASN'T EVEN PRETENDING TO TRY TO SLEEP. IT WAS nearing 3:00 A.M., but her mind wouldn't turn off. She heard the hum of the AC in Teresa and Jim's room running and glared at the wall. They'd gotten an AC all right, but it was reserved for Teresa's bedroom. Alonda'd been pissed, and Teresa had tried to say that they could open the door to her bedroom and fill the living room with the air from the AC, but the cold never seemed to make its way from their room into the rest of the house. So Alonda still lay at night either soaked in sweat or sharing her bed with cold, damp paper towels that made her bed soggy and gross.

She couldn't get the art gallery out of her mind. The energy of it, it was sending shocks of electricity through her brain. And it was so cool to see Lexi in her element—well, in a different element than Alonda had seen her. She pulled Lexi's face to her mind's eye, the way it was flushed with excitement, her eyes dancing with joy as she answered questions about her work. The way her smile took up her whole face when she was happy.

Alonda's thoughts were interrupted by the buzzing of her phone on the nightstand.

She picked it up, squinting as the light came on and stung her eyes through the dark.

LEXI: Hey, thanks again for coming through.
ALONDA: Wouldn't have missed it for the world.

Lexi sent back a smiley emoji. Alonda smiled back at it. The heat was still sweltering in her room. She knew that heat couldn't take up physical space, but that's how it was feeling, as though it was.

ALONDA: How you feeling about the show?
LEXI: Mostly good.
LEXI: but also it feels weird now that it's done
LEXI: like, so much of my energy went into waiting for it to
   happen but now that it happened, I dunno what to
   do with all that energy.

Alonda nodded at the phone. She could get that.

Somehow the heat felt more unbearable. She wanted to get out, to breathe in the fresh air.

She climbed out the window, up to the roof. The world was dark and a little cool, sea salt stinging her nostrils. It smelled different at night, the ocean, especially in summer.

LEXI: So what're you doing up? Too hot?
ALONDA: Yeah, kinda. I went up to the roof. Cooler here.

Without walls the air could move freer. She looked up at the sky. It was cloudy, overcast and gray. As usual. She scrunched her nose at it.

ALONDA: Hey, you ever like. Wish you could see the stars?
LEXI: I see stars here

Alonda rolled her eyes.

ALONDA: Nah, I mean for real stars. Like, a bunch.

LEXI: You can see constellations sometimes

ALONDA: Nah

LEXI: Yeah. If you know what you're looking for, for sure.

ALONDA: I can barely see them peeking out.

LEXI: 'Cause you're not looking long enough. The longer
you look at the sky, the more stars you can see.

ALONDA: I don't think so

LEXI: It's true. Sometimes you just gotta look long enough
to see something more clearly.

ALONDA: so wise

LEXI: it's just true! Trust me, I'm an artist. I know tf I'm
talking about lol

Alonda laughed at that.

ALONDA: ok ok, imma look. Brb lol

Alonda looked up at the sky and then back down at her phone.
It buzzed.

LEXI: Bet you looked back at your phone immediately.

ALONDA: Nah!

LEXI: Right.

ALONDA: . . . okay yeah.

LEXI: Look up!

Alonda looked back up at the sky. Still looked gray and cloudy.

But she kept on looking, straight up instead of at the lights in front of her.

She squinted her eyes a little. A small star appeared, winking out at her from the clouds. She hadn't seen that before. Another appeared to its left. Another above it. Below it.

Shit, Lexi was right.

It's not like there was a cascading of stars or nothing; it was more that there was tiny pinpricks of light, all blinking their ways through the clouds. Still far apart from one another but close enough, too.

Sometimes you just gotta look long enough to see something more clearly.

Shit.

Alonda shifted in bed again. It had to be the thousandth or millionth time since she tried going to sleep, since she'd climbed back down and in through her window again, but she hadn't been keeping proper count. She grabbed her phone, checking the time. Almost five. The sun was starting to light up the sky. And she couldn't sleep. She didn't feel tired even though she logically knew she should be tired. She should be exhausted. But it was like the stuff on her mind had made its way into her body, shaking her body and keeping her awake.

She turned over onto her side, punching the pillow a thousand times in a row, but that didn't do anything but dent her pillow.

She breathed in and tried to silence her thoughts, to push them to the side. She listened to the world instead. Everything was mostly quiet in the way that Brooklyn's never fully silent. The buzzing from the late-night Coney Island crowd was floating through her open window, but it's not like they was so loud. The soft clanging of the train rumbling, the sound of traffic rolling down her street, the AC humming in the next room.

Nah, she couldn't blame this on the noise.

Alonda knew that nobody could see her, but she still glanced over at her door to make sure it was closed. Closed and locked. Nobody could see.

She took a deep breath and slid her hand under her sheet and down. She had never really done this before. She was usually good at silencing her body when it got like this, at going to sleep or thinking about a math test, but tonight was different. Tonight, this was something she wanted to do.

"It's okay," she whispered out loud to herself. Her own voice soothed her nerves somehow. "It's okay."

Alonda's hand twitched a little bit and starting moving again.

Her hand moved a little faster and a little faster, until

she breathed in sharp and deep and her body tensed up suddenly as though it was getting ready to take off, to fly right off the bed. Warmth flooded her body, a warmth that felt different from being outside in the sun, different from sweating after a run, a warmth that came from inside her, a warmth that was hers.

Her whole body felt relaxed, almost like the bones had left her skeleton and she was just a rubbery mess of flesh. She smiled a little and closed her eyes, listening for the backdrop of the dawn and within minutes, she was asleep.

☆ 23 ☆

"ALL RIGHT, EVERYONE, I KNOW IT'S HOTTER THAN THE SURFACE
of the sun out today!" Pretzel's voice crackled through the air. He
had gotten a megaphone, but Alonda wasn't sure if it made his voice
louder and clearer or just louder and harder to understand.

"But I'm gonna need you to keep up your energy, I'm gonna need
you to give it up for Rize's reigning champion—make some noise
for King!"

Alonda stood in the center of the ring, hopping from foot to
foot, pumping herself up for their match as King entered to his
music, cheers filling the atmosphere.

There were more people here than ever before. Even though
Alonda tried not to notice, it was almost impossible not to notice
now; their energy sparked the whole playground, electrified the air,
and Alonda soaked it all in, let it course through her as she readied
herself for the match.

King motioned to the crowd to quiet down, and a hush rippled
through them like a wave. He started to speak.

"All right, Alondra. I hear you wanna fight me. What gives?"

Alonda crossed her arms and shook her head.

"Why're you standing there pretending like you ain't heard?"
she asked. "I know Lexi talked to you!"

King shrugged, his voice light and playful. "Maybe I wanna hear you say it in your own words."

Alonda let out a huge, exaggerated sigh, pretending to be annoyed, but really, she had to fill the audience in just in case there was people attending who didn't know about this piece of the story line they had come up with.

"Lexi won't let me get a rematch with her till I prove myself. Like I *need* to prove myself," she scoffed, shaking her head a little. "But she said the only way she'd lemme get a shot at the belt is if I defeat the best. I mean, the second best," she said, jabbing at King, trying to ruffle his feathers. "So I gotta fight you. And win."

"Welllll . . . ," King said, dragging out the word as far as it would go, "I guess I can give you a fight. I don't got anything else on my schedule. Can't do nothing about the 'winning' part, though," he said, shaking his head.

"All right," Alonda said. She reached out her hand to shake his, but he pretended not to see it and kept going, the cockiness growing louder and louder in his voice.

"I guess I'll give you the once-in-a-lifetime opportunity to fight me. This'll take, what, five minutes?" he asked, pretending to look at an invisible watch on his wrist.

"Um, wait, no," Alonda said. "No, I mean, yeah, I need to fight you because Lexi said she wouldn't let me try for the belt unless we did, but you don't gotta go acting like you're doing me a favor."

"Sure," King said, laughing a little.

"You wanna fight me or what?" Alonda asked, putting her hands on her hips.

King came over to her, bent down a little, and patted the top of her head with two sharp pats. "You're real cute when you get all defensive."

"Okay, that's it," Alonda said, pulling her hair up high.

King started to laugh. "Oh yeah, what do you think you're gonna do—you see that?" he said to the crowd, his back turned to her.

Alonda took the opportunity to run at him and, with a bounce, jump onto his back, wrapping her arms around his chest, her legs around his waist. They'd practiced this move so many times, King barely flinched, but he sold the hell out of it, trying to shake Alonda off him, to get her to fall to the ground.

"And Alondra has King tied up in a bear hug, aaaaw," Pretzel said, turning to the crowd to try to get them to *aw* along with him. She twisted around on King, knocking them both to the ground safely.

Alonda quickly got to her feet while King rolled on the ground, milking the fall but also catching his breath. "Hey, we coulda done this the easy way," Alonda said, monologuing a little bit to give him time to recover. "You coulda just said, 'Oh yeah, Alondra, you deserve to go up against the Incredible Lexi because you're one of the best.' But you didn't say that, did you?" she asked, sneering at him. He gave a little nod, telling her he was ready to go on.

"Nah, you didn't. So I just have to say thank you," she said, walking closer to him so she was standing over him. "Because now, now you've given me something to prove."

"What're you talking about?" he wheezed out.

She squatted down, right in front of him, and slowly, deliberately, gave his head two sharp pats. She could hear the crowd laugh, heard someone shout, "Oh shit, she got you!" which forced Alonda to hold back a laugh that threatened to bubble up her throat and out her mouth.

"Okay, then," King said, and he kicked his legs out, and Alonda dropped to the ground.

"And Alondra falls to the ground like a sack of bricks, the fall knocking the wind right outta her while King stands up, he stands up and Oh, OH, he's picking her up, he's lifting Alondra up over his shoulders, oh shit! It looks like he's going to try to drop her—but Alondra has other plans, she's wiggled out, she's on the ground again, it's okay, everyone, everything's good," Pretzel said, turning away from the two of them again.

While Pretzel's back was still turned to the two of them, Alonda ran over to a giant textbook that she had hidden in the ring. King laughed. "What're you planning on doing with that?" he said.

Alonda lifted it up high, menacingly. "What do you think I'm gonna do with it?" she asked.

King held up his arms, shielding himself from the book. "Oh shit, no, that's cheating, you can't hit me with it!"

Alonda smiled and said, "School's in session" right before she ran at King, raising the textbook, but before she could hit him, she threw the textbook to the ground behind her so it made a loud THWACK. She threw herself to the ground right after, holding her head, feigning pain. "Ref, Ref!" she yelled from the ground. "He hit me!"

"What! No, I'd never!" King said as Pretzel came over to check on the damage.

"You did this?!" Pretzel yelled at King.

"She's lying, she's lying!" King said.

Alonda just kept moaning on the ground, milking it for all its worth and a little bit more.

The crowd was losing its shit; they were laughing and clapping and wooing.

Alonda used the fact that King was confused and distracted to knock him down to the ground. He fell hard, and Alonda put her hands on her hips and shouted, "¡Sin Miedo!" before she jumped down on top of him, grabbing his legs and pinning him to the ground. Pretzel counted it out—

"One, two—"

The sound of the bell.

"And your winner, Alondra! The Fearless One!"

He grabbed Alonda's arm and raised it in victory. She grabbed his megaphone and used it to shout, "I'm coming after you, the Incredible Lexi! Let's just see how *incredible* you are. You're next."

The crowd had left their mess behind. Alonda didn't know why it was so hard for people to clean up after their damn selves, disrespecting a space that felt so sacred to her, really boiled her blood. She was cleaning it up best she could while she waited for King; picking up and throwing out cans and stuff was one thing, but no way was she gonna touch a gunky napkin.

"Hey!" King's voice broke her cleaning spell. She turned to look at him, freshly showered and glowing with joy.

Damn.

"You was so great out there today!" King said, picking her up and twirling her around. Damn, he was so happy, Alonda could barely look at him. She didn't wanna be the reason his shine was gonna dampen.

"Listen—" Alonda started once he put her down, but he kept going, determined to make this the hardest thing she was ever gonna have to do in her life, probably.

"You wanna go get some pizza or something? I can grab us some cotton candy to split."

"King, wait," Alonda said. That stopped him in his tracks.

"Yeah?" he asked, looking toward her. The shine was already starting to slip out of his eyes.

"Can we talk?" she asked.

"We . . . are talking," he said tentatively, almost as if he could predict what was about to come next.

"Yeah, but I mean . . . look, I think we gotta . . ." Alonda's brain felt like it was short-circuiting now. Damn, but she had practiced the words in the mirror, why did things feel right before they became real?

"Gotta what?" King asked.

She took a deep breath in.

"I think we maybe gotta talk about us. Not . . . being an us no more."

King took a sharp breath in and looked up.

"You serious right now?" he asked the sky.

"I just—"

"Lay it on me," he said quietly, sitting down on the curb. He was looking at his hands, cupped together, quiet as he waited.

"Come on, it . . . it ain't like we been getting along the best, lately," she said. "And we don't even go to the same school, anyway. Fall's less than a month away, school's less than a month away, when it's all started up again, when're we gonna see each other?" Alonda said. She was gonna get through this, the exact way she practiced. No matter how *Afterschool Special* she sounded.

"Wow, that's just like . . . a lot of reasons," King said. It sounded harsh, but he wasn't looking at her at all, just playing with a twig by his feet, dragging it across the concrete. "Sounds like you really thought this out."

"'Cause that's the way I am," Alonda said softly. "I've got scenarios for every scenario, so that if one pops up I didn't think about, I might still got it covered. My brain don't stop running around in circles and trying to see things from every angle."

"And I don't," King said.

"And that's fine," Alonda said. "Your brain works different from mine, which is great, it should work the way that's best for you. You shouldn't have to twist yourself up to fit into my world. Just like I shouldn't have to twist myself up to fit into yours. We should just . . . fit."

"I guess," King said, still not looking at her.

Alonda sat down next to King on the curb. At least if she was sitting next to him, she couldn't see his sad face. Silence fell over them again, but this time it was different. It felt like the air was weighted with words but neither of them knew how to say any of them because maybe there truly was nothing to say.

"I'm sorry," Alonda blurted out. She didn't know why she was apologizing, it just slipped out, like a sneeze.

"Nah," King said, still twiddling the twig, "there's nothing to apologize for. It's like you said, probably for the best or whatever. My broken heart'll see that in due time. Maybe my ego, too, a little," he admitted.

Alonda bumped her shoulder against his gently. "Oh please, like your ego could really be destroyed by this," she said with a small, teasing laugh.

"Not *destroyed*," he admitted, "but like . . . I dunno. I'm . . . gonna miss you . . . ," he said, his voice trailing off.

They dissolved into silence once more, the thick heat of August swallowing up their words. It felt like a different silence, one that wasn't itching at Alonda to fill it, one that felt full, fuller than it usually did.

They'd probably be better as friends.

"You think I really got a chance, though?" King asked, bursting the silent bubble.

"At what?"

"Making it as a pro. Wrestling for real."

"Why's it such a big deal to you?" Alonda asked. "You still got a year of high school to go, not like this can lead to something immediately, you know?"

King got that serious look across his brow, the one he got when he was thinking heavy.

"Nah, it's not—like fine, okay, I dunno what I wanna do with the rest of my life. That's true. But my parents, they keep pushing me that I'm gonna go to college. Especially my mom. Like, that's it, that's the end goal, college, no questions or conversation beyond that. But I keep thinking, what if there's another way forward? A different path to take, and I felt like, maybe, if I could make this a different path . . ." He trailed off, words disappearing onto the playground.

"And I love it," he continued, more quiet, his voice not a whisper, but not talking regular either, somewhere in the in-between, somewhere he was only letting Alonda into. "I know it's not real, but it's real to me. It makes me feel like . . . even though I'm not being me, I'm still being more me than I usually get to be."

Alonda let his words hit her heart. She kinda knew what he meant.

A truth that made sense.

She let his words echo in her head as she looked out into the playground, into the little world that they'd been able to call their own.

August meant that summer was already almost over. It meant that the real world was gonna look different again. And even though it was the right thing to do, to break up with King, she was gonna miss it, a little. Endings were weird like that; even when she knew they was coming, there was always a sad feeling to them.

"Hey, I'm just gonna get going," King said, standing. Alonda nodded and stayed sitting on the curb.

"I'll see you Saturday," Alonda responded.

"Yeah. See you then."

She watched as King walked away, toward the boardwalk, watching until he blended in with the rest of the crowd. The streets were still busy with tourists and beachgoers, all of them still in the height of their summers. None of them felt its ending yet, not like Alonda did. What was fall gonna look like, when they all went back to school and never saw one another again? Alonda tried to push those thoughts away, tried to silence them, labeled them as Future Thoughts. She was always trying to write the future before she lived it. She wished her brain didn't work like that. When she was wrestling, she had to be in the moment. Couldn't be thinking about worries or concerns, just what was right in front of her at any given time. She wished she could live her life like that. She was sure there was a way to. She just wasn't sure how.

☆ **24** ☆

IT WAS DARK.

Late.

Alonda squinted, but she couldn't see nothing.

What time was it?

Felt like deep into the night. That past-midnight-but-still-hours-before-dawn time.

Why was she awake?

Something had woken her.

What had woken her?

Had a dream pushed her mind awake the way they sometimes did?

No, there was noise. Yelling?

Yeah, yelling.

She groggily opened her eyes. She could hear it clearer now, yelling coming from the living room.

"And I'm telling you, I don't wanna hear it, you understand me?!"

Alonda snapped herself awake. That was Teresa. She was yelling.

She squinted at the darkness. She could make out the low rumble of Jim's voice; it sounded like he was begging, pleading. Teresa responded louder, "I don't care, I don't want you here, get out!"

Alonda made her way over to the door and softly opened it a

crack. Jim was on the floor, begging like a baby. She could hear him now,

"You don't understand, it was a mistake."

"Nah, I do understand mistakes, I understand 'em well, and what you did? Was not a mistake. Was it a mistake her number floated into your cell phone?"

Alonda's blood went cold. She knew she should close the door, mind her own business—but wasn't Teresa her business? She stayed at the door, listening.

"Was it a mistake you called her, was it a mistake you wound up at her place how many times? And was it a mistake she didn't even know I existed?!"

"You don't understand," he tried saying again, but Teresa wasn't hearing none of it, and why should she, Alonda thought to herself, he wasn't saying anything worth hearing.

"A mistake is spelling my name with an *h*, a mistake is getting on the uptown train when you meant to go downtown—this shit wasn't a mistake, and you can walk your sorry ass right out my house."

"It's the middle of the night," Jim said, but Teresa just laughed.

"Go ask your girlfriend if she's got some room. You can't stay here 'cause this ain't your home, not anymore."

"But, Teresa—"

"No," she said. She had stopped yelling; her voice was low and serious. "No," she said again, "I told you from the millisecond I met you that I wasn't gonna put up with that shit, not in my house, not in my life. You'll get your shit, don't worry about that, but there is no second chance for you. Get out."

Jim's whole body deflated like a balloon; a man who knew he

couldn't fight a battle he couldn't win, that he didn't deserve to win. He opened his mouth one more time, but no words came out. And with that silence, Jim finally turned and walked out the door. Teresa slammed it shut.

She put her back against the door and looked up at the ceiling. Now that Jim was gone, the fury that had given her face such light dimmed.

Alonda accidentally nudged the door open farther. Teresa looked. Saw her.

"You should be asleep," Teresa said.

Alonda nodded. "I know."

A quiet moment. The sound of the portable fan, twirling around and around.

"How much did you hear?"

Alonda shrugged. "You were loud."

Teresa nodded.

Alonda tentatively stepped out of her room, closer to Teresa.

Teresa slid down against the door until she was sitting on the floor.

After a moment, Alonda joined her, sliding down as casually as she could.

They sat side by side.

The humming of the fridge as it kicked on.

Their breathing, filling the air.

"You want some water?" Alonda asked, unable to take the quiet any longer.

Teresa shook her head and smiled softly. "You don't need to do that."

Alonda widened her eyes in mock innocence. "What? Me, doing

something?" Teresa pretended to swat her away, but pulled her into an awkward side hug. Alonda breathed in her scent, the familiar but indescribable smell of Teresa filling her nose, the familiar scent of home.

"I'm sorry," Alonda said, but Teresa pulled away, shaking her head.

"You don't have to be," she said. "I had to do it. Shoulda never let him live here in the first place," she said a little bitterly. "I knew he wasn't— Whatever. Foolish of me . . . ," she trailed off, her voice getting softer. Alonda stayed quiet. Even though Teresa finished speaking, it felt like she had more to say.

"Ah, but it don't matter," Teresa continued, breathing deep. "It don't matter at all."

"Yeah, but still," Alonda said, turning her body to face Teresa. She could see tears glimmering at the edge of her eyes. "You don't have to pretend like it don't hurt."

"I can't cry in front of you," Teresa said, mostly to herself. Alonda shrugged.

"You don't gotta cry," she said, "but you can if you wanna."

Alonda sat facing forward again, her body next to Teresa's.

She sat next to her, and though she didn't turn to see if the tears had fallen down her cheeks, she could feel her shoulders shaking a little, could hear the sniffles, the familiar sounds of someone trying to hide their hurt.

☆ 25 ☆

"I CAN'T BELIEVE I FORGOT MY KEY," LEXI MUTTERED UNDER HER breath as Alonda struggled to get her own key to work. It was sticking in the lock more and more, shit. They'd have to do something about it.

"Thanks for letting me crash at your place," Lexi continued, looking at her phone. "My mom should be home soon—she'll be able to let me in."

"Yeah, no problem," Alonda said, shaking the key inside the lock. *Pop*—the key finally turned. Success! She opened the door slowly, taking a look around. The door to Teresa's bedroom was open—didn't look like she was home yet. Good. She opened the door a little wider and ushered Lexi in.

It was definitely the middle of August with these big, wild rain showers coming out of nowhere and passing through. She could practically smell the start of school in the raindrops. Usually that made Alonda happy, but lately the start of school also meant the end of a lot more than just summer.

"Make yourself at home," Alonda said, quickly doing a sweep of tidying to the room. It wasn't so messy, not really. Good. She turned to look at Lexi.

Lexi was still standing there awkwardly. Rain was dripping from her hair, her clothes soaked through. Looked like she had gotten caught in the brunt of the storm. Alonda had been able to duck under some scaffolding as the skies opened up. She'd been watching the rain before she got Lexi's text, asking if she could crash.

"Where's your bathroom?" Lexi asked. "I'm dripping all over."

"Don't worry about the drips, I'll grab a paper towel, bathroom's down the hall, can't miss it," Alonda said. Lexi walked carefully, but water still fell from her clothes, leaving a little trail of droplets for Alonda to sop up behind her.

Once she was sure everything was dry, Alonda went back to the living room and continued her haphazard tidying.

"What should I do with the towel?"

Lexi's voice interrupted Alonda's thoughts, startled a gasp out of her.

"Sorry, I thought you heard me come out—"

"No, it's fine, I'm just not supposed to have anyone over when I'm here alone, so I'm, like, a little, I dunno, jittery? I guess?" Alonda said, grabbing the towel.

"Your mom seems intense," Lexi said. "She's got you all jumpy like that."

Alonda grunted. "Teresa ain't my mom, not really," she said. It came out more harsh than she meant. Damn, she hadn't even meant for it to come out at all. Now she was gonna have to explain. She took a deep breath in, still working on drying the spot.

"I mean, I love her and everything, she's cool and all, she's great, but I had a real mom and she just ain't it, that's all," she continued, softening her tone.

Lexi sat quietly, listening. Alonda waited for her to come out with the thousands of awkward questions people usually had when they found out her mom wasn't around, but Lexi wasn't voicing any of them. She was just looking at Alonda, letting her talk. And for some reason, that silence, that's what made her wanna answer, wanna talk about Mami.

"Yeah, she died," Alonda said, letting the words come out slowly, "a while ago, but yeah. Yeah."

"Oh. I'm sorry," Lexi said quietly.

The spot seemed as dry as it was gonna get, but Alonda kept patting it. Better to look at the floor than look at Lexi right now. Didn't want her to see her hurt.

Thunder rumbled, low and deep like a yawn.

Alonda stopped patting the spot. Leaned back on her heels.

"It was a blood clot," she said softly. "And she died like . . . I guess it's a full decade ago now. And sometimes I try to convince myself I don't miss her, but I miss her every day."

Lexi didn't say anything, but Alonda could feel her listening. Somehow her silence made it easier for Alonda's words to come out.

"I never watched wrestling before she died," she blurted out. "But when she died, I dunno, I just kinda stopped talking for a little while. Teresa would try to get me to talk, but I refused. Swallowed up all my words. Took me to a doctor and everything, and she was just like, 'Give her space, she's lost her mother,' you know? Even though I knew Mami wasn't lost. She was gone, but I didn't misplace her. She was just . . . gone. Does that even make any sense?"

Lexi nodded.

"And I'd sit in front of the TV, and Teresa would let me because she really didn't know what to do. And Big Ricky, he moved downstairs into my old apartment, he'd usually come up and watch me when Teresa was out at work or whatever. And he'd put on wrestling. And at first I wouldn't pay attention, it was loud and weird, but then, I dunno, I couldn't get enough."

Lexi just nodded. She was listening. Alonda hoisted herself onto the couch and picked at her flaking manicure before going on.

"But also, it don't matter because that's why I love wrestling. Because it's like, they're all superheroes, kinda. Like, real superheroes, even though it's all fake. They're strong. In real life strong. And this shit's made me strong. Like"—she flexed a bicep. Lexi cocked her head a little, but she still didn't say anything. Still listening.

"And so then I got a little obsessed, it was all I wanted to talk about, and so I'd talk about it, and, I dunno, in a weird way wrestling, it kinda makes me feel like I'm with her? Even though she wasn't even around to see me get obsessed with it."

The air felt open between them.

Alonda breathed it in.

"My name was supposed to be Alondra. That's the real reason why I chose it," Alonda said. It's one of the things she could hear Mami say, in her voice. She could even pull up Mami's face saying it. It made Alonda smile, to think of it. "Mami'd been going back and forth between Alonda and Alondra and she said as soon's she chose Alonda, she knew it shoulda been Alondra. I know it's just a one-letter difference, but one letter can make all the difference. And wrestling is all about being a bigger version of yourself, right? I mean, it works best when there's a seed of truth in the character. Because wrestling is really all about the truth. Whether you're the good guy or the bad guy, there's seeds of truth that go into a character. And that's pretty awesome, I think."

Lexi was looking at Alonda, something funny in the back of her eyes. Alonda felt self-conscious. "What?" she asked, casually wiping her nose. Maybe she had spit on her lips?

Lexi just shook her head. "The way you talk about wrestling, it sounds like poetry," she said. She wasn't making fun of Alonda. She was just saying the truth.

The butterflies that had been sleeping soundly in Alonda's stomach chose that moment to come to life, swirling around like they was caught in a windstorm.

"Yeah, so I dunno, anyway," Alonda said, looking desperately for something else to say. "Sucks about the r-rain," she managed to stutter out, trying not to let her nerves jangle her vocal cords too badly. She didn't know why she was so jittery. It was Lexi—it was just Lexi—on her couch.

"Yeah, I guess we're gonna have to cancel practice tonight if it keeps raining like this," Lexi said, scooting closer to her. The rain was pushing a cool, wet breeze into the living room, and Alonda had been close to shivering, but now that she could feel the heat radiating off Lexi's body, she was starting to sweat. Or maybe that was just the rain.

"I dunno, might just be a passing shower," Alonda said. "Might be over by five."

"Our matches are the best," Lexi said, moving a little closer. She smelled sweet and a little bitter, and Alonda wasn't sure if it was her lotion or deodorant or if it was just her scent, and it was crawling into Alonda's nose, burying itself into her memory. "Everyone's excited about our rematch."

"Yeah, I think they are," Alonda said. She was trying not to look at Lexi but couldn't help but look at her. "Michelle said you're her favorite," she blurted out.

Lexi smiled big. "Yeah?" she asked. Damn, Lexi was so beautiful all the time, and when she smiled, the beauty shifted into not more beauty, but different beauty.

"Yeah," Alonda said, moving a little closer. "Yeah, she really liked the whole telekinesis thing we came up with. Maybe . . ." She hesitated before pushing through. "Maybe you can, like, read my mind or something. Like, for real."

"Sometimes it feels like I can read your mind," Lexi said, laughing low. "Like, in the ring. I know what you're thinking before you do it, and then we wind up doing it." Alonda was hypnotized by her lips.

"Like," Lexi continued, her gaze so intense, it was like she was trying to dig a hole into Alonda's eyes, "it makes me feel safe with you. I feel safe with you."

They were both staring, looking at each other. Alonda was barely breathing. Her heart was a drumbeat in her ears.

"Can you read my mind right now?" Alonda asked.

Lexi nodded. "Yeah, I think so."

"Okay." Alonda nodded. Her head was inching toward Lexi's. "Okay. What's it thinking?"

"I dunno," Lexi said, her hand inching toward Alonda's. Her thumb brushed the side of her hand. "You tell me."

The moment hung in the air between them.

Alonda couldn't see anything but Lexi's eyes.

Couldn't feel anything except her hand against hers.

"Is it okay if I kiss you now?"

"Hell yeah," Lexi started to say, but her words were caught in between Alonda's lips as she breathed them in, deeply.

And she tasted like Lexi, a taste that had no words except for her name. And Alonda wanted to taste it and taste it. She kissed Lexi back so hard that their teeth clinked together and if she had been thinking clearly—or at all—Alonda would have been embarrassed, but she was too exhilarated to be embarrassed. She'd known Lexi'd done this before, but damn, Lexi had definitely done this before.

And suddenly it was like her body knew just what to do, knew where to put her hands; it was true, she and Lexi could communicate without speaking, they always could—or, communicate without saying too many words. Lexi kept checking with her, kept whispering out an "Okay? Okay?" looking for consent, consent that Alonda was all too happy to grant.

Lexi flipped Alonda over to put Alonda on top of her, pulling her head down to keep kissing while her hands kept exploring Alonda's body, pausing only to ask, "Is this okay? Is this okay?" before she did, to which Alonda enthusiastically said yes. Alonda realized that this was what she had wanted all summer, being with Lexi, it was everything, and shit, it felt good, no, like, it felt really, really good and she wanted it, this is what she wanted, what she had wanted and she looked up and

Teresa was standing in the doorway.

"Oh fuck," Alonda said, rolling off the couch and hitting the floor.

"Yeah, oh fuck," Teresa said, looking at the both of them. Alonda didn't know what word would describe Teresa's face. *Rage* was too weak a word.

"Hi, nice to meet you," she said to Lexi, sarcasm wrapping itself around every word.

"She was locked out and it was raining and—"

"I know you don't think I've been under a rock."

"Teresa, it's not, it's just—"

"So nice to meet you, you may leave now," she said pointedly to Lexi.

Alonda stood up, but Teresa turned to her, that fury still in her eyes. "Alonda, you know I do not mean you, you sit back down right now, I am talking to your friend—"

"Lexi," Lexi said, finishing her sentence. "My name's Lexi, and I was just gonna go, so . . ." She was already halfway to the door, stopping only to shove her sneakers on.

Damn, she was quick.

"Got everything?" Teresa asked. Alonda just sat on the couch, looking at her hands.

"Yeah."

"Good, bye!" Teresa gestured toward the open door for Lexi, and she practically ran out. The door slammed closed, and they was suddenly alone.

Teresa looked at Alonda, not speaking.

Well, not speaking with words; her face was speaking a whole montage of silent questions. She was in jackpot mode, the way that she got when there was so many things rushing to the tip of her tongue to yell about her brain couldn't make up her mind which one to go to first.

Alonda tried to take advantage of the moment.

"Listen, I can explain everything, she was just locked out and it was raining and I figured—"

"Who was that?"

"Lexi."

"Right, I got that. And who the hell is Lexi?"

"My friend."

"You do that with all your friends?"

"No!"

"Then are you gonna tell me who that was or what?!"

"I dunno!" Alonda yelled, walking away to the kitchen. She hadn't planned on it, the words just exploded out of her like her heart was a furnace keeping them warm that got overheated. She was hot, tired, and full of feelings, full of—

"I thought you was hanging out with a guy!" Teresa shouted back, following her into the kitchen. She was blocking the way out, though, so Alonda was trapped. "What happened to him?!"

"Why, you mad she's a girl?"

"What?! No, Alonda—"

"Then leave me alone!" Alonda shouted.

"I'm just confused, Alonda. Will you give me a minute to catch up?"

"What's there to catch up on? What do you need to know?"

"Who the hell was that girl, and don't give me any My Friend Lexi crap, you ain't mentioned her once all summer, so either she's a brand-new friend or you been lying to me—"

"God, she came over when I had friends over to watch the fireworks—just because you were too busy hanging out with *Jim* to come up and meet her doesn't mean I've been *hiding anything from you*," she said hotly. She knew she wasn't being fair, but neither was Teresa. "I haven't been *lying* to you, I just don't tell you everything!" Alonda shouted.

"You explain to me what happened right now or—"

"Or what, you'll kick me out?" Alonda threw back at her.

"Oh please, I ain't kicking you outta nowhere. In fact, you won't be leaving this house, you're gonna stay in your room till I decide you can leave it."

Alonda felt her body go cold. The match.

"You can't do that," Alonda said. "I've got work—"

"Yeah, and you'll give me your schedule and I'll be making sure you're there and then home again," Teresa said. She was as tall as Alonda, but damn, when she was angry, she was a giant.

"I have a thing to do tonight," she said, quickly backtracking.

"Yeah, what thing," Teresa said, crossing her arms.

"A thing."

"You're gonna have to do better than that."

"I wrestle and we got practice!"

Teresa's jaw dropped. "You do what where? What are you talking about, wrestle?" she asked, each word getting louder and louder. "Where?"

"Out on the playground—"

"On the playground?!" she practically screamed. "In the park? You *wrestle*?" Teresa's face was turning red with rage. Normally Alonda would back down, but she wasn't even close to being finished.

Alonda nodded defiantly. "Yeah, we wrestle out on the playground, on the Astroturf."

"You could get hurt!" Teresa yelled.

"Yeah, and I do get hurt!" Alonda shouted back. "I've got bruises, and I even cut my arm open, but so what, I love doing it and I actually happen to be the crowd favorite and we got a match—"

Teresa was shaking her head before Alonda could finish. "Oh no, you do not got no nothing of the sort. I can't believe you, Alonda. Has this been going on this whole time?"

"Yup," Alonda said, her voice gaining more and more power the more she spoke it. "I been wrestling all summer, and nothing bad happened except the fact that I was having the best time I've ever had, and now you wanna go and rip it all away from me, you wanna take it from me because you don't want me to be happy."

"Okay, that ain't true—"

"You're never happy with me because I'm not my mom and you wish that I was and you wish she was still here instead of me!" The words burst out of Alonda like water, words she'd never said out loud, that she hardly allowed herself to even think, and she realized she was crying. Why was she crying when she was so angry? It's like her anger had turned into tears. "You wish it had been me, not her, you do, and I know if you coulda chosen, you woulda chosen that she lived instead of me, and I know I woulda chosen it, too." Now she was sobbing and wasn't even sure her words were making sense.

Teresa looked frozen. She had no idea what to say.

"Tell me it's not true—you can't, you can't!" Alonda shouted.

"I . . ." Teresa's voice trailed off into silence.

Alonda finally ran past her, straight into her bedroom, slamming the door so loud she was sure it made the walls shake at least a little bit, and she fell into bed crying until her sobs finally rocked her to sleep.

"Pretzel here with a very important message from Rize Wrestling.

"It is with our greatest sadness that we have to announce that Alondra has decided to take an early retirement, to spend time with her family and whatnot. We will miss Alondra and all the contributions she gave to Rize and wish her all the best of luck in her future endeavors, I guess."

26

"ALONDA."

Teresa's voice was soft at the other side of her door.

It'd been three days since the Incident, as Alonda was officially referring to it in her head. She'd successfully been avoiding Teresa, only tiptoeing out of her room to use the bathroom or grab food from the kitchen. Her bedroom was a whole house right now, her world shrunk to four corners, a bed, a dresser, a way-too-full closet, and a janky desk.

Worst about it all, she could still hear the group from her window, outside, wrestling. She was supposed to be out there, with them, doing their thing, but they'd all be forced to reshuffle. Alonda didn't realize she'd care as much as she did, but the whole thing felt like the worst thing.

"Sweetheart, can we talk?"

Alonda considered ignoring her, plugging her ears with her buds, putting music on and drowning her out like she had been.

"Come on, don't be mad at me," Teresa said. It sounded like she had stomped her foot on the other side of the door.

Alonda made a face. "Who's mad?" Alonda asked. She had learned sarcasm from Teresa, may as well use it.

"Can you let me in, and we'll talk about it?"

"You gonna let me wrestle?" Alonda asked.

Teresa sighed, annoyed, and put on an overly patient voice. "That's not what we're gonna talk about right now."

"I already told them I had to stop," Alonda said. "That not enough for you?"

"Come on, please," Teresa said, a little bit of pleading creeping into her voice. "I just wanna talk about everything that happened. Can you at least open the door? I'll talk to you from the door frame if you want, don't gotta come in and intrude on your space or nothing."

Alonda sighed deeply into her pillow, a sigh that was masking a scream. "It's open," she mumbled, and the door opened.

Teresa stood in the doorway, looking at Alonda weird, with a look she didn't recognize—a little sad, a little anxious.

"My mom never let me have any privacy when I was a teenager," she said. "Woulda gone ballistic if I shut the door—this used to be my bedroom, you know." Alonda nodded. She knew, a hundred times she knew. "And Ma, she'd make me keep the door open, even at night. Once she even took it off its hinges, hid it in the alley. That old-school way of thinking, of doing things, not good, but it was what it was." She was rambling. Alonda just gave her a look.

"Yes, did you want something?" Alonda asked.

Teresa shifted a little, still looking nervous. "May I come in? And sit down?"

"Thought you said you could talk from the doorway," Alonda muttered.

"Yeah, but—this ain't how I pictured this talk going."

"What talk?" Alonda scoffed. Her heart froze a little bit in her chest when she saw what was in Teresa's hands.

Folded-up papers.

Crib notes.

Shit, she was gonna talk to her about sex.

"On second thought, please leave," Alonda said.

Teresa shook her head. "Come on, Alonda, we gotta talk about this sooner or later. Putting it off hasn't helped anyone, clearly."

"Please, Teresa," Alonda begged a little, "I don't wanna—"

"I'm not gonna lie, I had to look up some things from the internet," she said, walking into Alonda's room and sitting at the edge of her bed. Alonda wanted to bury herself under her pillows. "I had a different kinda talked prepped and ready to go, had practiced it and everything, gotta admit, I don't really know about this stuff at all—"

"What're you talking about?" Alonda asked, confused. Teresa took a deep breath in.

"Listen, sweetie, I don't care that you're gay—"

"No, but I'm not gay," Alonda said.

Her words stopped Teresa. "Oh, I'm sorry," she said, "I mean a lesbian—"

But Alonda was already shaking her head. "Nah, that's not what I mean, either."

Teresa looked a little confused. "Okay . . . But . . . it looked like . . . you were having a good time with that girl—"

"Lexi."

"With Lexi—"

"Yeah!" Alonda said over her to spare them both from anything more. "But I'm not gay. I'm . . . I'm actually, it's not like—" Damn, why was it so hard to find the words, they were all flowing around her brain but before she could put them into order, Teresa interrupted.

"Oh," Teresa said. It looked like she understood suddenly. "You're confused."

Alonda's heart started to race, harder than before.

"Nah, Teresa, I'm not confused."

"Listen, no matter who you wind up liking, boys or girls, I'll love you."

"But . . . I do know. No, I mean—"

It felt like Teresa was stamping out an ember, like there was a choice to make rather than it just being a truth. Her truth. She knew it wasn't a choice, she knew that it moved through her whole body like the waves of the ocean at Coney Island. And it would always be a part of her, and that was a fact that was a part of her as much as the facts about chemistry and physics, the fact that she'd always love Teresa and that she'd always love her mom even though she wasn't here, it was a fact and that's why it was important, that's what made it important. And that was enough, it was more than enough, it was everything.

"Teresa, I'm bisexual," she blurted out. She let her words come out fast, before Teresa could respond. "And I don't even know if that's the right word for it, or if there's something more 'Right,' but for now, it's exactly what feels right, what feels real to me. And yeah, I'm happy that you're gonna love me no matter what—I mean, I know that you would, but I also know not to take that for granted"—she felt like she was rambling but with a purpose, gaining more and more power the longer she talked—"but also I know that I'm not confused about that part, that I'm not straight, I'm not gay, I'm bisexual. Okay?"

She was watching Teresa's face while she talked; at first, it looked like Teresa was trying to interject, to give her opinion or say something soothing, who knows, but the longer Alonda talked, the more Teresa's face calmed, the more it seemed like she stopped, stayed still, and listened instead. She was just listening.

Teresa looked at the papers in her hand.

Looked at Alonda.

"So what you're saying is . . . you're gonna need two of these talks?" she asked, and Alonda burst out laughing. Teresa started laughing, too.

They laughed together, and their laughter bounced off the walls of the room, stifled only by their hug. At least something was gonna be all right. That felt good.

Teresa looked over Alonda's shoulder, out the window, and flinched. "You really like doing that?" she asked. Alonda looked to where she was gesturing. Rize was in the middle of their match, the one Alondra was supposed to be headlining. Lexi was lying on the ground, Spider walking around with his arms in the air. He probably had just body slammed her to the ground.

"Yeah, I love it," Alonda said. Teresa sighed.

Looked at Alonda.

Back out the window.

Back to Alonda.

"Go," she said.

"Seriously?"

"Yeah, just . . . be careful—" Alonda gave her a kiss and was already running out the door, out toward the playground.

"And still Rize Wrestling Champion, give it up for the Incredible Lexi!"

Alonda approached the crowd, her heart thumping in her chest. Lexi and Spider had just finished their match, and, even though it had been set up to look like Spider was gonna win, Lexi came from behind and won. She had the belt flung over her shoulder. Alonda tapped Pretzel on the shoulder. His eyes went wide.

"What're you doing here?" he asked. "I thought you were grounded forever!"

Alonda just gave him a smile. "Play along," she said, grabbing his megaphone from him and lifting it to her mouth. It let out a scream of feedback, which made everyone look over to her. Lexi turned around, her eyes as wide as her smile became.

"Well, well, well," Alonda said, her voice crackling with the static of the megaphone, "I know you didn't think you could all get away with doing a match without me!"

"Rize Fans, it looks like Alonda has made a stunning return!" Pretzel shouted, cupping his hands to his mouth to make his voice be as loud as it possibly could.

Alonda sneaked a glance at the crowd and could see them in various states of surprise, buzzing with excitement. Kimmie was jumping up and down, clapping her hands, and even from across the group, Alonda could hear her saying, "I knew it, I knew it!" in her squeaky voice, could hear the loud, deep "Oh shit!" that Big Ricky let out. He'd brought his own folding chair, a plastic bowl of popcorn sitting in his lap. King was standing next to Tania. "You getting all this, right?" she could hear him ask. "Shush!" Tania said, pushing him away a little. "I wanna see what's gonna happen!"

Lexi looked shocked but was shifting her weight from foot to foot, which Alonda knew meant she was excited. Lexi didn't even hesitate, didn't miss a beat. "What are you doing here, Alondra?" she asked in her pompous voice. "Get bored in your retirement? So you felt the need to show up here unannounced, unwanted, because, why, you watched everything on Netflix or something?"

Alonda shook her head and brought the megaphone back up to her mouth, but the feedback was stronger than ever. She threw it to the ground (she could hear Pretzel give out a "Hey!" of annoyance as it bounced off the Astroturf), and she walked closer to Lexi, letting her voice be as loud as she could possibly make it. "I don't need a megaphone to get my point across!" she shouted, and a bunch of cheers came up from the crowd.

The Incredible Lexi raised her arm, shushing the crowd. "Let the New Girl speak," she said. "Go ahead, I am listening."

"Hey," Alonda said, walking closer, "I need you to know something, 'Incredible Lexi,'" she spat out, her air quotes as big as she could make them, the crowd hanging on her every word.

"You're only champ . . . because I *let you* be the champ!"

Everyone went wild. She could hear some people shout out, "OOOH!" loud, and she could see Michelle holding her whole face in her hands like WHAT, and Kimmie was shouting, "You are the champ, Alondra's the champ! Alondra's the champ!" which got the whole crowd chanting, "Alondra's the champ, Alondra's the champ!"

Lexi held her arm up. A hush descended over the crowd.

"You know, the real reason I think you left wasn't so that you could retire, like you so claimed," Lexi said, gently placing the belt at her feet. "I think you left because you were too scared to face me."

A ripple of "Ooohs" raced through the crowd.

"Well, I guess you haven't been listening as hard as you claim," Alonda said, walking closer to Lexi, putting all her heart and fire into her words, "because if you were, you'd realize I'm no longer the Fresh Face, I'm no longer the New One, I . . . ," she said, taking a pause that stretched out before them.

"I am the Fearless One."

Alonda put her hands on her hips.

Raised her eyebrow.

Smiled.

"Sin miedo."

And she moved forward to strike at Lexi, but Lexi did a double backflip, away from Alonda. The crowd was screaming now, nobody knew what was going to happen, but Alonda and Lexi knew, they had practiced this canceled match and they were ready.

"Come and get me!" Lexi said.

"You running away from me, Lexi?" Alonda shouted, taking her time as she moved closer to Lexi, moving to strike again, but stopped. Lexi brought her hand up, and Alonda was caught in the force field of her powers.

"This ain't a fair match!" Alonda shouted, but Lexi just smiled. "Hey, you have your strengths, I've got mine!" Lexi said, and with a flick of her wrist, Alonda was forced to cartwheel backward, away from Lexi.

"Hey, you know the rules!" Pretzel shouted at Lexi. "No telekinesis if you wanna compete for the belt!"

"That's not fair!" Lexi turned to Pretzel and started arguing, which gave Alonda the chance to walk up behind her and grab Lexi's arm. Lexi twisted out into a cartwheel. Damn, she was good at those acrobatic kinda moves!

Lexi landed on her feet and reached out to strike Alonda several times in a row. Alonda pretended to absorb each hit, though each one was really Lexi clapping her own hands together to make the sound of being hit. But each hit got them closer and closer to the gate, which Alonda felt against her back. She covertly grabbed the gate and gave Lexi a quick nod. She was ready for this.

Lexi pulled Alonda's feet out and was holding her horizontally. The crowd was losing it; Alonda knew that there was even people who were just walking down the street who had stopped to watch now, people hanging out their windows to see them all.

"And now—I can't believe it, never in all my years of wrestling have I ever seen anything like this, Alondra has wrapped her legs around Lexi and OH MY GOSH, ARE YOU SEEING THIS, Lexi is holding on to Alondra, but Alondra has twisted out and brought Lexi down to the ground, she's on the ground now, ONE, TWO—but no, Lexi's kicked out, she's kicked out, a reverse kick out and has Alondra pinned now, ONE, TWO, THAT'S IT! The Incredible Lexi is still Rize Champion!"

Pretzel pulled Lexi up in victory while Alonda stayed on the ground, catching her breath. Right before Pretzel pulled up Lexi, she had whispered in Alonda's ear. "I'm glad you came back." Yeah, Alonda was glad she had come back, too.

27

ALONDA STOOD IN THE KITCHEN, INGREDIENTS ALL SPREAD OUT
before her on the counter, looking at them like they could get up
and walk away at any moment. She was a pretty decent cook, nothing like Teresa, but still, she knew how to do things beyond fry-
ing an egg or boiling pasta. But today was different. Today, she was
finally gonna make sofrito.

Mami's sofrito.

Yeah, the diary hadn't been full of revelations or nothing and
Alonda had been ready to stop reading through when she had
skipped to the back of the book and saw it.

The sofrito recipe.

Mami used to put sofrito in almost everything. It's a base for
cooking things like soups, stews, beans, rice, even the nachos she
used to make. And even though Teresa was a great cook and tried to
replicate Mami's food, there was always something missing about
her dishes, and Alonda knew it was the sofrito (fresh sofrito, not the
watered-down store-bought kind she'd found at the supermarket).

This was the recipe in the diary:

What you're gonna wanna get is:
2 bunches cilantro

1 bunch culantro (but if they don't got, use
*   + + cilantros)*
2 red peppers
a green pepper
1 onion
a handful garlic
a handful ajicitos (if you can't find, use
*   another red pepper)*
some olive oil

And even though it wasn't an exact science, Alonda was gonna try to replicate it.

She just didn't wanna mess it up.

She took a deep breath, the paper out in front of her. She'd practically memorized the steps and everything, had the blender out. But she was still mad nervous.

She picked up a pepper. Brought the knife down to cut it and—

BANG, BANG.

Alonda started, looking toward the next room where the banging was coming from, and saw Teresa trying to carry her big AC through her door and into the living room. She was wrestling with it, trying to keep it from slipping through her arms and crashing to the ground.

"Oh my God, Teresa, hold up!" Alonda shouted, darting toward her and grabbing the other side of the AC. "Why didn't you ask for help?!" she demanded, helping her straighten the thing out.

"Didn't wanna bother you," Teresa grunted out.

Alonda rolled her eyes. "Please," she said, shaking her head a little. "Here, I got it," she said, and pulled it away from Teresa. She'd gotten mad strong during the summer, and the AC really wasn't that heavy.

It was a little heavy, though.

"Where d'you want this?" Alonda asked, shaking a little. Teresa pointed toward the window across the room. "Figured we could use it out here," she said.

Teresa opened the screen, and Alonda carefully placed it through the open window. Somebody from years ago (probably Teresa's ma) had nailed a wooden block into the sill, and Alonda carefully placed it on top. Teresa put the slides in, making sure it was sturdy and in place.

"There!" Teresa said, turning it on. Cool air blasted out, combating the stickiness of the day. "Shoulda done this from the start. Never listen to anyone when you should be trusting your own heart," she said, raising her arm, letting the air dry out her armpit.

Alonda felt her heart pull a little bit. The AC kinda blocked her view of the playground.

Teresa was sniffing the air. "Why's it smell so good in here? Like"—she sniffed again—"cilantro and garlic?"

"Oh!" Alonda said, running back to the kitchen. "I'm just cooking."

"You making sofrito?" Teresa asked, seeing the ingredients. Alonda nodded.

"Damn, you haven't even started and it already smells so good! I don't think the kitchen has smelled like this since Ava . . ." Her voice trailed off.

"I miss her," Alonda said softly. She said it to a pepper, but really, she was talking to Teresa.

"Yeah," she heard Teresa say. "Yeah, I really miss the hell outta her."

"I wish you'd talk about her more," Alonda said, looking at Teresa.

Teresa nodded, her eyes looking watery behind her mascara. "Right," she replied, "I know I should. And I wanna. I guess . . . I dunno, things was so different when I was growing up. Ma never talked about nothing real, nothing deep. Always shoved it away, deep down. Even when I wanted to talk about something, she'd change the subject. She was good at that . . . ," she trailed off, shaking her head a little. "And I guess I picked up on the habit till it was something I didn't even realize I was doing. And sometimes we don't talk about things because we wanna pretend like they don't exist. 'Cause talking about them, it can tear open the hurt we spend a lotta time pretending ain't there. But it's always there." Teresa stopped, clearing her throat a little before continuing. "But your mom . . . Ava . . . God, she wouldn't want us to not talk about her," she said with a watery laugh. Alonda nodded, smiling through the tears that were creeping up the back of her throat.

"You know, she had a girlfriend. Once." Teresa's voice was so low, Alonda wasn't sure she had heard her. But as the words hit her ears, Alonda felt her mouth open a little. Teresa nodded. "At least she was the only girlfriend I knew about. When she told me, I . . . I didn't get it," she said. "She tried talking to me about it, but I . . ." She shook her head, her voice trailing off. Alonda felt her heart pounding. "I called her confused and—I think she stopped telling me things. We used to tell each other everything, but . . . I think that put a crack in us. Because I didn't wanna talk about something I didn't get. I never wanna do that with you," she said. Her eyes were still watery, but her tears were staying back.

Alonda nodded, her tears dripping down her cheeks. Teresa opened her arms, and Alonda folded herself into them.

"Oh," Alonda said, pulling out of the hug, "before I forget, this is for you," and she handed her the little sheet of paper. Teresa's eyes widened at the sight of Ava's handwriting.

"It's yours," Alonda said. "I mean, I'm obviously making a copy of it, I already took a pic and put it on my Insta, but this version, it's for you." She pushed her hand back toward her. Teresa gave her a look, turned it over.

At the bottom of the page, Ava had written *For Teresa*. Probably a reminder to herself, a reminder to pull it out and give it to Teresa, a task easily forgotten, one that had been stuck in the pages of that little diary.

"Shit," Teresa said, her voice choking. She looked at Alonda and back down on the paper.

"I know," Alonda said. And she knew she didn't really know, but inside her, she understood exactly all the words Teresa couldn't say. "I know."

Alonda didn't know what else to say or do, so she just pulled a bunch of the leafy green cilantro to the sink, started washing it.

Teresa looked up at her. "You need help? You know I love to chop."

Alonda laughed. "You got the time? We haven't cooked together in a minute . . . ," she said, trailing off, but Teresa was already grabbing her apron from its hook and tying it around her waist.

"Yeah, come on, I'm in the mood to chop some stuff!"

"Yeah, sure, I could always use a sous chef here," Alonda said, pushing some garlic toward her.

"It's still not gonna be exactly like hers used to, though, like, these measurements aren't a real science, all of them," Alonda said, and Teresa shook her head with a small smile.

"Nah, it won't be like hers, not really. 'Cause you'll make it yours."

Alonda smiled a little larger. "Yeah, I guess that's true. Now, come on, I wanna use this to make nachos later, so get to chopping, please!"

☆ **28** ☆

ALONDA WAS LYING ON HER BED, STUDYING THE CEILING OF HER
bedroom. Damn, there were more cracks in it than she'd ever
noticed before. All her thoughts were running around her brain
and she was trying to follow them when there was a knock on her
window.

Alonda felt her heart grip inside her chest a little bit—shit, was
it a bird or something?!—but when she looked she saw

"Lexi?" she sputtered out, sitting up immediately. Lexi was
crouched on her fire escape, squinting to try to make Alonda out
through her curtains. She jumped up and ran to the window, opening it wide. "What are you doing on my fire escape?! That shit's not
safe!"

Lexi smiled a little bit and threw her a wave. "It's an emergency."

"What? Is something wrong with Spider? King?"

"Nah, nah, nothing like that—can I come in?"

"Yeah, obviously," Alonda said, opening the window. Lexi jumped
through.

The two of them looked at each other kinda awkwardly. They
hadn't seen each other since that last match and hadn't really
talked about . . . anything. Lexi shifted from foot to foot.

"So . . . what's up?" Alonda asked, trying to be as casually cool as possible.

"Hey, yeah, I know that we should probably talk about, like . . ." She gestured between the two of them.

Alonda felt her cheeks go warm. "Yeah, for sure—" Alonda started to say, but Lexi talked over her.

"But also, right now, you gotta come with me," Lexi said. She was hopping from foot to foot a little bit, bouncing up and down. Alonda raised her eyebrow.

"You gonna tell me why?"

Lexi shook her head. "You just gotta trust me."

Alonda felt her head nodding. Lexi's face broke into a huge smile. "Okay, awesome, great, okay, let's go!" She grabbed Alonda's hand and pulled her through her door.

The two of them stopped short.

Teresa was sitting on the sofa doing a crossword puzzle. She raised an eyebrow.

"Fire escape?" she asked lightly.

Lexi cleared her throat. "Hello, ma'am, I'm—" but Teresa was already waving her hand at her.

"Don't ma'am me, I'm Teresa. And you're Lexi."

Lexi nodded. "Yeah, and I'm here to take Alonda to a very important event."

"You gonna yell at me because of the fire escape?" Alonda asked, but Teresa just made a noise like *oh please*.

"What, you think you invented sneaking out of the fire escape? I was your age once, too," she snapped, looking back at her crossword puzzle. "Just surprised it took you so long to figure it out," she muttered. Alonda's mouth dropped open.

"I'm gonna take that as your blessing," Lexi said, pulling Alonda toward the front door.

"It's nice to meet you, Lexi," Teresa called after them.

The sidewalks closer to the boardwalk were crowded with bodies that Lexi deftly weaved her way through, stopping every few seconds to make sure Alonda was behind her.

"Why's there so many people today?" Alonda grumbled to Lexi, who ignored her and pulled her arm toward the depth of the crowd.

"Just come on!" she said, pulling her on. Alonda glanced around at the crowd and saw there was a bunch of people all wearing shirts with wrestlers on them. Some of them were carrying around big plastic belts slung over their shoulders, others holding photos.

"Oh, today's the wrestling expo," Alonda said. She'd forgotten all about it.

"Where are you taking me?" she asked Lexi as Lexi continued to pull her forward.

"Here!" she said finally, pointing to someone seated at a table. Alonda took a look.

Lovely Loveless was sitting behind the table, signing some merch.

"No way," she said. "Is that—no *way*!" she said again. She thought she'd never have a chance to see her ever again, and she was sitting five feet away from her?

"Yeah, I guess today's your lucky day!" Lexi said. She gave her a gentle nudge. "I was walking through and I saw her and I ran over immediately— You gonna say hi?"

"I, uh, I don't really have anything for her to sign or anything," Alonda said suddenly, her words all running forward while she found her body pushing herself back. She couldn't believe she was seeing Lovely Loveless here. Right here. In front of her.

And now she didn't know what the hell to say.

"Just go say hi! What's the worst that can happen?" Lexi asked. "Like, you can really run up to her right now, wave your arms in her face, and run away; she'll never even think twice!"

"Really, you don't think that would be memorable?" Alonda asked. Lexi nudged her forward.

"Come on. Sin miedo, right?"

Alonda looked back at Lovely Loveless.

Took a deep breath.

Walked forward.

"Hi!" Lovely Loveless said, smiling big.

"Hey," Alonda said, her voice squeaking her words on the way out of her mouth.

"Cool hair!" Lovely said, pointing to Alonda's pink streaks.

"Thanks," Alonda said, and kept staring.

"Do you . . . have anything for me to sign?" Lovely asked. Alonda shook her head no. "You wanna picture or something?" she asked. Alonda shook her head no. Oh wait, she'd meant yes, wait—

"I mean, yes, for sure, I definitely, I want that, but also I just . . . I just needed to tell you . . ."

Lovely Loveless's big green eyes were locked on Alonda's own. Even though Alonda felt some people on line behind her were starting to get antsy, Lovely Loveless didn't try to rush her or anything. Just let her take her time.

"You really helped me," Alonda blurted out. "I mean, I saw you on YouTube? And like, your videos, they all, you made me, you helped me find my voice? I mean, you did, you helped me. And I just. Wanted to say thank you."

Lovely Loveless smiled bigger. "Oh, hey, I'm glad I could help."

Alonda just nodded a bunch of times. "Hey, why don't the two of you get together," Lexi said. She had her cell phone out and pointed at them, ready to take a picture.

"Sure," Lovely Loveless said, putting her head close to Alonda's, "let's do this!"

They posed for the picture, and Lexi snapped the photo.

"Looks like a magazine cover," Lexi said, flashing them a grin.

Lovely looked at Alonda. "Well, it was great meeting you—I didn't catch your name?"

"Alondra," she said. "My name's Alondra."

September

EPILOGUE

"THAT'S RIGHT, EVERYBODY, THIS IS GONNA BE RIZE WRESTLING'S last match of the season—"

"Yeah, but is it the last match forever?!" Big Ricky's voice rose up from the crowd. He was sitting in his usual seat, a couple of buddies set up in their own folding chairs next to him. A few others followed suit, Kimmie shouting, "Yeah!", her voice carrying. Alonda could see Pretzel hesitate, but only for a second.

"Well, all good things must come to an end—"

The crowd moaned.

"Like Alondra taking my belt away from me!"

A voice shouted, and Lexi's music started blasting through the speakers. Alonda couldn't help but laugh. Lexi was always good at an entrance. And distraction.

Alonda watched as Lexi walked into their ring, her arms raised above her head, taking her sweet time to get to the arena.

Lexi grabbed the megaphone from Pretzel and shouted into the crowd, "It don't matter if this is the last time, if this is the twelfth time, or if this is the first time again, those silly facts are just distracting shit to get us away from the main event. Alondra's out there and she's got my belt and she thinks that she can just keep it? I'm here to win it back fair and square. All good things must come to an end, and her reign is just about to end."

Would it really be the last time they all wrestled together? Might be.

It was fall, and they all had shit to do. School changes everything. Like, they all still hung out, but putting together a show? Doing everything that the endless hours of summer made possible and trying to fit it all in between college applications, homework, extra classes, it all just didn't seem feasible. They were all busy.

King was working, had a new gig down at the GameStop on top of his school shit, which apparently included tutoring. Pretzel was getting more caught up with Tania, and Spider was never around. He'd become more and more of a quiet mystery since the summer ended; he'd abandoned his comics and was spending most of his time together with everyone with his head glued to his phone. Lexi was already working hard at her portfolio, taking new risks with her art, and had gotten into that special art program that met on Saturdays, which basically meant she had six days of school. And on top of Alonda's already packed schedule of classes, she'd even joined track. It wasn't as good as wrestling, but she needed something to occupy her body; sitting still didn't seem to work no more—her cells were always itchy with movement. It was different, not knowing the outcome, just relying on herself, but at least it made her body sweat and feel.

Coney Island was starting to quiet down, started to lose the buzz of summer, replaced with the quiet of the off-season. Alonda still worked weekends, which were busy as ever, but with fall-themed decorations all around, a reminder that they'd all entered a new season, leaving behind the lazy days and filling them instead with the promise of ghosts and goblins and zombies. It still got hot some days, but the coolness was already beginning to creep its way into the air, almost like a shiver starting to snake its way down their spine.

They hadn't officially decided if this would be it for Rize. It was technically the end of their first season, but it might have been the end of their whole group, too. It was hard to imagine, but this had all been unimaginable just a few months ago, too.

"All right, Lexi, give me the mic!" Pretzel whined a little as he grabbed the megaphone back from her hands. Lexi laughed her dramatic, pompous laugh. Probably to mask some real laughter floating under there.

Pretzel lifted the megaphone back to his mouth. Took his deep breath in.

"And introducing her opponent—"

Less than a year, and her whole world had been altered without her even realizing it was happening while it was happening.

"Coming at you all the way from Coney Island—"

One last match, then.

"I need to hear you make some noise for ALONDRA: the Fearless One!"

Alonda walked out to her music, raising her arms and soaking up the cheers. And this time, she didn't pretend she was entering a professional ring, didn't try to change the cracked concrete or the dulled black padding, didn't try to erase the buildings around her or make the music from the speakers louder, or change the people who were watching. She was wrestling here, on her home turf, in Coney Island, in Brooklyn, on a piece of land that clung to the state known as New York. Rize Wrestling might not exist past the summer, they might never come back, but none of that shit mattered because right now, she was here, right here.

Right where the concrete met the padding, she stopped and threw her body into her signature cartwheel, catapulting herself to the center of the ring, toward Lexi. The crowd cheered, and instead of trying to knock them to the back of her mind, she listened harder. Heard their cheers, their unintelligible "Woos!" that melted into random "Yeahs!"

Was it possible to bottle up a moment? Bubble Wrap it in memory and place it on a shelf inside her brain so she could access it whenever she wanted?

Nah. She'd never be able to relive any of these moments, not for real. All she had was living them now. It's probably a beautiful and painful thing about life.

She turned to face Lexi.

Lexi, who she adored, but who right now was her bitter enemy.

Lexi, who was waiting patiently for her to enter and settle herself, but who kept a look of impatience on her face for the crowd.

Lexi.

"The following contest is scheduled for one fall."

"One fall!" the crowd chanted back.

A hush fell over the playground.

Alonda's heart thudded in her chest.

"At the sound of the bell—"

A smile passed back and forth between their eyes.

"And one, two—"

Ding.

ACKNOWLEDGMENTS

Wow, I can't believe I wrote a whole book! This has been the hardest thing I've ever done and it wouldn't have happened if not for the following humans:

Thank you to my incredible editor, Trisha de Guzman, who took a chance on me and lovingly helped me nurture this story into existence; you made this book, and me, better with your kindness, patience, and brilliant mind.

Thank you to my agents at Gersh, Joe Veltre who helped broker the deal, and Skyler Gray who believed in me as an artist when few did.

To the many eyes and hearts who read the many drafts of this book and offered me feedback: Jonathan Alexandratos, Iyvon E., Ashil Lee, Nina Ki, Freddy Padilla—you all gave me the confidence in my voice. A very special thank you to Amara Janae Brady who not only read an early draft, but who was there in so many ways while I wrote this story—your voice mail forever lives in my heart. And thank you to my wonderful sensitivity readers Kayla Dunigan, Marlyn Matias, and Bari Robinson; you all helped me create fuller characters and a more complete world. Any missteps are mine and mine alone.

Taylor Reynolds, my best friend who listened to my slow descent to madness as I wrote this book and always made me laugh to bring me back. Dana Baliki, whose kind, gentle guidance helped me overcome the crippling fear of getting it wrong. Matt Barbot, you're great. And Jen Browne, whose words of encouragement I've carried with me each draft—none of this would be real without any of you, thank you all.

Ren Dara Santiago and Elena Araoz; the work you did on the play helped me find the heart of the book. Thank you both.

I would have written nothing if it hadn't been for the loving, patient support of my family. My Mama, Aida Vasquez, who was so understanding of me while I struggled to write this book. My sister-in-law Sandra Cardona, who was the first person who told me to take the leap of faith necessary to be a writer. And my sister-in-law Katyria Ramos whose humor and love helped me make it through the homestretch in more ways than one. Gracias, te quiero mucho.

My nieces, Kimberlee & Carolina; you both mean the world to me. Every word I wrote was an "I love you" to each of you.

Finally, my parents, JoAnn and Dennis Femia, who knew I'd be a writer before I even knew how to write, and who have done everything in their power to make my dreams come true. Hope I made youse proud. And Freddy Padilla, love of my life, who knew I always had a voice, even when I wasn't so sure. Thank you, babeo, love you.